THE INCLUSIVE BREED

JAMES S. KELLY

THE INCLUSIVE BREED

JAMES S. KELLY

ISBN: 978-1-963565-12-6 (Paperback)

Library of Congress Control Number: 2024907001

Printed in the United States of America

Published by

info@thequippyquill.com
(302) 295-2278

THE MOVING WORDS REVIEW

BOOK INFORMATION:

Title: The Inclusive Breed

Author: James S. Kelly

Genre: Historical fiction Review date: Jan. 5, 2024

BOOK REVIEW:

"The Inclusive Breed" by James S. Kelly is a gripping historical novel set in the American South during the era of slavery. The story revolves around the Sutters, a family who relocates from Texas to Alabama, and their complex interactions with the world of plantations and slavery. Central to the narrative is the Sutters' cotton plantation, Bridlewood, and its diverse cast of characters, including the Sutter family, their slaves, and neighboring plantation owners.

Kelly's storytelling shines in its ability to weave a rich blend of relationships and experiences.

The novel explores themes of love, friendship, societal norms, and the harsh realities of slavery.

Particularly noteworthy is the portrayal of the deep and forbidden bond that develops between Marsha Lee Sutter, a member of the plantation-owning family, and Odelle, a slave. Their relationship challenges the rigid social structures of the time and drives much of the novel's emotional depth.

The author excels in bringing to life the setting of the American South, with vivid descriptions of the plantation landscape, the brutal realities of slavery, and the social intricacies of the era. The narrative is well-paced, balancing moments of tension and drama with character development and historical context.

One of the strengths of "The Inclusive Breed" is its multidimensional characters. The Sutters and their slaves are portrayed with complexity and nuance, avoiding simplistic or stereotypical depictions. The book also does not shy away from the moral ambiguities and challenging choices faced by individuals in a society structured around slavery.

In a nutshell, "The Inclusive Breed" is an entrancing and thought-provoking novel that offers a window into a tumultuous period in American history. James S. Kelly has crafted a story that not only entertains but also invites reflection on the enduring themes of human dignity, love, and resistance in the face of injustice. The novel is a must-read for anyone interested in historical fiction and the American South's complex legacy.

themovingwords.com

Contents

OTHER BOOKS
BY
JAMES S. KELLY

WESTERNS

A MAN OF BREEDING
A BREED APART
THE WOUNDED BREED
THE DOWNTRODDEN BREED

MYSTERIES

I DIDN'T FORGET
INTERNED
NOT IN MY BACKYARD

CIVIL WAR

MAGNOLIA

VIETNAM WAR

A LONG WALK HOME

ACKNOWLEDGEMENTS

SPOUSE

PATRICIA

CHILDREN

STEPHEN
MARK
NANCY
MICHELLE

EDITOR

MIKE PETERSON

CHAPTER 1

The most magnificent and beautiful plantation in Western Alabama was owned by Jesse and Carolyn Sutter; they named it Bridlewood. Both Sutters were born in Texas and raised on a cattle ranch in the Panhandle of Texas. Their two families lived close to each other; twenty five miles was considered close in Texas. Eventually their children were introduced to each other at a spring cattle event and then nature took its course. Jesse was seven years older than Carolyn and spent some of his early twenties aboard a pirate ship working out of Cuba. It was there that he met Frank Wilcox where both spent some time with the pirate Jean LaFitte.

The two friends were into smuggling, cards and pretty women. Though their initial time together lasted only two years; they vowed to maintain contact. When the Sutters grew tired of the dust storms, the raids by Comanche War Parties and the hot dry weather of the panhandle in Texas, they decided to accept Frank and his wife's standing invitation to visit them at their plantation, called Hickory Hills in Eastern Alabama.

Not only did they like Hickory Hills Plantation but they fell in love with the plantation style of living and were eager to make a change. It took several years to sell their cattle ranch and emigrate from Texas twenty five years earlier. Within a few months they found one thousand acres of prime land and called it Bridlewood.

The first thing Jesse did was learn about cotton; the second thing he did was learn about slavery and he learned it well. At the peak of the south's renaissance, the

Sutters had one hundred fifty slaves working on their estate. Their cotton business flourished, his social status rose and he became the most respected man in that part of the state. Many of his friends thought he could be a US Senator; some thought he could even be President.

It took the Sutters five years to complete the construction of their house and all the support buildings needed for a cotton plantation. It was nearly an image of the Wilcox plantation. The main entryway leading to the mansion was lined with Magnolia Trees. A visitor's first view of the home was of the lofty columns and intricately carved railings on the porch and the large windows and shutters on either side the gardens surrounding the house and leading to a small pond adorned with colorful flowers and neatly trimmed hedges.

The two couples visited each other at least once each year. The Sutters had been successful in the cattle and mustang business in Texas and had enough funds to build up their enterprise in Alabama while taking their time before showing a profit.

Frank Wilcox married much later than Jesse. His wife was from a wealthy family but she became very ill after losing a child in childbirth. Although she recovered, the doctors advised the Wilcox' not to have any children. Mrs. Wilcox lived only to the age of twenty seven. Frank was devastated and drank a good deal after her death.

Carolyn produced two spirited children. The first being a male heir to the estate and two years later a charming and active female who was the apple of her father's eye. His first born James took after his father, followed him everywhere and tried to emulate all his father's expressions and mannerisms. This wasn't lost on a proud father who spoiled the boy in every way he could.

From his early years, James was taught to ride, shoot and stand his ground. He was to be the future master of Bridlewood. Marsha Lee was tutored at home, taught to be a lady and encouraged to have a keen eye for a young man that would provide her with a comfortable lifestyle in the future.

There weren't many children from the wealthy families nearby, so James and Marsha Lee played with children of the workers on the estate, which were mostly black slaves. James liked to wrestle and he was generally the best at his age, except for Odelle Jones, the son of a slave. Most of their tussles would end in a draw. The two young men were so friendly with each other that it didn't matter to either, who won.

Marsha Lee loved to follow her brother around their estate. When his friendship with Odelle grew, she naturally followed the two boys around annoying them to a point where they tried to hide from her. She was undaunted and most times was able to find their hideout. Eventually the two boys gave up and welcomed her into their group. The three could always be seen together, whether fishing, swimming, riding or just throwing rocks at snakes.

As the trio reached their teenage years, James and Odelle were inseparable and could be seen riding horses on the estate or hunting small animals. Odelle was generally included in family functions and occasionally invited to eat with the two children. As they grew older, the boys would occasionally go off hunting for a few days.

Most times they'd bag a deer; or come home with a few partridge. During this time Marsha Lee started to come of age and although James didn't recognize it, Odelle did. His mother saw the problem early on and warned her son that his playmate wasn't for him and he better be careful. What she saw in her son's eye was a hanging offense in these parts.

The other black boys could see what was going on and liked to tease Odelle about his white girlfriend. He'd retaliate by getting into fights with one or more of his group. Sometimes he'd win; other times he sports a black eye or a swollen jaw. None of the teasing occurred while James was present, so he was oblivious to the insinuations about Odelle and his sister. It should've been Marsha Lee that Odelle's mother warned about a relationship. The young woman was absolutely enchanted with her black playmate and loved to tease him. She didn't realize what her little flirtations could be doing to the young man. At thirteen, Odelle was in love; at sixteen he was in heat.

One day Marsha Lee and Odelle went swimming. James was in town on an errand for his father and the two were left alone. They were in the pond splashing each other as teenagers do. Suddenly, Marsha Lee stumbled into Odelle as she was coming out of the water. He reached out to prevent her from falling and in so doing she fell into his arms. She blushed as he held her close and when he kissed her, she kissed him back. It took a few seconds for it to dawn on her what happened and she pushed him away and ran home.

The young woman was careful after that incident to avoid being alone with Odelle. The young black man didn't understand why she was becoming so distant. He became moody and got into more fights with other blacks. His relationship with James Sutter was still positive, but Odelle wasn't being invited to dinner with his two playmates anymore. His mother tried to counsel him but he wouldn't listen. She was afraid nothing good would come from his fixation on Marsha Lee.

Soon, young men coming to Bridlewood were taken with the pretty young woman. Her father and mother saw the change in Marsha Lee and when she reached her sixteenth birthday, they threw her a party and invited every male and female teenager from the elite families in the area. The party was held outside near the swimming pond. The plantation's carpenters built tables and a platform for dancing. It was to be the centerpiece of the festivities; nearly 100 teenagers attended.

Many of the black teenagers had jobs as waiters; others did the setup and cleanup. Odelle was assigned as a waiter, which he performed well. After dinner, Marsha Lee danced with at least half of the young men attending, including Jerome Templeton the nineteen year old son of Marshall Templeton, a notorious loudmouth and brawler. The father successfully won two duels, using pistols. Both contests were over words said to someone's wife and both opponents eventually passed away. Rachel Farms owned by the Templetons, was five miles east of Bridlewood. The younger Templeton was older than the other boys at the party and Marsha Lee was mesmerized that he was taking such an interest in her.

It was late spring and the temperature in the days was in the middle eighties and didn't cool off very much in the evening. When Jerome suggested they'd go for a walk to cool off, she readily agreed. The landscaping around the main house and the pond which was within two hundred yards of the house was lush and contained many paths, bushes and trees. When they reached a clump of trees about one hundred yards from the house, they stopped to enjoy the small breeze that had come up. Marsha Lee was leaning back against a magnolia tree while dabbing her chest with a white handkerchief. Jerome took this opportunity to press his hips against hers and kiss her softly on the mouth.

Though the kiss was a surprise to her, she rather enjoyed it, though she wouldn't let him force his tongue into her mouth. She remembered her mother's warning about that. Jerome looked down and smiled at her as he slipped the straps of her dress off her shoulders, exposing her breasts which he began to fondle. She was in a panic mode and tried to shove him away but he was too tall and too strong. He continued to squeeze both her breasts while smiling down at her. All of a sudden he was pushed away from her and he landed on his back getting his white dinner jacket dirty. She glanced to her left and saw Odelle and she assumed it was he who shoved Jerome away from her.

Jerome rose and looked around. All he could see was a young black man close to Marsha Lee. He yelled at Odelle, "I'm going to beat you within an inch of your life."

Odelle seemed numb to what happened, though when Jerome rushed him, he struck out with his right hand and Jerome went down on his back again. Marsha Lee finally lifted up the straps of her dress and tucked in her breasts. She'd been so caught up in the moment that she didn't realize her chest was bare while both boys fought over her.

Jerome was screaming obscenities at Odelle as he scrambled to his feet and lunged at his agitator. He took a swing at the young black man but went down on his back again under several blows delivered by Odelle. Several men rushed up. They'd heard the noise and came to see what happened. Two men grabbed Odelle's arms and held him as others helped Jerome up. Jesse Sutter arrived with his foreman. Will Thacker, and ordered Odelle to be taken to the barn. "No", screamed Marsha Lee.

The seven men who were on the scene stopped and looked over at her. "No father. Templeton took liberties with me and tried to take off my dress. Odelle stopped him."

No one seemed to know what to do. Marsha Lee repeated her statement and her father put his arm around her and said, "that's okay honey; I'll take care of this."

Jerome yelled out. I want that son-of-a-bitch whipped right here. Jesse Sutter looked at the young man and hit him as hard as he could with his fist and broke Jerome's nose. The two men holding Odelle didn't know what to do so they continued to hold onto him.

"Release Odelle and take young Templeton up to the house." Sutter ordered.

Sutter looked at Odelle. "Thank you. I'll thank you properly tomorrow."

Jesse Sutter knew that trouble would be on the way as his staff cleaned up Jerome and put a bandage on his nose, The young man was swearing at Jesse, who offered his hand. "My father is going to kill you. He's the best shot in the state. You're going to pay for this humiliation."

The master of Bridlewood instructed his foreman to go with three armed men and take young Templeton home "Come right back. If there's trouble, don't be afraid to use your weapons."

Odelle was brought to the mansion the next morning and all four of the Sutter's thanked him for his assistance to Marsha Lee. They presented him with a suit of clothes and a nice shirt. His eyes lighted up when he saw the suit.

The Overseer delivered the young man to his home and told the help that his nose had been injured. Luckily, the older Templeton wasn't at home. Everyone at Bridlewood knew the issue hadn't been resolved. Two days later a rider appeared at the front door of Bridlewood asking for an audience with Jesse Sutter. The meeting was short and a note from Mr. Templeton was delivered to Sutter. "My master begs a response to his request," the rider said

Sutter read the note, told the rider to wait on the porch while he wrote a response. He went into his study and composed a reply. Ten minutes later he returned, handed an envelope to the rider and wished him a good day. Templeton was asking for a meeting with Sutter to discuss the issue of his son's injuries. Sutter responded that he and his son were available at ten the next morning.

The apprehension that Jesse Sutter felt was understandable. Marshall Templeton was a formidable adversary and one who acted at times without rationale. Sutter intended to have his foreman and son James attend the meeting. Will Thatcher had been his overseer for ten years. He was smart, loyal and gave firm direction to all his employees and slaves. But best of all, he didn't overreact. He seemed to take things in stride without creating situations that got out of hand. James was his heir and although young, he always looked at things as they were and not as he wanted.

Templeton, his son and overseer arrived on time and were ushered into Sutter's large office. Templeton's overseer was a man near sixty years of age and had seen his best days. There was enough room in the office for everyone to be comfortable. The chairs were arranged in a circle with the three Templeton representatives facing the Sutter group. Refreshments were provided on a table to the side. Jerome Templeton had a significant bandage over his nose that almost restricted his vision. He seemed to be in pain.

Templeton didn't waste any time after the preliminaries. "I asked for this meeting today to seek satisfaction for my son's injuries. I'm appalled that he was hit unnecessarily several times by one of your slaves and no one came to his aid. "

It was on the table and Sutter now had to consider how he'd respond. "What form of satisfaction are you seeking?"

"I want an apology from you sir for striking my son and I want you to transfer ownership of the slave Odelle Jones to me."

The room was quiet waiting for Sutter to respond. "I certainly apologize for breaking your son's nose. Perhaps I overreacted at the time, but after discussing what happened with my daughter, who was nearly violated by your son, I think not. The question should be, what is a good daughter's reputation worth? She's sixteen years of age and this was her first party. Your son is three years her senior and more experienced than she. When we invited the children of other plantation owners, we expect them to represent their parents and act within the confines of good behavior. Your son did not adhere to those standards and as such was treated fairly by me. Odelle Jones grew up with my children and acted as a representative of mine in protecting my daughter's honor."

Although Sutter's response was delivered calmly, there was no question in anyone's mind in that room, that he was not persuaded by Templeton's demand. No sooner had Sutter responded when young Templeton blurted out. "That little bitch led me on."

He might have had more to say, but he didn't complete the remainder of his statement because James Sutter, although younger and shorter, lunged at him and knocked him and his chair over. Templeton's overseer, who was sitting close to Jerome was hit by James' leg and fell backwards; he hit his head on the floor. James was on top of Jerome Templeton and pummeled him with his fists beating his face to a pulp. Marshall Templeton tried to intercede but William Thacker was out of his chair quickly and got between James and the senior Templeton. James continued to hit Jerome in the face until Jesse Sutter picked him up around the waist and lifted him off the younger Templeton and put him in one of the chairs. Jerome lay unconscious on the floor behind James' chair.

Marshall Templeton put his right arm around Thacker's waist and tried to throw him aside. Thacker was too strong and held onto Marshall's arm, turned ninety degrees and broke the older man's arm. Everyone turned toward the two as they heard the bone in Templeton's arm break. He cried out in pain and slumped into the nearest chair. Jesse Sutter called for some help from his household staff and directed a servant to go for his doctor. He and Thacker tried to attend to the older Templeton's arm. They both felt it was broken. The elder overseer was still on the floor though he was starting to stir. Several of the male servants helped lift him up and put him in a chair. One of the women staff members put a wet cloth on the back of his head.

James helped the doctor pull the senior Templeton's arm straight and reset the bone. He broke a leg off a kitchen chair and used it as a wooden brace on Templeton's arm and bound it with some cloth wrappings. Sutter grabbed some brandy and gave Marshall a glass to ease the pain. Young Templeton was groggy as the doctor and Sutter's overseer helped him up and settled him in a chair, The young man's face was a bloody mess. The doctor did his best to remove most of the blood but the young man looked hideous and was barely coherent.

After two glasses of brandy, the older Templeton said, "all of you will pay for this and I'm going to kill you." He pointed at Thacker.

"Sir, I'm no gentleman. If you challenge me, I'll pick knives and I've never lost a knife fight. I'm bigger and stronger than you. So, keep that in mind." Thacker responded.

In spite of the animosity shown between the two plantation owners, hospitality was at stake. All three men from the Templeton Plantation were injured and Mrs. Sutter would not let her husband send them home in that condition. They were given guest rooms in the house and because of their injuries; all three were served meals in their rooms over the next two days. Jesse Sutter made sure that the Templeton trio didn't have any weapons. For security, he stationed a servant in the hall for the entirety of their stay. Both Sutter men and Mrs. Sutter visited all three men each day to be sure they were well taken care of. The doctor was concerned about the younger Templeton's face and voiced his concern to Jesse that the young man may need an operation.

Prior to leaving, Marshall Templeton asked to speak to Jesse Sutter in private. "I can't go home in this condition and face my family. I must have a concession so that this incident doesn't turn into a blood feud between our families."

"What do you have in mind?" Sutter asked.

"That prized roan you've shown at several of the county racing events would be an ideal peace offering. All the damage other than your daughter's reputation was done to my side. What do you say?" Templeton was smiling.

Sutter knew he could ignore the request, but something inside him said, why not a peace offering. "I'll have my groom get him ready and you can take him with you." The two men shook hands.

CHAPTER 2

By the time Marsha Lee was eighteen, she had two serious suitors calling on her at Bridlewood. One of the young men, named William Jeffries, was from a distinguished southern family and the heir to the family plantation in Eastern Georgia. The other young man, named Harold Surries, was from a sailing family in Louisiana. Both had visited Hickory Hills owned by Frank Wilcox and his wife and heard about the blonde beauty. Frank personally made the introductions for both young men. Each spent a week at Bridlewood courting Marsha Lee. Either one would be suitable according to Marsha Lee's mother, but for some reason Marsha Lee wasn't in a hurry to make a decision.

Carolyn Sutter wasn't raised as a debutante. She herded cattle with her husband and helped with the annual branding, and when she spoke everyone listened. One day she had a heart-to-heart talk with her daughter. ''There's a window of opportunity for every young woman to attract a suitable young man. Once that window shuts, the number of suitors decreases and the cost of a dowry to attract a suitor is larger. Take care that you don't become too choosy and have to accept someone you don't care for.''

It wasn't that Marsha Lee wasn't listening to her mother. Neither of the young men struck a chord in her. She liked them, especially the one from the sailing family; he made her laugh. Something inside her told her to wait; neither was the right one.

The situation with the Templetons seemed to be a thing of the past. In fact, the Sutters hadn't seen the Templetons since the day they took Pleasant Breeze, Jesse Sutter's prize horse. However, the grapevine kept them informed; Jerome married a girl from Atlanta with a substantial dowry.

Odelle had been promoted to the mansion's staff and was responsible for Jesse Sutter's daily schedule. He saw the family at breakfast and just before they sat down for dinner. Although he had access to the entire home, it was understood that he couldn't go upstairs where the family resided. His mother had constantly impressed upon him that Marsha Lee wasn't for him and to stop thinking about her. It was easy for someone to say you should do something or someone wasn't for you. But, reconciling good advice with your emotions was difficult. Odelle thought about Marsha Lee on a daily basis and made every effort to see her. How he held his feelings in check so far was a mystery to his mother.

There were incidents when the two young people were alone, but in each case, neither made any overt movement toward the other. There seemed to be a tacit agreement between the two that any relationship was strictly forbidden. What changed that mental set for both was never determined. It could've occurred the day Marsha Lee went on a buggy ride with her mother. When Odelle helped the young woman into the carriage, he held onto her hand longer than necessary. This was followed by Marsha Lee squeezing Odelle arm when she sat down in the carriage. There seemed to be some sort of code being passed to the other that no one but the two seemed to notice.

The slave quarters were about three hundred yards from the main house. Odelle passed by the pond to and from work on a daily basis. One evening he was working late and on his way home; he saw Marsha Lee coming out of the water. She immediately stopped for a second when she saw him, but then continued on her way to her house. As she got abreast of Odelle he touched her arm and she stopped. He didn't wait; he put his arm around her waist and kissed her on the mouth. She resisted and tried to pull back but he held her to him. Soon she gave in and put her arms around his neck and kissed him back.

Odelle led her behind the trees, undressed her and they made love. When they were finished she raised her concerns. "We can't do this. It's forbidden and I know they're watching us. There can't be a life for us."

"I can't let you go. I love you and I think you love me. We could go north. I'd be free and we could be together." Odelle said.

"That wouldn't work. Besides, we have no money and we don't know anyone up north that would take us in. You have no skills and I most certainly haven't been trained for work. I've been told since birth that I must find a husband who'll support me similar to how I live now. We'd be destitute within a year even if I used the money given to me by my father and mother."

"Well, we can't stay here. I don't want to be here if and when you marry. I couldn't stand that."

"If they catch us together, they'll hang you and then where will we be?"

"I don't care what they do to me as long as you love me. Can we meet here tomorrow at the same time? Odelle asked.

"I won't promise, but I'll try." The actual affair started then, though it had been in the back of their minds since the incident at the swimming hole.

Over the next five months they tried to be discrete, moving their rendezvous to other places and changing the times of their meetings. But as time went on they became impatient and discretion was ignored. Neither seemed concerned at what would happen if they were caught. Their passion was so great that eventually they would slip up. That came one night when they were alone in the cotton gin building, one of their frequent meeting places. They'd just finished making love and were lying side by side on top of two cotton bales when someone came into the building with a lantern.

The two lovers tried to dress quickly while trying not to make any noise, but Marsha Lee's shoe fell to the concrete floor below and that made a slight noise. But it was enough to alert the intruder and he called out, "who's in here?"

They knew the voice and tried to hide by crouching low on the bale and being quiet. However, the intruder was persistent and when he saw the shoe below the cotton bales he stopped and called out, "whoever is up there better come down or I'll call for more help and forcibly bring you down."

Marsha Lee showed herself. "James it's me. I was tired and laid down on one of the bales and fell asleep. My shoe must have come off. Why don't you help me down?"

"How did you get up there?"

"I had a ladder that I pulled up so I wouldn't be disturbed."

James caught some movement behind his sister as she was leaning over the bale waiting for him to help her down. "Who's there with you Marsha Lee?"

"Why no one? Give me your hand."

"There's someone with you. I must see who it is."

"Please James, let it pass and help me down. You're my brother, not my parent."

James grabbed a small ladder leaned it against the bale and started up while holding the lantern in front of him. When he spotted Odelle lying down on the top of the bale, he looked at him in disbelief. "Come on down Odelle."

The future master of Bridlewood was shocked. "Marsha Lee, I want you to go home. I'll deal with you later."

"I'm not going anywhere. You have no authority over me or what I do."

"If you want me to get father here, I will."

James waited until his sister left before he turned his attention to Odelle. He slapped him across the face. "How could you violate our friendship? I have no choice but to tell my father what you've done. Go home and report to my father at ten tomorrow morning. If you choose to run away, I'll turn the situation over to Mr. Thacker. As of now you're relieved of your duties in the main house."

"Doesn't our friendship mean anything to you?" Odelle asked.

The answer was quick. "Not where my sister and our family's reputation are concerned."

Marsha Lee ran into the house past her mother and went directly to her room. Carolyn Sutter called after her daughter but either she didn't hear her mother or she ignored her. Carolyn could see that she was distraught. She followed her daughter upstairs and into her large bedroom and asked her what was the trouble. The young woman was lying across her double bed sobbing. "James caught Odelle and me in the cotton gin warehouse."

Carolyn wasn't quite sure what her daughter meant, so she sat on the bed and rubbed her daughter's back. "What does that mean that he caught you and Odelle together?"

The young woman turned and crawled into her mother's arms. ''James caught Odelle and me on top of a cotton bale."

Carolyn was shocked. "You can't be serious. After all I've told you about having any kind of relationship with a black man on our plantation." Carolyn lashed out and slapped her daughter across the face and the young woman buried her head in Carolyn's lap.

"How long has this been going on?"

"Not too long, maybe five months, but we've been in love since we were very young."

"Oh my god. When did you have your last period?"

"I don't know. I'm a little late."

"Your father is going to hang Odelle, and if he doesn't want to, I do."

Marsha Lee wasn't dumb. "What if I were to marry the young man from the sailing family and Odelle could stay here? No one need know."

"You may be with child. We can't take the risk that would ever get out. This is a closed society we live in. It has rules and it gets angry when its members violate those rules."

James walked back to the house and opened his father's office door, "May I talk to you dad?"

Jesse Sutter could see the serious expression on his son's face. Although he was tallying up this month's income and expenses, he put down his pencil and invited the young man to come in and sit down.

The color drained from the father's face as he heard his son relate the situation that James had come across. The senior Sutter couldn't believe his daughter defiled her heritage and actually lay down with a negro. As soon as his son finished, they heard a rap on the door to the study and he snarled, "come in."

The tears were still on her face as Carolyn Sutter joined her husband and son. She proceeded to tell them the rest of the story. "You mean she could be pregnant?" Jesse asked.

"I believe she may be. She's added some weight and her breasts are larger."

"I'm going to kill Odelle." Jesse Sutter snapped at the other two.

"I believe the punishment should be severe, but Marsha Lee and I grew up with Odelle. He was our playmate. You and mother treated him as though he were part of the family. I hate what he's done, but I don't know if I could hang him." James said.

Sutter was dejected and he needed to be by himself. "Is there anything else to add to this sordid situation?"

Mother and son shook their heads, no. "Since Odelle is coming here at ten tomorrow, let's call it a night and meet for breakfast at eight in the morning. We'll decide then what we'll do. James, I want you to get Thacker for me now. I want him to put Odelle in chains before that smart kid figures out a way to escape."

James did as he was told and within fifteen minutes, the overseer was sitting in the plantation's office facing Jesse Sutter. For a moment he was worried that he was in trouble. The owner was discreet. "Something has come to our attention that is very serious. I want Odelle Jones put in chains and locked up immediately. If he runs, I'll hold you responsible."

It finally dawned on Odelle the magnitude of his and Marsha Lee's actions and he knew they were going to hang him. After he left James, he went to the pond area and sat on one of the many logs circling the small swimming hole. He had to think. It wasn't only him. She wanted to do it as much as he did. In fact, lately she was initiating most of the rendezvous. He had to leave here as fast as he could. When he entered his wooden shack, his mother was just sitting down to eat. "Are you hungry Odelle, I have some nice stew ready for you"

She got up to get him a plate of food, but he grabbed her arm. "James caught us."

"What do you mean?"

"Marsha Lee and I were in the cotton gin warehouse and James came in and saw that we were on top of one of the bales." His mother's hands went to her face and she felt faint and had to sit down.

"What did James say to you?"

"He said he was going to tell his father and to be in his father's office at ten tomorrow morning. I don't know if they're going to hang me but I can't take a chance.

I'm leaving tonight. Can you get some food together for me? I've got to go."

Thacker was out of the chair immediately and through the door in search of Odelle Jones. He didn't know why the master had given the order, but he sure as hell wasn't going to ignore it. He found Odelle with his mother in her shack and the young man tried to evade Thacker and bolt through the door. The overseer was too quick and too strong and when he grabbed Odelle, he followed up with two blows to the young man's head and laid Odelle on the floor. Thacker fastened chains to Odelle's arms and legs. His adrenaline was working overtime. He reached down and picked up the young man and threw him over his shoulder. The mother screamed and got on her knees. "Please don't hang him. Please have mercy."

Odelle woke up as they were half way to one of the root cellars on the plantation. Thacker dropped him on the ground and got out his keys. "I don't know what you did, but I'm just following Mr. Sutter's orders."

Thacker put him in a root cellar used to store fruits and vegetables. He tied the chains to a sturdy pole in the center of the damp room, checked to be sure they were secure and set some apples aside for Odelle. He had no idea what this was all about and he didn't want to know. He went back to his cabin and fell asleep.

The morning breakfast was absent one of the family. Marsha Lee was restricted to her room until further notice. The three that sat down at the kitchen table were somber and talked very little. They knew that the help listened in on their conversations and they weren't ready to divulge what was going on to the entire state. They ate quickly and walked into Jesse Sutter's office. "I've thought about this all night; I hardly slept. Odelle will be sold to a plantation in the southern part of the state. I'll have Thacker take care of it. Only he and I will know where Odelle is, or at least where he's going initially. I really want to hang him but I know he's your friend James, so I won't exercise that option."

"Dad, I've thought about this all night. He's not going to last anywhere else. He's been treated like family here. Wherever he goes, he'll probably be a field hand and will rebel. I don't see him lasting anywhere else but here. Is there any way that he can be punished and remain here?"

"He violated our family. Even if he was white, I'd probably call him out for what he's done to my daughter. She's probably with child."

"We can't keep him. If she has his child, everyone here will know immediately that he's the father and soon our neighbors will know. He's got to go or be hanged, but I understand how you feel."

"I'll vote for either, though right now I'd like to hang him." Carolyn said.

"James finally agreed with his father that Odelle had to go and it was better that Marsha Lee didn't know where he went."

She didn't sleep that night but got up and sat in her rocking chair thinking about her lover and what her father would do. When she heard some noise out front,

Marsha Lee looked out her window toward the swimming pond. She saw their overseer bringing Odelle to the house. Her lover was in chains and could barely walk. From what she could see, he didn't appear to have been physically abused, but that could be deceiving. She came out of her room and from the upstairs balcony she saw Thacker drag Odelle into her father's office, just to the left of the front door. She didn't care if she was restricted to her room, she was going to see her father and plead for Odelle's life.

She burst into her father's office and saw Odelle standing in front of her father's desk. She went to her lover and threw her arms around him. "I'm just as much to blame as he. If you're going to hang Odelle, you might as well hang me. I don't want to live without him."

James grabbed his sister and pulled her away from Odelle and restrained her in the chair next to their mother. Carolyn put her arms around her daughter and held her tight. Jesse Sutter although near fifty was quick of mind. He turned to Thacker. "Don't you repeat anything you hear in this room or you'll answer to me."

Thacker knew immediately what this was all about and knew that his future was being decided at this moment. He looked at the master of Bridlewood. "I haven't heard anything and I won't hear anything. I'll honor your request."

Jesse Sutter turned to his daughter. "You might as well know what I'm going to do. Odelle is being sold to a plantation in the southern part of the state. They won't know why I'm selling him, but if he escapes and come back here, I'll hang him. Mr. Thacker will transport him to his new home this afternoon. Only he and I will know where he's being sent. If Odelle divulges anything about why we're sending him away, and I find out about it, I personally will kill him."

As Odelle was led away, Carolyn Sutter consoled her daughter and then took her back to her own room. "Will I ever see Odelle again?" She asked her mother.

"I think that chapter in your life has been written."

CHAPTER 3

He'd been given additional instructions before he left and he wasn't going to disappoint the owner. The ride to the southern part of Alabama took nearly four days. He removed the restraints from Odelle's legs but left the bracelets on his hands. At night he chained the young man to a tree. Thacker was most vulnerable when he took the irons off Odelle to relieve himself. Jesse had given him a handgun and told him in front of Odelle to use it if he had to.

Although the journey took longer than planned, Thacker and Odelle talked a lot on the trip. The young man said he had no animosity for anyone. He followed his heart and now he had to pay for it. Odelle was open about what happened and although Thacker didn't want to get involved, he was mesmerized by the tale that Odelle told. According to him, they'd been in love since their early years and although he was the aggressor initially, it was she who kept the fires burning inside them. They talked about going to New York City but the six hundred dollars she had in her personal possession wasn't enough. They thought about stealing three of her father's prized horses and selling them, but they didn't think they could pull it off.

Marsha Lee, according to Odelle, told him the only way they could continue their love affair was for her to marry and see Odelle on the side. She'd settled on a young man from a sailing family until they were caught by James.

When they reached Mobile, the overseer found a slave exchange/trading office and quickly made a deal. The two men shook hands and Odelle asked Thacker to tell everyone that he was sorry and that he loved Marsha Lee and always would. Thacker spent the night in downtown Mobile, had a few drinks and hooked up with a woman. He accomplished what he wanted and started home the next day. He didn't get much for Odelle because his master told him not to bargain. When he got back home, Sutter asked him if everything went okay. Thacker said it did and neither man ever talked about it again.

For the first month after Odelle was sent away, Marsha Lee remained in her room, ate very little and refused to converse with her father and brother. Finally, Carolyn was able to talk some sense into her and she started eating. There was no doubt she was with child and the closest that Carolyn could surmise was that there would be a birth in two months. When the event occurred, there was very little fanfare and only one black woman attended her. A baby boy was born and to everyone's surprise, he was white. The only distinguishing features that could set him apart from another white baby boy was his kinky black hair, his wide nose and his dark eyes.

Marsha Lee was quite sick from the ordeal of childbirth and one of the house slaves who'd recently lost her baby, nursed the child. Jesse and Carolyn came to the conclusion that the little boy had to be raised a slave and they made arrangements to have the child taken to their slave quarters. In retrospect they should have sent the child to another plantation.

The same black girl who nursed Marsha Lee's baby was the one the Sutters decided should raise the child. The Sutters delivered the young boy to the woman within two months after Marsha Lee gave birth. There was no doubt among the African population that this was a half white child and Marsha Lee was its mother. In addition, everyone knew that Odelle Jones was the father. Having half breeds on a plantation wasn't unusual, because most plantation masters and or their sons treated all female slaves as their personal property. But having blacks' mate with white females was unusual. It was nearly two years before Marsha Lee came out of her depression. Jesse Sutter tried to marry her off to several sons of the elite who were in need of a substantial dowry, but she wasn't interested.

It was nearly four years since the birth and Marsha Lee was becoming a spinster. If she didn't accept a mate soon, she could kiss away her chances of a suitable marriage. Her mother impressed that point on her until Marsha Lee turned the other way whenever she saw her mother approach. During the four years since she gave birth to a boy, she never raised the issue of her son and where he might be. That all changed one day. She was walking past the pond and nearing the slave quarters when she saw a white boy throwing rocks into the pond similar to what she used to do with James and Odelle.

The young boy seemed shy and started to run off as she approached. She stopped and put her hand to her mouth. It had to be her child. She knew they gave it away, but it never dawned on her that the baby was still on the plantation. The little boy went into one of the shacks and Marsha Lee followed him inside. She'd never been in the slave quarters and the smell appalled her at first; then the utter poverty made it worse. There was a woman and a man sitting on a crate inside. Both were very dark

Negroes. A makeshift bed made entirely of straw was up against one wall and a table with a couple of pots was on another. There was no interior plumbing of any kind, only a small stove to keep out the cold. "Whose child is this?" Marsha Lee asked the woman.

"He's my boy Miss Marsha."

"But he's white, he can't be yours?"

"I nursed him from birth. He's mine."

"What's his name?"

"Joshua Jones."

The three looked at each other for some time before Marsha Lee left and went up to the mansion to talk to her father. He was, as usual, in his study going over reports. He looked up as she walked in without knocking. "Is that white boy that the slave Henrietta has, mine?"

"As far as I'm concerned it's hers." her father countered.

"We'll see about that. He's mine and you know it. I want him brought up here. I'm not going to have my child living in filth."

"He stays with his slave mother."

Marsha Lee went to the slave quarters, picked up the white child and walked back to the mansion. The baby was crying and trying to get out of Marsha Lee's arms. The woman and male who'd been in charge of her son trailed after her; the woman was crying and the male was begging for the return of the child. Marsha Lee's mother met her at the front door and ordered her daughter to give the child back. "He's my child and I'm going to keep him, even if you force us to live in the slave quarters."

She marched up the stairs with the child on her hip and ordered the maid who was cleaning that floor to prepare a bath for her child. The maid stood motionless until Marsha Lee yelled at her. "You better get moving or I'll take the whip to you."

Over the next week Marsha Lee and Joshua kept to themselves, ate in her bedroom and when they left the room, Marsha Lee was always with the boy. The adjoining room that Marsha Lee used as a changing room was made over into a little boy's bedroom. Her mother and father were stunned. They decided to give it a week and see if their daughter got bored and allowed the child to return to the slave quarters. James tried to talk to his sister but she wouldn't listen. In fact, any discussion resulted in his sister going into a rage. Occasionally, she'd wield a knife and the others stayed out of her way.

It wasn't that her parents gave in, they exhausted every option they could think of without any resolution. They brought in their minister, their doctor and an outside psychologist who pronounced Marsha Lee sane. Soon the young boy had the run of the house and attended meals with the family. Marsha Lee was in charge and it was as though she was exacting a form of revenge on her parents. The young man's skin was white, his hair was kinky, his nose wide and his eyes dark. He had all the facial features of a Negro, except his skin was white. Marsha Lee brought in tutors to school the young lad and soon

Carolyn and Jesse were praising him at every turn. They hadn't named him, so they continued with the name the black couple gave him, Joshua Jones.

When Joshua was ten years old his grandmother Carolyn Sutter died after a long illness. Although mother and daughter clashed over Marsha Lee's determination to keep her son, the mother was her strength and confidant and treated Joshua as though he were her grandson. Jesse Sutter was devastated and was a recluse and James became the master of Bridlewood. With her mother dead and her father suffering from that loss, Marsha Lee became more erratic and at times dangerous. There were times that James had to restrain her and send for the doctor to medicate her. As the dosage was increased, she had very little interaction with the family and Joshua was lost; he looked to James for direction. At the same time, James felt the responsibility of the plantation falling on his young shoulders and didn't have time for courting; he never got around to marrying. Joshua looked to him as his father and James spent more time with the boy treating him as his son.

As Marsha Lee became more ill, Joshua continued to spend more time with James. He maintained his studies with the tutor but sought James' approval rather than Marsha Lee's. James taught Joshua all the things his father taught him. They spent time riding and hunting; a bond developed between the two that would never be broken. Joshua was being groomed to be the next Master of Bridlewood.

One day James was on his way back from the slave quarters and as he was passing the pond where he and his sister swam with Odelle, he saw something floating in the water and stopped to investigate. Before he fished out the object, he knew it was his sister. He knelt down alongside her and cried. What a beautiful person she was before the Odelle affair. He loved his sister and was sorry for anything he did that brought her to this end. Joshua was devastated and looked to his uncle entirely for support. Although Jesse was still alive, it was James who was Master of Bridlewood and the father Joshua needed.

Young Sutter was a good administrator and Bridlewood flourished under his guidance. But the prospect of an oncoming war, his father's failing health and what to do with the plantation if he had to go to war, distracted him.

Surprisingly, Jesse and Joshua became very close. Joshua needed parenting since his mother became ill and died. Jesse was coming out of his shell and had to have something to do. The two became a comfort to each other. Jesse became a proud grandfather and looked forward to his talks with his grandson. The two went hunting or fishing at least three days a week. James was so happy to see that something had breathed a new vigor into Jesse that he transferred some of the management to him, who though aging could still give some needed advice and alleviate some of James' concerns.

As the prospect of war between the states escalated, James saw it as his duty to join the southern cause. He was commissioned a Captain with his own detachment of Alabama reserves. Joshua was fourteen and wanted to join the reserves and serve with James. His uncle couldn't tell him why that wasn't possible so he used the rational that Joshua had to help his grandfather run the plantation while James was away.

Thacker was a big help, but that's what he was, the help. James could not emotionally lean on the man; he sought his father's guidance. Although Jesse was lucid and willing, he could only handle so much. James, with his father's permission, decided to sell Bridlewood. He just couldn't handle everything that was on his plate. He bought a small thirty-acre farm nearby, transported a few of the slaves there and moved his father onto the farm with Joshua. The remaining slaves were sold at a premier price. He bought some cattle and decided to grow corn and other vegetables.

Because James intended to keep the farm after the war, he set up a burial site for the family on a remote section of the property. He directed Thacker to have Carolyn and Marsha Lee's remains excavated and brought to the farm. Jesse was content, had plenty of help and with Joshua's and Thacker's help, he could handle the management of the farm.

There was still one thing that needed to be corrected before James went off to war. He knew his father had done the proper thing by removing Odelle from Bridlewood. But this was his childhood friend, his sister's lover and Joshua's father. He wanted to make things right, even if society wouldn't forgive him. Prior to the move, James had a heart-to-heart talk with his overseer. "I know that only you and my father know where Odelle was taken. I want you to return to that site and bring Odelle here. It's only fitting that he finishes his days with us."

"If I don't tell you, will I still have a place on the new farm?"

"It depends on how you get along with Joshua. He's going to inherit everything and he'll have enough money to run this place long after the war is over. You'll be working for Joshua."

"I get along fine with him and have no problem if he's the owner. I know who his mother and father are. My main concern, at my age, is to have a place where I can be of some use and my employers respect me. To show my good faith, I took Odelle to a plantation outside Mobile. I can find the place but I don't know if he's still there. I also don't know if they are willing to sell him back or what they'll want for him."

James gave Thacker $200.00 and told him to bring back Odelle. "If you need more to obtain Odelle, tell them you'll sign a note for the difference and I'll send it to them soon after you return. Don't forget to get an address."

James was a pragmatist. He knew that the war was inevitable and could not be won by the south. The proceeds from the sale of the plantation were placed in a bank in Philadelphia. Money would be sent to Jesse on a quarterly basis. Within a year, Joshua took over the day-to-day operation of the farm but still relied on his grandfather for the major decisions. He was sixteen years old as the war went into its second year. Soon it was Joshua who was receiving the money from the northern bank and depositing some of the money into a local bank to pay the expenses of the farm. Actually, he deposited just enough money in the southern bank for timely expenses and kept the rest under his mattress in case the war came to the south. Joshua was astute and with his uncle and grandfather's guidance, the farm was showing a profit growing vegetables and raising cattle. Soon dementia took Jesse to another world. He never returned.

One month after he left to find Odelle, the overseer returned with a middle-aged man, who though in apparent good health was very quiet and subdued. It took him several months before he could openly talk about his experience. He didn't recognize Joshua, especially since the boy appeared to be white, but accepted him as his son. Joshua had been told of his heritage and that Odelle was his father, but he looked to James as being that person and would always do so. He was kind to Odelle but kept him at arm's length. Odelle was more like an elderly uncle. Besides, Joshua saw himself as white; he could not accept the fact that Odelle could be his father.

James came home every six months to check on his father and nephew. Joshua was growing into a fine lad but he still had some of Odelle's facial features. Some people looked at him longer than usual but none challenged his authority when it came to the farm. It was in the last year of the war when James came home for good; he'd lost a leg and had multiple wounds that required daily attention. It was Joshua and Odelle who attended to James. The two older men, one the biological father and the other the natural father started to talk and reminisce about their younger days. They didn't talk about Marsha Lee but Odelle made sure there were always fresh flowers on her grave.

James knew he was dying and decided to adopt Joshua as his son. He talked to Odelle and told him that he loved Joshua as though he was his son and wanted to adopt him. "It really is best for him and everyone's future."

After Odelle gave his blessing, James petitioned the local court and with Joshua's concurrence the adoption was accepted by the local magistrate and Joshua Jones became Franklin Sutter. It took a few months before Joshua could accept his new name and especially his status.

When James died of gangrene from the amputated leg, Franklin cried and would visit his grave on a daily basis. Prior to his death, James made Franklin promise that he'd take care of Jesse, Thacker and Odelle. In addition, James continued the quarterly payments from the northern bank but designated Franklin as the beneficiary upon his death. The young man soon would be rich.

Jesse died as the northern army was at the front gate; it wasn't from anything in particular. It was just his time. The slaves ran off fearing all the stories of horrors that had been circulating about the Yankees. But Franklin, Odelle and Thacker remained and were able to tend to the cattle, but they couldn't control the endless theft of their stock by desperate people. Some of the people were their neighbors and they were hungry. James and then Jesse were buried on the farm in the family plot next to Marsha Lee and Carolyn. Very few attended; most friends or acquaintances had moved on ahead of the advancing Union Army. Franklin choked up when he thought about his mother, grandfather and James who were buried side by side.

Odelle and Thacker were apprehensive when they looked to a seventeen-year-old half white young man for guidance and support. Their future rested in his hands. Franklin was more mature than they expected. He replaced the stolen cattle and sold the vegetable crop at a profit. He improved some of the buildings and met his tax bill when the carpet baggers tried to steal most of the properties in the area from the destitute southerners.

Thacker was extremely helpful when buyers or sellers objected to negotiating with a seventeen-year-old. The older man was grateful that he had a home. He was always at Franklin's side if there was a problem. For that Franklin would always be grateful. Thacker took over for James and helped bring Franklin into manhood. During this period of time Franklin tried to raise Odelle's self-esteem by asking his advice on various matters and putting him in charge of the cattle operation. His father was making progress but it would be slow. Once Odelle asked about Marsha Lee and he cried when Franklin told him what she was like and how she died.

Franklin went to see his childhood home and took his father with him; however, Bridlewood was nearly destroyed. The mansion that he grew up in was burned to the ground and most of the other buildings were ravaged. Franklin thought about the foresight that James had in selling the plantation at the peak of the market, thereby leaving him with an inheritance that few whites would have as the war concluded. Up until this time, Odelle had been stoic, but today he shed real tears. Franklin gave him space, especially when his father went inside the nearly destroyed Cotton Gin building. When Odelle was finished, they left Bridlewood for the last time.

CHAPTER 4

It was the spring of 1865; Grant and Lee were facing off in a prolonged trench impasse near the Confederate Capitol of Richmond. Sheridan was pursuing another Confederate Army up the Shenandoah Valley at the same time. The south was short on money, ammunition and manpower. The Presidential Election between Lincoln and McClelland was in doubt. Many were conceding the election to McClelland, the democratic candidate.

Lincoln knew the polls showed him way behind and the only thing that could save his administration was an overwhelming victory over the confederacy. Jefferson Davis, the President of the Confederacy, was firm in his conviction that there had to be two countries while Lincoln steadfastly would not consider such a solution, even though many in his party wanted a negotiated settlement. If he considered the two-country solution, he'd in fact allow the south to win the conflict. The north was winning the war, why give into the south and the slave traders?

Washington was an embattled city with the streets covered with mud, animal feces and even dead bodies. Those in DC felt vulnerable. There was a great fear that the south would mount an attack and the government would have to flee. Many in Lincoln's own party were undermining the president. Some of his cabinet held secret meetings to try to gain support for impeachment. The dichotomy was that while the elite in the Union Capitol were fearful of its survival, they were trying to force its leader to make concessions. In addition, the same people were having numerous balls and large events. The elite were dancing as much as they could, while men were dying.

In another part of the country, thunder erupted and flashes of lightning illuminated the water filled sky; a bolt of lightning hit somewhere on Hickory Hills Plantation. It wasn't just rain, it was a deluge and the roof of the shanty William Todd called home leaked like a sieve. Water covered the dirt floor and the wind driving the storm played a dark melody as it whistled through every part of the partially wood framed shack.

The slaves could see fire south of them, probably caused by lightning striking some rotten building. He was tired, but it was the pain that kept him awake. William was bleeding from the lashes to his back and especially his hands as he tried to defend himself from the rage of the overseer, Augustus Swanson. Over twenty-five slaves were forced to watch the flogging as though it were a funeral. As soon as Swanson left to get something to drink, two of the male slaves lifted William out of the mud and placed him on a makeshift bed while one of the black women placed a blanket over the beaten man, who was shivering in spite of the summer heat and humidity.

But Swanson hadn't got his fill; he returned with a rage and when he saw the young slave lying on his bed, he went berserk. It was as though he was blaming William for everything that went wrong, including the storm. "Where'd he goes?" Swanson yelled out as he brought his whip down on the slave's legs continuously.

William tried to defend himself but that made Swanson continue the assault until he couldn't lift the whip anymore. It was as though Swanson was the victim as he staggered out of the shack and made his way to the overseer's house.

When some of the female slaves were sure that Swanson was finished with the brutality, they slipped back into the shanty and gave William some water and washed his wounds. Bass Blake had escaped and Swanson was blaming William for aiding him.

The overseer was one of cruelest of his lot in the state of Alabama. Hickory Hills Plantation in the eastern part of the state, a five-hundred-acre estate that employed Swanson had a high percentage of runaways. It was an acute problem, such that Frank Wilcox, the owner, threatened to fire Swanson if any more slaves escaped. In retrospect, if Wilcox had fired Swanson and replaced him with a more reasonable overseer, the plantation would've been more productive and fewer slaves would've escaped.

Bass had been the first in the last thirteen months to make the attempt. He'd been planning his escape for a year. It was only recently that he confided in William and asked for his help. William begged him to wait until the end of the war, which was fast approaching. But the desire for freedom was overwhelming and was the main factor motivating him.

"It's inevitable. Look at the number of casualties the south is incurring, let alone that it's too dangerous for a slave to make his way out of the south. There is no place to go and no one to help. Besides, Swanson would be unrelenting in his pursuit. He would unleash the dogs and if they didn't kill you, he would."

"I can't wait any longer and Swanson better pray that he doesn't catch up with me."

The number of dogs a plantation kept chained up would be the main impediment for any slave to overcome. William thought long and hard before he agreed to help his friend. Those who tried to escape were shot when they were recaptured; those who assisted in any way would get a severe beating, reduced rations and extra work.

There was no moon the night Bass escaped; the skies were overcast and rain was certainly on the way. There would be no shelter from the elements, no food to sustain him and nobody that he could trust. He'd be on his own. Even his relatives would turn their back on a runaway slave; others would turn him over to the authorities if they had a chance, especially if there was a reward.

However, the grapevine communication system which passed information from plantation to plantation faster than white slave owners could comprehend, told Bass where the Union Army Lines were. If he could make it to the union lines, he'd be free. Of course, he might have to enlist in the Union Army and fight for the north but that paled in comparison to the degradation he experienced as a plantation slave. The grapevine also said the war was almost over and for everyone to play it safe. The ugly truth couldn't be hidden from them any longer. Their masters and their master's sons were coming home injured or as causalities.

The better educated or skilled the slave was, the better his or her chances to escape were. Bass Blake was an accomplished horseman, accurate with a firearm and wasn't afraid to speak his mind. In order to control him, his master Frank Wilcox wouldn't allow anyone to teach him to read or write. Little did the master know that Effie the housekeeper was not only Bass' lover but also his teacher. By the time Bass left, he could read the printed ads the plantations circulated throughout the area identifying runaway slaves.

There was little doubt in his mind that he'd try to escape. The only bit of reluctance he suffered was what would happen to William when they found out he was gone. Swanson knew the two were friendly and Bass was sure the overseer would take his anger out on the young slave. He wouldn't kill him nor maim him; William repaired all the shoes on the plantation, making him a valuable commodity, but Swanson would make him wish he didn't help. Somehow, someday Bass would make it well with his friend.

CHAPTER 5

Blake had been at Hickory Hills since his teens and worked his way up from cleaning horse stalls to the trainer of some of the finest thoroughbreds in the South. His owner taught him to ride and subsequently train the plantation's horses. He gradually became well versed in the gentlemanly art of horse racing. Under his tutelage, at least two of their stock consistently won at racing events throughout the state. Because of his skill, Bass would travel with his owner to the other plantations hosting a racing meet. He met some of his slave counterparts and learned where the law was located in those locations. This was important information for someone who'd been planning his escape for two years.

Because he had an important, though non-paying position on the plantation, he came across things that the average slave wouldn't be privy to. One day he was preparing a horse for a race seventy miles away in a small town on Alabama's northern border. His owner was watching the workout with Bass while fussing with some papers that he left on a wine barrel when he went to relieve himself.

When Bass was sure he had a few minutes to spare, he walked over to the barrel and unfolded a map showing the slave states and Oklahoma. It looked like some kind of Army map. He knew his master was wounded in the war and had been furloughed from active duty; he probably brought the map home with him. Whatever the case, it listed the main roads and principal cities in the southern states. His time was limited, so he memorized about six cities and three main roads in

Tennessee because it neighbored Alabama and Arkansas. Lucky for him, he was able to get back to his horse before the master returned, picked up the map and stuffed it in his pocket.

The grapevine said Oklahoma was the place to go if you could reach it, but it didn't recommend a route. It was a free territory and closer than going by the underground railroad to New York. He knew he had a small head start but heard the dogs that were chasing him as he entered the low land. Soon, he came upon a large marsh area which had been flooded from the recent heavy rains. He knew he could hide in there for a short time because the dogs would lose his scent, once he was in the water.

Gus Swanson sent messengers to most of the plantations in the area letting them know of the runaway slave. Next, he retrieved some clothing from Blake's room and threw it in the compound holding ten dogs. When he unleashed half of them, they immediately headed for the cotton field in the northern part of the plantation. The other half were leashed and held by one of the white overseers, Joe Cooper. Each carried a twelve gauge shot gun. Swanson suspected that Bass would head to the nearest marsh and try to hide inside that area for at least a day. He knew every inch of that land and was confident that he would catch the escaped slave. As an added incentive, he promised Joe Cooper, twenty dollars when they caught Bass.

The only weapon Bass had was an old six inch kitchen knife that he hid in one of the cotton fields. He retrieved it on his way out but didn't know if it would be of any use. He was bound and determined not to be taken alive. If he had to kill, he would. He reached what he considered the midpoint of the marsh and climbed a Sycamore tree, then hid in the foliage and listened for the dogs.

Swanson and Cooper arrived at the marsh about an hour after Bass entered the wetlands. The hounds found where the runaway slave entered but the area was too big to search. Swanson tried to encourage the dogs to continue into the water covered marshland, but most refused. However, two waded into the middle of the marsh, but Swanson lost sight of them within ten minutes. Cooper put a leash on the remainder and started around the wet area, hoping that he'd flush Bass out of his hiding place. Bass could hear the hounds that Cooper was tending but he didn't see them. One thing was for sure; their barking gave him a good indication where they were.

Thirty minutes later one of the dogs swam up to the tree Bass was hiding in and started barking. How that animal found him was a miracle. The question was, how was he going to handle it? It wouldn't take Swanson or whoever was with him much time to realize the hound had Bass cornered. He pulled some large pieces of bark off the tree and threw it at the animal several times. When he thought he had the animal confused, he dropped down on top of it and slit its throat. The dog cried out and then slowly slipped under the water line, leaving a visible crimson ring.

Quietly, Bass exited the marshland and continued on his way west toward Arkansas. He heard sporadic barking in the distance but it didn't appear the hounds were gaining on him. He was wet, hungry and tired; he didn't know where he was going to sleep tonight, let alone find some food. Traveling at night had its benefits. Other than a stray dog, there was little to alert anyone that he was in the vicinity. Nighttime would be a good time to steal food and clothing.

One of the houses on the outskirts of the village left their laundry to dry on a clothes line. Although they were woman's clothes, he took them anyway. He spied an apple tree in the yard and picked six and what he didn't eat he put in his pocket. It was near dawn when he found a place in a meadow between some high shrubs and lay down to sleep. He changed into the woman's dress and tied his shirt and pants around his waist.

Augustus Swanson was not someone who'd give up on a runaway slave. He and Joe Cooper walked around the marshland until the hounds found the spot where Bass exited the water and made his way west. It was three hours later when Swanson and Cooper entered a village and listened to a woman tell her neighbor someone had taken her clothes off the line. Gus was tired but he snarled, "Gotcha."

Being a slave, Bass was used to coming awake in the middle of the night. He didn't know how long he slept, but he distinctly heard the hounds and knew he was in trouble. It took him a few seconds to get his bearings and realize he was wearing women's clothing, but off he went as quick as he could with his original change of clothes tied around his waist. As he went deeper into the brush, he could hear a roar up ahead and loud barking behind him. He guessed the overseer had freed the dogs from their leashes and they'd soon be on him. He didn't know how close they were but he ran for his life.

Soon, he came upon a creek that had swelled to its banks from the heavy rain and was flowing quickly. Just then Cooper fired his shotgun at him. It missed but Blake braced himself for a round from Swanson's shotgun. He felt something go by his left ear as he dove into the rushing creek. The flowing water pulled him down as it rushed forward. He wasn't sure but he thought they fired at him again. He tried to surface but some debris was tangled in his dress and holding him down. With all his remaining strength, he tore the dress, kicked out and broke water long enough to fill his lungs before the raging stream pulled him back down.

He banged up against several large rocks and the remnants of his dress caught on debris that was flowing his way. He was able to surface long enough to breathe two or three times. He didn't know how long he'd been in the water but he pulled himself up on the far bank and lay down on the wet ground. The dress he had on was torn to shreds, so he took off what was left. Although they were wet, he put on his pants and shirt and started to move on. As he looked back across the creek, he was fired on by Cooper and Swanson and he dove for cover. Two more shots rang out and dirt splattered around him. He got up and ran away from the creek. Cooper and Swanson couldn't cross the creek. It was too high and too treacherous. "I'm going to catch you and then I'm going to hang you." Swanson shouted after him.

The last volley from Swanson's shotgun made the adrenaline run through his veins. Over the next day, he was careful to avoid the main roads and cities by utilizing back roads as much as possible. In order to run a large farm or plantation with slaves, some had to be allowed access to town. Not all the chores could be done by the white managers. Bass had been on the run for nearly a week, stealing food from wherever he could and sleeping far from any of the main or secondary roads. Today he spotted a wagon being driven by a black male with a black female sitting alongside him.

He was cautious as he approached the wagon, looking in all directions to be sure there were no white persons in the area. The wagon was coming toward him as he signaled that he wanted to talk. He was mildly surprised that the driver stopped. Bass acknowledged the woman and asked if they could give directions toward Arkansas. "Are you a runaway? The woman asked.

"What makes you ask that question?"

"We've seen most of the slaves in this area and you don't remind us of anyone we know."

"I haven't eaten in the past day. I wonder if you have some food to spare?"

They looked down on him as though trying to assess his intentions and at the same time wondering if they'd be punished if they were caught talking to him. "We have some apples in the baskets in the back. You can take a few if that'll help."

He walked to the rear and reached in the back of the wagon and took what his hands could carry. "If I was a runaway, would there be any help around here for me?"

"We don't know of any. Just to let you know, there's an ad in the newspaper giving a reward for your capture. Your main concern is the many slave catchers in the area; most have at least one bloodhound. They catch a lot of runaways." The woman said.

"There're many forests and woodlands in Western Alabama. Once you reach that area, it'll be easier to evade capture. We have to go; we can't help you; be careful who you talk to." The black male said.

The two rode off and didn't look back. Bass understood their reluctance and moved away from the dirt road and hid in the deep growth. He was moving entirely at night and using the daytime to catch up on some sleep and plan his next move. The problem was that he was most vulnerable during the daytime, especially if he slept.

His assumption was that Swanson had given up and taken the hounds back to the plantation. Bass guessed that the newspapers and slave catchers would be his prime concern. He had a knife, but if he could get a gun, his chances of escaping would increase dramatically. He finished an apple before he lay down to sleep and ate another before he started his nightly trek.

As he made his way west using the North Star to guide him, he heard dogs in the vicinity and tried to steer clear of them, but they seemed to be coming in his direction. He quickened his pace but the sounds were becoming louder; he started to run. All he could think about was Augustus Swanson and his dogs. Even though it was sure death if he was captured, he favored that over being eaten alive by vicious hounds.

There were many trees in the medium sized forest he entered, with a few large sycamores. He decided to climb one of the larger ones and take his chances. The barking was getting closer and he could hear male voices urging them on. He tried to make himself as inconspicuous as possible by using the leaves in the tree to hide him. Soon he heard someone running and thought he saw a man run under his tree and continue in a southerly direction.

Before he knew it, four hounds were running past his tree followed by four men with lighted flares. They were screaming, "stop" as they ran past his position. Subsequently, whoever was running had taken to the trees and the bloodhounds had him treed. Several shots were fired and Bass could hear a man pleading for his life. Two more shots were fired and a man screamed out and someone yelled, "shut up" and the dogs went quiet.

Although he was fifty or sixty yards from the scene, he could hear some of the dialog. It became apparent that a slave had been shot and probably killed by four men with bloodhounds. "What are we going to do with the body?" He heard the men talk among themselves. He couldn't determine who was talking.

A deep voice said. "I'll bring back a wagon. We'll throw him in the bog."

"I need to get the dogs back to the plantation. Mr. Adams said we could use them to hunt the slave but to bring them right back after we caught him." Another of the men said.

"How are we going to split the reward?"

"Four ways is okay by me."

"We need to leave someone here to guard the body, in case some of the blacks come and move him."

Three men with their hounds walked back the way they came, leaving one man to guard the dead slave. When they passed under his tree, the dogs stopped, looked up and started barking. One of the handlers yelled at them and used the whip to keep the dogs moving forward. The sweat ran down Bass' face and a shiver went up his spine as he watched them walk away.

He knew this was an opportunity to get a gun and he wasn't going to be denied. The distance between he and the man guarding the body of the slave was far enough that any casual movement of the branches as he descended to the ground wouldn't raise an alarm. He took his time moving from tree to tree toward where he heard the gun shot. He was twenty feet away before he saw someone sitting on the ground leaning against a tree with a rifle over his knees. Bass was a good sized man for the times, standing nearly six feet two inches tall and weighing one hundred eighty pounds. But what was remarkable about him was the lightness of his movement. He'd been chastised by his owner on two occasions for sneaking up on him. He didn't try to surprise his master; it was just the way he moved.

He could hear the man with the gun humming to himself as Bass crept closer. When Bass was sure he could surprise the fellow holding the gun, he moved quickly and sprang at his adversary knocking the rifle from his hands. The man yelled out in surprise and started to get up but he didn't have a chance. Bass was too strong and quickly delivered two damaging blows, one to the neck and the other to the temple and the man lay lifeless on the ground. Bass checked for a pulse; there was none.

He found some change in the man's pockets and a small handgun tucked in his belt. He removed the ammunition from around the deceased's neck, and picked up the rifle. Intuitively, he knew there'd be an additional bounty on his head because he killed a white man and more slave catchers would be out trying to win the larger reward. But he was starting to feel more comfortable with his chances to make it to Oklahoma. He rested a few moments, gathered his thoughts and walked away.

Two men minus the dogs came back in a one horse wagon and drove up to the spot where they left the man to guard the dead slave. When they found their friend dead on the ground and his weapons missing, they jumped out of the wagon, spread out and each walked about one hundred yards in a different direction away from their dead companion. Within a half hour they met back at the scene. "You know those hounds were looking up in that tree back there and barking and we ignored it. Someone could have been hiding in that tree. I think I remember which tree it was." The older of the two said.

They walked back to the tree and the younger of the two climbed up the tree. The other man handed him a lighted flare. "There are several small twigs that are broken up here. Someone must have heard what happened and after we left, attacked Jeb and killed him." The man crawled down from his perch and dusted himself off.

"There was an ad about a fugitive slave from West Alabama that went missing about ten days ago. If he was in good shape, he could've made it this far and now he's armed. We better notify the sheriff and that plantation from where he escaped. Jeb's father and his brothers are going to be angry as hell when we tell them what happened. They've got a couple of dogs and may want to go after the fellow who did this. I pity him when they find him.

The two picked up the slave and their friend and started back. They dropped the slave in the bog nearby and the lifeless man sunk into the mire. When they delivered the body of their friend to his parents, the mother howled and the father screamed at the two. "What happened?"

The two had a difficult time telling the slain man's parents what happened because the father and his other two sons kept interrupting them. At one point they feared for their lives. It was midnight and they wanted to go home. The father of the slain man insisted they at least go back to where his son was killed; reluctantly they went with him. The ground was soft and although it was nearly two in the morning, they used flares and were able to find footprints of a solitary individual heading northwest. They went back to their home to get supplies. It was going to be a long night.

CHAPTER 6

The Pendrake clan, headed by Benjamin Pendrake, owned a thirty acre scrub farm in North Central Alabama that paled in comparison to the many well-groomed plantations in the area. As such, they and their clan were looked down upon by the more elite plantations owners as pure white trash. However, they were considered useful when it came to tasks that others didn't want to do. Their main source of income was catching slaves. Yet, Ben along with his sons Rufus, Jed and Clyde and six bloodhounds were considered to be nothing but thugs by the general populace. They were big, sloppy and illiterate. Everyone tried to give them enough space. If you had a disagreement with one of the Pendrakes, their entire family was at odds with you. But, when it came to chasing down runaway slaves or wanted criminals, they were the first to be called.

This latest incident where their son Jed was killed impacted the close knit family hard. Ben didn't show any emotion; all that was needed was produced by his wife, Amy. Since their expertise was in tracking down slaves, it didn't take them long to gather enough supplies for three days and be on their way. Bass was unaware of what was happening at the location he left. His plan was to travel at night and sleep during the daytime. The Pendrakes would be coming day and night. They had a special incentive to catch this slave.

It was late when Bass decided to stop and catch some sleep. He wasn't sure what the total reaction would be when the dead man was found. He expected the sheriff and local deputies had been alerted and would be out patrolling their districts. He didn't feel bad about killing the man, for he was one of four that killed the slave. After a restless three hours of rest, Bass was alert. Something wasn't right, but he wasn't sure what it was. Since he was near the Tennessee River, he decided to follow its path until it meandered north.

The Pendrakes knew the area quite well and since they had been involved in at least six captures of runaway slaves, they went about their pursuit in a businesslike manner. They used the time that Bass was asleep to make up a lot of the distance lost initially. When Bass heard the hounds, his instincts kicked in and he was alert; the bloodhounds were tracking him. He stayed close to the river with the intent of jumping in if the dogs caught up with him, which he knew would eventually happen. Carrying the rifle was slowing him down, but he needed it for protection.

Three shots rang out and the dogs started barking; it was as though men and hounds were right behind him. He didn't look back but took a zigzag route to the river and dived in. Two more shots went over his head as he went under water and tried to swim away from the threat. The current was carrying him downstream. But every time he raised his head above water, he saw one or two men with their dogs running parallel to the river. His only recourse was to stay in the water. A hundred yards later he caught a break. It was as though the river split into two sections. He was to learn later that the river went around both sides of a sandbar. Bass took the easterly current and momentarily was out of sight of his pursuers.

His main threat was the bloodhounds. If he could neutralize them, he'd have a chance against the slave catchers. The split in the river lasted about a half mile. Bass exited the river about two hundred yards before the two forks rejoined. There was a grove of trees to his east with some outcropping of rocks. He made his way up a small hill and settled behind some rocks. He cleaned his rifle and revolver and checked his supply of ammunition. He had enough for about four shots. He knew they'd release the bloodhounds when they were near a crossable part of the river and he'd have about time for two shots. He'd have to make that work.

He set his revolver on the rock in front of him and raised his rifle as though he was waiting for an attack. Fifteen minutes later, the two hounds came at him in tandem. He waited until they were within twenty yards and shot the hound on the right. Immediately, he dropped his rifle and had his right hand on the revolver when he was hit in the chest with a fury he'd never experienced. He kept his composure as he fell over backwards while the hound's momentum carried it about ten feet away. While on his knees, Bass turned and shot the animal in the head and it fell over dead at his knees. He'd been in this position before. Only, the other time it was a bear and again it took two shots.

Time was of the essence. He reloaded the rifle and revolver and put the smaller weapon in his belt. The owners of the dogs would soon be here and they were armed. There was also the possibility that people in the area would join the hunt. This was slave country; there would be no sympathy for his cause. It was dangerous to wait, but he needed a few minutes to gather himself, before moving on.

When the Pendrakes came upon their two dead bloodhounds, they were livid. The father shouted obscenities while one of his sons broke down and cried. The boys raised the hounds from pups and considered them part of the family. The father wanted to move on but acceded to his sons' wishes and buried the two bloodhounds.

Without their tracking animals, they were at a disadvantage, but Ben was adamant; their family pride was at stake. As soon as the hounds were buried, they were on their way. Their tracking expertise was limited. Although they could tell which direction Blake initially took, they were unable to determine which trail he selected next. Soon they were out of their element and unable to have any degree of certainty that there were following their prey. After a half day of wandering around without direction, they decided to go home.

The fleeing slave was exhausted but unwilling to stop, even though it was daylight. He paralleled the river south for a mile before he found a place where the river narrowed. Although it was still flowing above the bank, he was able to swim twenty yards, grab some branches that were hanging low in the water and pull himself ashore. Blake was tired and hoped that those who were running the bloodhounds would stop for a bit before pursuing the chase. He estimated he was still in Alabama, as he continued west.

His pace was limited by the denseness of the shrubs and trees. Though he continued west throughout the night, he didn't feel that he put much distance between himself and those pursuing him. When dawn came, he found a thicket of scrub shrub around a vegetable patch and lay down. He knew he shouldn't but he closed his eyes to rest and fell into a sound sleep. He thought it was hunger that awoke him and not the two voices that seemed to be nearby He tried to listen but he couldn't make out what they said. Soon they moved away; he didn't know whether they were white or black.

No one seemed to be around so he grabbed a couple of tomatoes and checked his surroundings. It appeared that he was on a small farm. He could see a house, several corrals with a few head of cattle inside and a small two story hay barn. He crawled close to the barn and still didn't see anyone so he became bolder and entered the barn. He climbed a ladder and crawled behind about ten bales of hay, cocked his rifle and lay down.

Thacker and Franklin watched the Negro from their kitchen window and wondered what he wanted. "He looks like a runaway. What do you want to do?" Thacker asked.

"We could use some help if he's not a fugitive."

Thacker shrugged. "Why don't I wait an hour to see what he's going to do and then sneak up on him? He may be asleep. I'll bring him to you and we can then decide what we want to do."

"Take my father with you. If the wakes up before you grab him, my dad may be able to talk him into giving up."

"Good idea. I'll go tell Odelle."

Thacker found Odelle in the front of the house and told him what was going on. Why don't you go with me? You may have a calming influence on the man."

"Let's do it."

Ten minutes later they stopped at the front of the barn and Odelle agreed to go up the inside ladder while Thacker set a long ladder near the second floor opening and both went up simultaneously. Bass heard them and waited. He didn't know if they were armed so he waited until he could see them. He was surprised that it was a black man coming up the inside ladder while a white man was coming up from the outside. Neither displayed any firearm so Bass decided to wait and see what they planned.

When Odelle stood up and approached him, Bass said. "I'm armed but I don't want to shoot unless you force me. What do you want?"

Thacker was standing on the top rung of his ladder and was outlined in the open door on the second floor. "We mean you no harm. We don't know if you're a runaway or someone who's lost."

"I'm not lost."

"We have a small farm and need some help for about a month to move our cattle and pick the vegetable patch. Maybe we can help each other out. If you're interested, why don't you come down and talk to the boss. We're not armed."

Bass didn't take too long. He got up, followed Odelle down the ladder and carried his rifle with him. Odelle was a little shorter than Bass but Thacker was the same height. He said, "Let's go meet the boss and see what works for us."

They entered the kitchen and Franklin was there to greet them. He asked the three to sit down. "I'm Franklin Sutter and I'm the owner of this farm. This is my father Odelle and our manager. Will Thacker." Bass looked at Franklin and Odelle when he heard they were related.

Franklin looked directly at Bass. You look tired. I'll bet you're a runaway. Nobody comes here so I believe we can protect you. All our help has left, primarily because the Yankees are coming. I'd like to offer you our hospitality and protection for a month's worth of work on our farm. What do you say?"

Bass was confused and looked at Thacker, then at Odelle and finally at Franklin. "You look white to me; how can this man be your father?"

"It's not too complicated. My mother was white and for practical purposes her brother adopted me and left me this farm. "

I can protect myself, but I'm hungry most of the time. If you can provide adequate food, I can work."

"None of us are good cooks so we all pitch in and do the best we can. We have plenty of meat and you saw our garden which we work daily. We recently butchered one of our cows. We're having steak tonight."

Bass fit right in with the other three. Occasionally, they'd see a stranger ride by or walk near the farm and Bass would stay out of sight. As the weeks went by, he became less cautious and started talking freely with Odelle and sometimes Thacker. Franklin was a puzzle to him and he couldn't quite comprehend a half white young man in charge.

He finally asked Odelle what the story was between him and Franklin, so Odelle told him. "I fell in love with the daughter of the owner of the plantation. Her brother, who was my best friend, caught us one night after we made love. It turns out that she was six months with child, who turned out to be Franklin. I was sent away by my lover's father. When he was near death, I was brought back by the son, who subsequently adopted Franklin and left the estate to him."

"His features are as a black man but he certainly is white. How is the relationship?"

"We all get along fine."

One night they heard some noise coming from the barn; Thacker woke Odelle and he and the former slave decided to investigate. When they got near the barn, they heard some voices and the two dropped to the ground and crawled the rest of the way. They looked through one of the windows and saw a black woman with a small child hiding behind one of the bales of hay. She didn't seem like much of a threat, nor did the child. The two men got to their feet and Odelle lit the lantern that illuminated the two strangers.

The woman was cowering back against the side wall while holding the child close to her. Odelle went over to her and shone the light to see who else was with her. "Are you alone?" He asked the woman.

She cried and hugged the child. "Please don't hurt us, we didn't mean anything. I was looking for some food for my child."

Thacker looked to Odelle and smiled. "Come with us to the main house. We'll feed you and the child. "

Not knowing what to do, she reluctantly followed the two men to the kitchen of the small house. Bass and Franklin were awake by now. Franklin told her they meant no harm but they could tell she was scared at being along with four men of which two were white. He poured milk for the woman and child and sliced up some beef and cut a few slices of bread. The woman kept looking from one man to another while feeding her child. "Tell us why you're here." Franklin asked.

"The farm I was working at was burned to the ground by the Yankees and I had to run. My child was tired and hungry. That's why I was in your barn."

"What did you do at your farm?" Odelle asked.

"I cleaned the house and cooked for the husband and wife owners."

The four men looked at each other. Each must have been thinking the same thing, but it was Franklin who articulated their position. "If you need a place to stay and care for your child, we need a cook and housekeeper so we can get more work done."

"What if the Yankees come?" She asked.

"There're four of us and we're well armed. I think they'll leave us alone. I know you're nervous but we're honorable men and won't bother you. You and your child can have one of the rooms upstairs. What's your name?"

"My name is Mary and my boy's name is Samuel. His father is dead."

"Well Mary as far as I'm concerned, you're a free woman and I'll pay you to do our cooking and cleaning. You can start tomorrow, if that's okay with you." Franklin said.

The woman looked at Franklin and said. "You're part Negro, aren't you?"

"Yes, I am and I own this land. This man is my father." He pointed at Odelle.

"Thacker was our overseer when I was on the plantation and Bass is like you; he needed a place to rest for a short time." Franklin pointed to each as he talked.

The four men got up early, worked the vegetable patch until noon and then set the cattle out to graze. Mary had lunch ready and after lunch the four went out again to pick vegetables. They followed this ritual for six days and took Sunday off to rest, play with the child and map out their strategy for the next week. They knew the Union Army was close at hand. They could hear the noise of the cannons and knew it was just a matter of time before they were at their doorstep.

One morning six Union Soldiers came onto the farm carrying rifles and they heard Mary scream; the four came running with their rifles loaded. They surrounded the surprised Union Troops and asked them what they wanted. A Corporal said, "We don't mean you any harm, but we're hungry. Do you have any food?"

"Stack your rifles up against the house and our cook will feed you. When you're full, I'd like you to leave. Like you, we don't want any trouble." Franklin said.

The Corporal looked at the other five, leaned his rifle against the house and went into the kitchen. The other five followed his lead and the new cook fed them eggs and beef. When the soldiers were done, they thanked the four who'd been sitting outside with their rifles just in case there was trouble. Mary handled the situation with calm while her little boy was fast asleep upstairs. Franklin knew there'd be other incidents similar to the one today, but the four men were armed and appeared to be able to handle situations that arose.

After a month, Bass became restless and wanted to move on. He had his mind set on Oklahoma and that's where he was going. No one came looking for him the month he was with the others. The other four were sad to see the former slave leave, but they understood. They planned to wait out the Union coming and the war ending. Then they'd make their decision on what they wanted to do.

Bass knew he made the right decision in accepting the protection of the farm that Franklin owned. Still, his main problem was food. He was a big man and had an appetite. He'd been gone a week when he came over a slight rise in the terrain. He saw a small town in the distance and several fields planted with vegetables. If he was lucky, he wouldn't go hungry tonight. The thought of fresh vegetables was more than he could ignore. He found an old bag and systematically filled it with vegetables. Though it was the middle of the day, Bass thought the risk was worth it and besides he'd been with the others for a month and had no problem. Perhaps he was lulled into complacency...

After filling the small bag, he made his way to where the field ended and the brush began. Just as he left the planted field, he was struck from behind and fell to the ground. He was able to rise but was beaten savagely by one man while another held a gun on him; soon he lost consciousness. When he woke, he was lying on a cot in a jail cell. There were metal bracelets on his hands and leg irons on both legs. He could hear men talking, while others were laughing. He started to get up from the bed but he was sore all over. His clothes were torn and his arms, face and legs were bloody. "I say my brother and I get the reward. We're the ones who captured him." One of men outside the cell said

"Well, no one would be able to collect the reward if we didn't help bring him here. I say we split it", someone else said.

Apparently, no one paid any attention to Bass as he lay on a filthy cot. The reward and who was going to share in it took everyone's attention. Soon a large man with a beard, a big belly and a badge pinned to a dirty shirt came up to the cell door and looked down at Bass. "We're going to hang you if your master doesn't come up with the reward in a couple of days."

He was fed some kind of slop, once a day over the next two days, but wouldn't eat it initially. By the second day, he was so hungry that he ate it and threw up in his cell. Two deputies made him clean it up and then wash the entire jail floor, with his restraints in place. Bass knew that he had to escape here. He couldn't wait for Swanson or whoever the owner of Hickory Hills would send. That was a death sentence. He did what he was told but watched how the deputies acted when the sheriff was out of the office. His best chance was when they took him out of the cell to clean up the jail,

By the third day the sheriff was suggesting that they hang Bass because his owners were never coming and if they did, they probably wouldn't pay the reward. After the sheriff said he was going for breakfast, the two deputies took Blake out of the cell and gave him a broom to sweep up the floor. He immediately lashed out at one of the deputies, hitting him over the head with the broom and the man went down. When the second deputy responded, Bass poked the end of the broom into his stomach and then brought the broom down hard on the back of his neck and the man fell to the floor.

Bass took their keys and removed the shackles on his hands and legs, tied up the two deputies and went through their pockets. He found two dollars and their deputy badges which he kept for future use. He dragged each by the collar into a cell and locked it. He retrieved his two weapons and checked the ammunition. The two deputies' horses were tied to a rail on the side of the jail. Blake went out the back door, mounted one of the horses, tied the reins of the other to his saddle and off he went. He didn't escape unnoticed. Two men were walking across the street to the barber shop and sounded the alarm, but Bass had a head start, two horses, two weapons and a strong desire never to be caught again. He didn't know if anyone came after him. He didn't stop for the first two hours.

Bass Blake rode away from the jail with an extra horse, extra saddle and two weapons. But most of all he was pumped up with confidence and knew he was going to escape. He felt stress as he approached a white man to sell the extra horse and saddle so he'd have money to eat. His coat was open displaying his guns. That probably helped reduce the tension. He was able to sell the horse and saddle though at a substantially reduced price.

What was obvious during the daylight hours was the number of Union Soldiers in the area and the number of blacks on the roads. In fact, Bass was able to travel freely, sleep at night off the main roads and join other blacks at campfires in southern Arkansas. But not everything was that smooth during his journey to Oklahoma. In the southern part of the state near the town of Camden, Bass was attempting to buy some bread at a small stand on the side of the road. He had some coin left and handed it to the woman selling the bread when four white men who were sitting on the side of the road came up to him and demanded to know where he got the money.

"None of your business," he said to them. Bass climbed aboard his horse and started to turn to his left when one of the men grabbed his arm and pull him out of the saddle. As Bass was falling, he grabbed his revolver and swung out. Luckily, he hit the aggressor in the head and the man fell over backwards. As Bass was getting to his feet one of the other men came around the horse and hit Bass in the head with his fist. The black man staggered but steadied himself quickly by putting his left hand on the horse. He hit the second man with his revolver and he went down.

The other two opponents charged Bass. He kicked one in the groin and backhanded the other with his revolver and all four were on the ground. Two were unconscious and two were moaning.

The white woman selling the bread suggested that he get out of there. Bass grabbed the reins, got in the saddle and off he went to Oklahoma. He arrived six months after he escaped from the plantation in eastern Alabama.

There were numerous camps along the road as he made his way to Oklahoma. Most were populated by blacks, but occasionally there would be six or seven white men with their families sitting by the fire in these camps. Here was where Bass kept up with news of the war. He hadn't realized the war was over and Lee had surrendered at Appomattox. When he was told that Lincoln had been assassinated, he had to ask who Lincoln was.

He rode the area where Sherman had made his March to the Sea. There were very few soldiers along the way, but with the surrender, the people around the campfires figured they'd all be coming home. At the next camp he heard that Jefferson Davis was in hiding. Bass was not familiar with this man or the events people were talking about. He only started picking up this type of news in the camps. To make any sense of all this Bass had to ask some of the people at the camps what it all meant.

This was a new world and a new life for Bass. Soon, he'd become a normal citizen and learn about government, elections and politicians. It would take him a year to realize he was free and had the same rights as the white people. Bass would learn much more in time and he'd learn it well.

CHAPTER 7

When Augustus Swanson returned to Hickory Hills Plantation without the runaway slave, his owner chastised him in front of some of his lower-level employees. Swanson was livid but kept his mouth shut and went to his cabin to clean up and brood. He didn't know how but he'd get even with Wilcox, but first things first. The next morning, he sought out William Todd who was working in one of the cotton fields. "I know you helped Blake escape, so I want to know what his planned route is."

"I don't know anything about his escape. We talked about things here on the plantation, but I don't know anything about any escape plan."

Swanson hit the slave in the head with the handle of his whip, and William fell backyards in the mud. "I'm going to keep after you; eventually you'll tell me everything or I'll skin you alive."

Everyone knew the war was coming to an end. More and more men from the neighboring plantations were being conscripted into the southern army. Consequently, there were fewer overseers and the rate of escape for slaves was increasing. Even if they were caught in another community, no one could be spared to go after them. Though he'd been furloughed because of his wounds, Frank Wilcox was called back to duty and the notice that Bass had been captured in Tennessee was ignored.

Swanson asked Wilcox if he could send someone to bring back Blake. "There's no one we can send. Even if I could free someone, Blake isn't worth the effort now."

With Wilcox going back on active duty, he reluctantly appointed Swanson as head man on the plantation, Wilcox' main objective was to meet the plantation's cotton quota for the mills in England. There was very little currency in the south other than what the Europeans would pay for bales of cotton. Swanson in his mid-twenties was not an educated man; he was what was known as an opportunist. When payment arrived from England, he pocketed nearly half. In order to make the books balance somewhat, he reduced the purchase of food supplies for the slaves under his care and made the books reflect higher food costs. Sickness from malnutrition was rampant, but who were the slaves to complain to. Things were so bad that those who were too sick to work were left to rot in their shanties. Five of the twenty five slaves at Hickory Hills died.

Swanson heard the cannons and with every new day, the sounds were getting louder. If the Union Army kept up this pace, they'd be at Hickory Hills within three days. He knew the time to leave was now. He gathered up his personal possessions and counted the gold he received for the cotton; it was less than he remembered, but he didn't have time to investigate where the missing gold went. He took one of the owner's prized geldings and made his way south to New Orleans. Some of the sleek blockade runners were still operating to Cuba out of that southern port. He bribed one of captains and ended up in Havana Cuba with enough money to think about his options.

Most of the slaves on the plantation didn't know what to do. This land had been their home for most if not all of their lives. The thought of the Yankees coming up their road caused many to fear for their lives. When that day actually came, they were told by the advancing army commander they were free and could leave. The trauma of that thought caused near hysteria among the former slaves. There was limited food at the plantation and the conquering army had none to spare. William Todd was the exception. He knew what Swanson was up to and found the hiding place the overseer used to store his ill begotten gains. William wasn't greedy. He took only one gold coin at a time. Within two months he had ten gold coins and was already formulating a plan to escape the south after the war.

The plantation grapevine wasn't peculiar to Alabama. Both slaves and the white elite throughout the south knew of the Underground Railroad's existence. What they didn't know was how it operated. It wasn't a railroad at all. It was a method of moving runaway slaves west, south to Mexico or as far north as Canada. To facilitate this operation, they employed people called conductors who guided the slaves on their way. Stations were set up to act as safe locations where slaves rested and were fed. A so-called ticket identified the slaves using the railroad.

William was determined to head north until he reached New York. He'd often heard the name because Wilcox and his wife frequently went there for business or pleasure. As soon as the Union Army moved into the area which coincided with Augustus Swanson's departure from the plantation, William said goodbye to everyone and started his trek north. Ex slaves or free black people were numerous on the roads heading north. Soon he learned where the next Underground Railroad Station was and where he could expect food. Occasionally, he'd be ahead of the soldiers of the north but most times he was in their wake and felt perfectly safe.

The former slaves would walk during the daylight hours and rest at night. There were infrequent stations serviced by volunteers, where the travelers could receive food. Most nights they slept along the road without any food. Several months later he reached the state of Virginia where the south was making a final stand. The main threat for those traveling north was the Confederate soldiers .

They could hear gunfire most days and occasionally one of their fellow travelers would be struck down while he was walking. It was dangerous for travelers and especially runaway slaves who could be shot indiscriminately by the retreating southern soldiers. William learned of the Great Dismal Swamp and was lucky to be led there and subsequently sheltered by the indigenous Maroons.

The first people to locate in the Great Dismal Swamp were former slaves brought to America in the mid-sixteen hundreds. Since there were no slave laws at that time, these people were treated at indentured servants. When their term was complete, as many as twenty self-liberated slaves set up residence in the swamp living on Mesic Islands. These were the highest and driest points in the swamps. As the population increased, trading was initiated between the surrounding white population and the so-called Maroons.

Soon many of the runaway slaves made their way to that part of Virginia where the swamp was located via the Underground Railway. The residents of the swamp set up a governing structure to control the Mesic Islands and ensure that all those coming to the swamp were treated fairly. At one point in time the population was as high as several thousand. Access was difficult, consequently, incursions by law enforcement wasn't practical. In essence, the inhabitants of the Great Dismal Swamp were allowed to live within their own community structure and self-govern without outside interference.

William remained with the Maroon people for a year. It was comfortable and he felt free. Since he was one of the slaves that could read and write, he took a leadership role in the community. One day he heard a familiar voice call out to him. It was Effie the housekeeper at the big house on the plantation. She'd been Bass Blake's lover and she asked William if he heard from his friend. "No. The last I saw of him was when he went over the fence in the north cotton field." This wasn't what William wanted and he left after a year, Effie and he were just friends. She'd become intimate with one of the other former slaves and with her ability to read and write, she became a fixture in the swamp. That was the last he saw of her.

It was one of the Underground Railroad volunteers that guided him out of the swamp and past the remnants of the battlefields. The war was over even if some of the diehards couldn't accept it. William made stops in Washington DC, Baltimore and then Philadelphia. He had enough walking and decided to stay in that city for a few months. The influx of the Irish due to the famine back home left few low-income positions available. However, his skill at repairing shoes as a slave and the fact that he was a former slave gave him a leg up with a Black owned businessman. He applied for a job with a black custom shoemaker, named Isaiah Springs and was accepted as an apprentice.

He didn't know why he decided to stay in Philadelphia, but after a month in the city with a job he liked, William was delighted he made that decision. He settled into the black section of town and met several other former slaves who were starting their lives over. Again, the exodus of slaves from the south had swelled the black population in the city to thirty thousand with over three hundred black owned businesses. The black community was organized and very active. They were able to stop segregation on streetcars in the city and by the early eighteen eighties, segregation was eliminated in the city schools.

His decision to make Philadelphia his home was based primarily on Sophie Howard, the daughter of a Baptist Minister. She was a teacher at an elementary school in the black section of town. They met at church where he was introduced to the Howard family by his employer. He had limited leather training at the plantation, but under his employer's tutelage and patience, he became a skilled craftsman and soon rewarded the owner's faith in hiring him.

When the Civil War ended, there was an immediate demand for clothing and shoes. The little shop he worked in became inundated with orders and had to expand. His owner took a chance on William and assigned him many of the new customers. William's confidence increased as did his skill and the company continued to prosper. His forte was riding boots. Since horses were one of the main modes of transportation, the demand for this product was constant. Soon many of the custom shoe orders were coming from out of state, as far away as Chicago, but recently from the Santa Ynez Valley of California. Springs hired additional workers, some of which were former slaves.

William and Sophie married in 1867 after a lengthy courtship and had two children, a boy and a girl As his skill increased so did his income and stature in life. They bought a nice bungalow in the black section, went to church on Sundays and became active in the black community. Their idyllic existence ended with the influenza epidemic in 1880. Sophie and his two children contacted the disease and died shortly thereafter.

No matter where he went or who he interfaced with, the image of Sophie and his family appeared. He couldn't face his customers and he couldn't face his neighbors. The community rallied around William but it was to no avail. He'd purchased a share in Mr. Springs' business after five years and now he wanted to sell. Springs was up in age and had always planned to have his interest in the shoe business transfer to William upon his death. The old man was reluctant at first but finally agreed to repurchase William's twenty percent interest. William wanted to get away from everything and start over again. He left Philadelphia in eighteen eighty-one and traveled by train to Chicago.

CHAPTER 8

The final days of the civil war were characterized by violence, people fleeing their homes and Confederate Soldiers trying to make any sense about what had happened to them. Millions of people were looking for food and what was left of their homes. Nothing was sacred as law and order became nonexistent. Union soldiers were capturing everything in sight but failing to provide any direction to the vanquished. Southern people were leaning up against buildings or sitting alongside the roads trying to figure out what to do. To say there was a breakdown in society was an understatement.

When the Republican Administration sent businessmen and law officials to fill the void and declare martial law, it only heightened the absence of a structure that once held the southern society together. Reconstruction of the entire society was needed but was somewhere in the future. The slave society was disbanded, but what were they to do. Their skills were in growing cotton and attending to rich plantation owners. It wasn't something that could readily be retrained; it needed time; it needed acceptance and it needed reality

Young Franklin was thrown into a situation that required more maturity than a half white seventeen year old landowner was expected to have. But with Will Thacker's help he was able to muddle through the initial shock that they all felt, because the others on the farm weren't that helpful. Marie was a very immature twenty two year old. How could she be anything but, since her entire life until this point was directed? Odelle still hadn't realized he was a free man and his input was non-existent.

Will Thacker knew some of the things that needed to be done but he was reluctant to overstep his bounds and make his owner feel that he wasn't ready.

In spite of the fact that none of the males had been in charge of anything before, they didn't give up. Franklin held a meeting nearly every day to get everyone's input as to what should be done. In spite of their indecision, they could see that their cattle and vegetables were their livelihood. If they were to survive, they needed to protect that investment.

One night. a gang roaming the neighborhoods, cut the fence about two hundred yards from their house. The gang gathered up some vegetables and took two of the cattle that were in the corral and escaped back through the fence they cut. Franklin heard them and roused Thacker and Odelle and the three ran after the gang and tried to stop them. All they got for their effort was to be beaten up and left in the mud. They knew some of the bandits but that wouldn't help. They picked themselves up and although they had many bruises, they vowed it wouldn't happen again. These gangs were organized; as soon as the robbery was over, the gangs would disappear into the countryside to either enjoy their illicit booty, sell the stolen goods or plan for another target. Many times, they returned to a place they'd previously robbed.

Storekeepers were faced with the same problem as those on the farms. Some still had ample supplies on their shelves, but few buyers and fewer with any money. If they didn't sell what they had, it would be stolen and they might as well shut down their business.

Young Franklin had been receiving money from the Bank of Philadelphia and depositing enough in the local bank to pay his help and buy whatever he needed to survive. The rest he kept in a safe place on the farm to be used when necessary. After the three men took a beating by one of the gangs, they vowed to each that they would protect their livestock and produce, Franklin found a store that had an excess supply of fence-posts and wire. He bargained well and purchased enough for the farm

It took them three months to dig enough post holes and string wire, but eventually they had the entire farm enclosed. Occasionally, sections of the fence were cut, but the three quickly repaired the damage. There were many dogs running around the area. People couldn't afford to feed their pets, so they set them loose to seek food on their own account. Odelle captured a large sized dog outside the farm and tied it up. Over a month, he fed it and worked with it to be a guard dog. When that experiment worked, he captured three more stray dogs and trained them all. Soon they had four that could be trusted to help protect the farm. The dogs were fed just enough to keep them attached to the farm. To supplement their food requirements, Odelle trained them to catch rabbits and ground squirrels

Not surprisingly there were plenty of weapons available from soldiers coming back home and in need of money. What Thacker wanted was six handguns, six shotguns and plenty of ammunition. He bargained well using hard currency and was able to have enough weapons on the farm to keep the gangs at bay. Thacker trained the other two to the point that each was a skilled marksman and could easily hit a target at one hundred yards.

Odelle slept in the barn, Franklin in the house and Thacker in a small building near the barn. It was Odelle who heard the dogs growl one summer night. He grabbed his shot gun and alerted Franklin and Thacker. Someone had cut the fence near the spot that had been cut before. The dogs had reached the fence and started barking but the intruders fired at the animals scattering them. By this time Franklin and the other two had reached the cut fence those who had cut the fence weren't there. The three ran to the vegetable patch and found six men picking in their garden. Four of them turned on Franklin, Odelle and Thacker. The three opened up with shotguns and killed the four robbers and when the other two robbers threw down the produce and started to flee, they were shot and killed...

They buried the six in a remote spot on the farm. The soil was good and soft and they buried them deep. They doubted anyone would come looking for them unless it was the other members of their gang. Thacker talked to the other two. "I know it bothers both of you to kill someone. But this is war. If we don't protect what we have and make it clear to everyone that we will protect our patch, we'll be overrun and be like the people leaning against the walls in town."

They had a few break-ins after that, but none that caused much damage or theft. A banker from New York City arrived and took over management of the local bank. The reconstruction committee in Washington DC wanted to stabilize the financial institutions so the south could recover much quicker. This was an advantage to Franklin, who was a little concerned about the amount of money he kept on the farm. With the number of break-ins, the money could be a liability. He put all excess funds in the local bank and established himself and his partners as a viable business.

Soon the carpetbaggers came and came and came. They were there to buy property at a bargain. They approached Thacker, thinking Franklin was his son, but the former overseer told them politely he and his family weren't interested. Within a week, the carpetbaggers came back with their bodyguards and tried to coerce Thacker. When Odelle and Franklin came up behind the visitors with loaded shotguns, the carpetbaggers decided to leave: they never came back.

Since the farm didn't plant cotton, they couldn't be assessed a Cotton Tax, which was a ploy by the carpetbaggers to take over poorly financed operations. But other taxes came up from time to time to put the farmers and share croppers at risk. Although land was given to the blacks during reconstruction, they were forced to turn to many former plantation owners to borrow money for equipment and machinery. The fees charged for the equipment were exorbitant and the borrowers had to work night and day just to make payments for the equipment. It was as though the old plantation life had a rebirth and the blacks though not slaves per se, were beholden and indebted to the richer white planters.

Although Franklin and his group weren't rich, they never turned away someone who would ask for food. Soon they added two more workers to handle their increasing herd and vegetable garden that had grown from five acres to ten. At least once a day a family, mostly black, would come and eat their fill at the table prepared by Marie and in return would work enough hours to repay the hospitality.

Chaos was everywhere. A day didn't go by without at least one killing either by Union Soldiers, displaced Confederates or gangs that were roaming the area, robbing everyone. The three stayed mostly at home with their shotguns ready for anyone that meant them harm. With the addition of two free blacks, they felt secure. If they went into town, at least two men would travel together and stay together until they came home. The five were armed and all were good shots.

As the year passed, there was a decided effort on the part of Franklin to build up Odelle's self-esteem. Too many years as a slave still weighed on his shoulders and he didn't know how to cope with freedom. Also, he didn't know how to identify with a son who was white and now a man of twenty five. He still looked to Thacker and Franklin for direction and was reluctant to initiate anything on his own. The three would pick vegetables on Thursday and take them into the farmer's market every Friday morning in town, about a mile away, where they'd sell their produce. Gradually Franklin bowed out of the chore and much of it fell to his father.

Odelle was responsible for gathering the produce, and with one of their employees, took it to the farmer's market on Friday. Odelle would deposit the proceeds in the bank before four o'clock. After three months, they all noticed a change in Odelle. He smiled a lot more and his confidence was apparent. He started playing with Maria's son. In fact, Franklin thought his father was sweet on their cook. One Friday in September, he and one of the black workers sold all the produce they'd taken to market. While his worker was cleaning up, Odelle deposited the proceeds in the bank.

As he was walking out of the bank, he was intercepted by a constable and asked for some ID. Odelle didn't know what he was talking about and started to walk back to his cart and join his worker. The constable ran after him and tripped him from behind. While Odelle was on the ground, his hands were tied behind his back and the law enforcement officer declared him a vagrant. When Odelle didn't return to his stand in the farmer's market, the hired man, named George didn't know what to do. He pushed their cart to the bank and asked around if anyone saw Odelle. No one did. Finally, not knowing what to do, he went home and told Thacker what happened.

Thacker waited an hour, thinking that Odelle met someone he knew, before he told Franklin that his father hadn't come home but the hired man had. Franklin sent Thacker into town to see if he could find Odelle. It didn't take him long to find out what happened. Odelle had been arrested. Franklin and Thacker grabbed their weapons and with their hired man rode into town. They stopped at Magistrate Harold Thames home for an answer.

Franklin had seen the handwriting on the wall and knew that he needed some friends in local government. When election time came, he was fortunate to support the winners of two elections, one for magistrate and one for superior court. Thames was having dinner but welcomed the three men into his house. When he heard the story of Odelle's arrest, he sent his house boy to the jail to bring Odelle there. Within twenty minutes the house boy returned to tell them that Odelle had not only been arrested but was leased out to Henry Whitney, a well know plantation owner.

"Franklin, I've done all I can tonight. First thing in the morning I'll talk to the sheriff and have Odelle released. I apologize but that's the best I can do. I hope you understand."

Having his father unlawfully arrested was more than young Sutter was able to accept. "No. That won't work Harold. I want my partner, and he is a partner on the farm, returned immediately. I want you to get the sheriff over here and tell him to go get Odelle Jones now. We're not leaving here without him."

Thames looked at the determined look in Franklin's and Thacker's faces and especially the shotguns they were carrying and acquiesced. He sent his house boy to get the sheriff and let him know it was important. The sheriff arrived within twenty minutes and the magistrate explained what happened and what needed to be done. "Harold, I'm not going to go out to Whitney's house and tell him we made a mistake. He paid a seven day lease fee and he'll want it back."

"Can't you tell him we made a mistake and sent the wrong man?"

"I'd do that if I could but I don't have anyone in jail I could send. And then there's the fee. I gave a portion to the constable who arrested Jones and then I gave him the night off."

"Tell Whitney there was a mistake, and he'll get his fee back within a couple of days and then bring Jones here."

"What if he won't give up Jones?"

"Then take him, you're the sheriff."

Franklin knew Henry Whitney when he was a boy. James and Jesse had dealings with the man and got along fine. But this was different and Franklin wondered if there'd be some repercussions from this incident. He wasn't surprised when Odelle, the sheriff and Henry Whitney arrived at the magistrate's home together. Whitney was livid. "Harold, I want my money back. I paid in good faith and I want it now. How could you send the sheriff to my home during dinner time and demand this Negro be released to him?"

Whitney looked over at Franklin and Thacker and asked the magistrate who they were. "This is Mr. Sutter and his foreman Will Thacker. Mr. Sutter is the son of James Sutter who owned Bridlewood. Whitney didn't say anything but nodded at Franklin
who looked out of the corner of his eye to see what Odelle would say?

"Our partner has been returned. We'll leave you Harold and my thanks to all that this incident didn't get blown out of proportion." The three left but they could hear the shouting inside the house when they were a half block away.

CHAPTER 9

The fact that the normal social structure in the south post civil war had been replaced with chaos would make anyone nervous about what was to come. The psychological impact to Odelle for being a slave for seventeen years could not be measured. The awkwardness of having to address your white son as your superior must have further lowered Odelle's self-esteem. He identified as a slave or former slave and yet his offspring was looked upon as white and was his employer.

Odelle was forty seven years old and he wanted to marry Maria and father children that were more like him than Franklin. It wasn't that he didn't want a father/son relationship with Franklin, but every time he saw him or talked to him, he felt inferior. Franklin had assured him that he was a partner in the farm and that it would be left to him sometime in the future. But Odelle's expectations were low. He could not fathom the reality of him owing this 30 acre farm and his neighbors accepting that fact. What would happen when Thacker passed on was foremost in his mind.

Although he could see some things that needed to be changed or improved on the farm, Odelle didn't feel it was his place to raise the issue and thereby criticize Franklin or Will Thacker... He knew he was free because that's what the law said, but was he really. He didn't think as a free man; he acted as someone submissive to the power structure. He feared that another constable would come to the farm and arrest him for no reason and lease him out to some plantation as though he was an inanimate object.

The plantation grapevine was still working, though more informal now since most plantations were destroyed. Many of the black population kept it alive and word spread very quickly. The one thing that united the former slaves several years after the end of the civil conflict was the rise of the Ku Klux Klan.

When the first burning cross was discovered on a black family's front yard, it set off a series of attacks on blacks that created fear not only on that segment of the population, but those whites who didn't subscribe to this kind of intimidation. If certain whites spoke out against the tactic, they were singled out and made an example of. It didn't take long for people to recognize that they should keep their thoughts to themselves. The old hierarchy was still in place and as intimidating as ever even though none of the Klan were operating in that area.

Money was the power behind the south after the civil war. Though the number of slaves that were free in the south were substantial, their sheer numbers didn't take into account that none of the blacks had any money; it was the old plantation owners who controlled the money flow. What difference did it make if the government gave slaves 40 acres? They didn't have the money to lease or buy equipment to work the land. Even if several slaves joined their parcels together, the problem was the same. After the war ended, it was common for plantation owners to divide their property up into forty acre plots and lease each parcel to former slaves. They'd lend their former slaves money to buy equipment or they'd buy the equipment and lease it to their sharecroppers to farm the land. The net result was the lenders would realize a nice income while the slaves barely broke even

Odelle was a ship out of water. He wanted to marry Maria but he didn't know if he could. Maybe his son would say no. He talked to Will Thacker and asked him what to do. "You're a free man, a partner on this farm and you don't need anyone's permission to ask Maria to marry you. If Maria says yes, then all you need is a ring and a ceremony. Have you asked her yet?"

"No, I was waiting to see what Franklin would say."

"Well, I told you what you can do and what your rights are, but you do as you want."

Odelle couldn't forget that James Sutter adopted Franklin and made him his son and heir. Therefore, Franklin wasn't his son; he was Odelle's employer. No matter what Thacker said, his mind was made up. Odelle went to Franklin to ask his permission. He couldn't get it out of his head that Maria belonged to his son and he had to have his approval. The old ways were hard to ignore. Franklin told Odelle to ask Maria and if she said yes, then he'd give the couple a nice wedding. When Maria said yes, Franklin asked to speak to her. He told her about his relationship with Odelle and that the farm would be transferred to him within ten years provided that the couple looked out for Will Thacker. "I promised Will Thacker that he'd have a home until the day he passed on."

Within two years there were two more members of the Odelle Jones family on the farm; both were boys and both were black. Franklin could see a decided change in Odelle's relationship with the two young boys. He was happy for his father and yet, there could never be anything but owner and hired man relationship between the two. He felt sad and wondered what he could have done differently when Odelle came to the farm.

Franklin began attending state legislature sessions. Initially, he sat and listened, but lately he asked questions and entered into a discussion with the legislators if permitted. Something about politics intrigued him. Soon he was asking some of his contemporaries what his chances were if he entered the political arena. Thanks to his mother Marsha Lee, he was an avid reader. He began reading the bills proposed by the legislature and speaking for or against them in open session. Intuitively, he hated what the average Scallywag and Carpet Bagger stood for; yet he was courting some of the Scallywags and asking them for their endorsement.

His first attempt to unseat a long-term politician met with failure. He lost by five hundred votes. He'd gotten on the wrong side of some of the issues and vowed to not let that happen again. During the next two years he started giving speeches to the various clubs in the area and polled what issues were important to them and what weren't. His second attempt was against a one term congressman, who had a lack luster term. Franklin won by fifteen votes and was on his way He wouldn't make the same mistake his predecessor made. His primary goal after being elected was to ensure he'd be returned to the US House of Representatives. Raising money for a campaign was a tenuous job and Franklin hired two full time people to attain a successful end.

Congressman Franklin Sutter was an impressive looking man, standing five feet ten inches tall and weighing one hundred eighty pounds. His dark eyes and black hair contrasted with his stark white features, but the name of Sutter was respected in the area. Although there were whispers that he was half black, it didn't seem to have any impact on the ladies in his district. He was sought out by the best families and was an attractive dinner companion for someone's daughter who was of marrying age.

One evening, he was introduced to Sally Ann Tucker at a congressional party hosted by his fellow Republicans. She was twenty-one years old and had her coming out party two years earlier. Her father was a lobbyist for one of the tobacco companies and she was a frequent attendee at these events. Neither she nor Franklin was interested in marrying at this time and the two began a two-year affair that was known only to a few people. Finally, Sally Ann's mother talked to her daughter and told her she was playing with fire.

The young woman broke off the affair and married John James Hunter, a freshman representative from South Carolina. The two saw each other occasionally and continued their affair in a very discrete manner for another year. Young Hunter had a reputation as an excellent shot and a quick temper, so Franklin broke off the relationship rather than come to her husband's attention.

In congress, Franklin was considered a mover and shaker. The tutoring that his mother insisted he have, gave him a step up on most politicians, and to complement those traits, he was quick and articulate. Soon, he was assigned to the Ways and Means Committee and served his apprenticeship under the wily congressman from the neighboring state of Georgia. Jonathan Weems. The long-time congressman was a power broker and took a liking to Franklin and shepherded him through his first term as a congressman. Franklin was to be his handpicked heir as Chairman of the House' most powerful committee.

Franklin returned for Will Thacker's funeral and transferred the deed to the farm entirely to Odelle and his two sons. The older man broke down and cried. "I know for a fact that my mother loved you and would have no other man after you left. It's a tragedy that our society prevented the two of you from being together. If she had her way you would never have left Bridlewood. James was against it and tried to intercede. I know this gift can never repair what you experienced. I just hope it will help make up for all your lost time. You now have something to leave to your family. My mother and your love are buried on the farm. Please see to it that her plot always has flowers." For the first and last time in their lives, the two men embraced.

Franklin knew in his heart that he'd failed his biological father. He kept him at arm's length and didn't consider him even a relative. He saw James as his father and although that was practical, it wasn't right... He wondered if he was prejudiced. It was true that he felt more comfortable in white society than black but he didn't know how to handle it. He accepted the cards he was dealt and made the best of it.

Franklin would always be grateful to Will Thacker. He was the glue that held the farm together and was always by Franklin's side as he grew into manhood. For Odelle, he served as a buffer between the community and the owner of the farm. Without him, Odelle wouldn't have matured to the level of being able to run the farm but more importantly, be able to take care of his family. For the first few years after Franklin went to DC, whenever Odelle went into town to contract business, Thacker was by his side. If Odelle stumbled, Thacker was there to give support; he never failed him. Franklin hoped that his father appreciated the man, who was the best friend Odelle would ever have.

Franklin moved to Washington DC five years earlier and would never live on the farm again. He squired several other women from well to do families around the nation's capital, but none interested him enough to marry. His benefactor told him that if he had ambitions to be a US Senator or perhaps even seek the White House, he had to have a wife who could help. Franklin knew his time in Washington was coming to a close. He knew that if his political ambitions got the best of him, his secret might come out, even though there were only a few still living that knew the truth.

There was something missing in his life and he hadn't found it here. After six terms in Congress at the age of thirty-seven years old, he sold his Georgetown Home and decided to go west.

By this time Franklin was a wealthy man. The proceeds from Bridlewood that fueled his Congressional ambitions, paled in comparison to the money he made in the stock market, real estate ventures and from tips on investments that naturally came the way of influential people in Washington.

CHAPTER 10

Frank Wilcox was livid when he returned to his plantation. Not only was the war lost, but he was broke. Swanson had run off with the proceeds from the plantation's cotton sales and all his slaves, except one had left. He was sitting on a five hundred acre plantation without any help. All his people both white and black sensed a lost cause and went someplace else. Within a month, the carpet baggers were taking over every place. Most of his neighbors had been foreclosed on and the sheriff escorted them off their own place that many built from scratch. Wilcox had a tax bill that he couldn't meet, so he took inventory of his stock and supplies. There were two hundred acres of cotton, ready to be picked. In addition, there were a few bales of cotton in the warehouse, some oat hay in the barn, three of his prized horses and some household furnishings.

Once he had a mid-sized but well-maintained plantation, now the entire estate was in dire need of preventive maintenance. The house, kitchen and garden were okay but the building housing the gin mill had a roof that leaked like a sieve. The warehouse where he stored bales waiting for shipment had the left side blown away by Yankee cannons. His prized smokehouse had been leveled to the ground and the slave quarters were nonexistent. The only thing that seemed to survive the war was his cotton field. Without anyone to pick the cotton it was valueless, unless he could find a buyer pretty quick.

He had enough food to last a couple of months and enough hay for the horses for two months. What he needed was some operating capital. His first stop was the

Bank of Alabama. He put on his best outfit, and went to see Jeb Northy. They'd been in the same southern brigade. Though Wilcox had been a prized customer and depositor, the banker couldn't help. "We don't have anything to lend. Most of our investments are in bankruptcy with little chance of recovery. Do you have any assets other than the plantation that you could sell?"

"There're some paintings my late wife bought, some gold and items such as candlesticks. Of course, there are the three horses."

"My suggestion is to sell all of that ahead of a tax sale which has started on some of the plantations. Get some money before they take everything you have."

"Who's buying?"

"There are a couple of northerners that have come down here this past week. They're opportunists but they have money. Seriously, I don't think you can save your house and land. Your best bet is to get some capital, move someplace else and start over. You'll find the two men at the cotton auction house. Their names are Worth and Reed. They'll bargain hard but they do have funds."

Wilcox made an appointment with the two men for the next day at his plantation. They bought the gold and silver plated items, some furniture and the three prized geldings; he was lucky to get twenty five percent of their reasonable value. He tried his best to get them to at least buy the cotton waiting to be picked, but they wouldn't bite on his propositions. He decided to take whatever they offered and go after Swanson. The word was that his overseer had headed to New Orleans, so that's where Wilcox was going. Even though he was still recovering from his war wounds, he was a formidable opponent for anyone. He planned to find Swanson, recover his money and kill him.

Wilcox was raised by a relative of Jean Lafitte, the famous pirate. Like the legend; he had a mixed education until he was a teenager. The only difference was that his so-called parent was an educated man who insisted Frank attend college. Growing up, he was a charming rogue and quick with his fists, a saber or a knife. When he was twenty two, he commanded a pirate ship and made a quick profit by attacking a merchant ship and capturing its rich cargo. With those funds, he got into an all-night poker game and came away with enough funds to set himself up in society along with the deed to Hickory Hills Plantation. His good looks and charm got him invited into the elite circles of Selma and he married well. She was twenty two years old and came with a substantial dowry.

Their marriage was childless and she succumbed to influenza when she was twenty seven. Though the marriage was short, Wilcox and his bride were very happy. He was glad that she didn't have to see the decimation in the south that the war exacted. She always had the best. She died before the war was over and never found out they were insolvent.

On his trek to New Orleans, the former plantation owner was learning what it was like to be poor. Without a horse, he had to travel by foot or catch a ride on a hay wagon; in some cases, he walked with freed slaves and their families. He ate apples, radishes and some pears that were given to him or he took when no one was looking.

He slept on the side of the road at night with a revolver in his hand and a Bowie type knife in a sheath strapped to his leg. Only once during his trek was there an attempt to rob him, but he was fortunate to hear them coming and when he fired a shot high over their heads, they ran off.

New Orleans didn't look like a city that had been under siege at the end of the civil war. The Union Army had been in control of the city the past four years and would remain so until eighteen seventy-two Their benign occupation was ignored by the population swelling from the influx of southerners who were looking for an avenue to escape from the war.

Wilcox recognized some men he served with and although they were helpful, none could tell him how to find Augustus Swanson. His acquaintances invited him to some clubs in the city that specialized in gambling and other amusements for men. He started playing poker for small stakes and found that he could hold his own and if he wasn't greedy, he could make a living. He met a southern widow who had some assets, mostly jewelry and was looking for companionship. Wilcox became her protector and confidant; she became his mistress. He hadn't lost sight of his goal to kill Augustus Swanson, but he couldn't find him. He was in a kind of a holding pattern waiting for some clue to evolve that would lead him to the scoundrel.

In the interim he played cards three nights a week and consoled his widow friend the other four nights. One night he was playing poker at one of clubs he frequented. Another player in the game was an English Capitan who ran cotton out of Cuba for the south to Liverpool, England and returned with munitions. He used New Orleans to bring his cargo in from Cuba. He remembered Swanson and believed he sold him passage to Cuba about four months earlier, but he hadn't seen the man since. To the best of his knowledge, Swanson was still on the island. As time passed, Wilcox became more interested in politics in New Orleans and started to forget all about his former overseer.

Though the south had lost the war, the white minorities still controlled what wealth was still available and consequently the legal structure within any community. Wilcox was approached by another former southern officer to see if he was interested in running for sheriff; the incumbent was too old and too corrupt. He and his friends wanted someone new. What Wilcox lacked in political experience, he made up with charm, good looks and easily got more votes than his opponent. With a new mayor, city council and county sheriff, he and his friends were now in control. If anything, New Orleans would be an open city for some time. Gambling and brothels were allowed to operate openly provided they showed their appreciation to the new power structure.

Within a few years Wilcox had his own club and a string of girls who serviced his clientele. Soon he was as rich as he'd been before the war and thought about going back to Alabama to see if he could recover Hickory Hills Plantation. But realism set in and he decided that his life was better now, so why leave. His lady friend was still very attractive and wasn't overly suspicious of the hours he kept. He married her after living with her for three years and bought a splendid home in one of the prestigious parishes. The desire to chase after Augustus Swanson dissipated. It became a thing of the past.

CHAPTER 11

When Bass Blake reached Oklahoma, he wanted to be sure he was there. He asked several people if it was true that this was the free state of Oklahoma. At least it was his promised land. For nearly two years all he did was hope that when he reached this country, he'd be free. He didn't let any grass grow under his feet when he was sure he was in Oklahoma. He immediately signed on at a cattle ranch in the center of the state. Mainly what he did was ride a fence line while staying weeks at a time in a shack on a remote part of the range.

He was happy to find work and save a few dollars, but he got lonely and decided to see what else was available for him. Over the next year he worked at three other ranches punching cattle and fixing fences. Subsequently, he stayed with two of the three Indian Tribes in the state, easily picking up their language and acting as tribal policeman when there was trouble on the reservation or campground. With his size and command of firearms, he was a natural policeman. Mostly what he did was put some of the tribe members in jail over night when they got drunk. The next day he'd let them go.

He missed Effie the house keeper at Hickory Hills and wondered if she'd made her way north as she wished. In his second year on the reservation, Bass married a comely Indian woman who was nineteen years old. He bought a parcel of land near Enid and built a two bedroom home. Lotus Petal bore him two sons, who he named William and Henry. He built some corrals, captured some mustangs and bought a few head of cattle. It was the first real home he had.

One of his skills was as a tracker. He developed a reputation as someone who could bring back escaped prisoners. He was in demand and would travel to any part of the state to catch an escaped prisoner. He could count on being hired four times a year to bring someone back. It stabilized his income in his early years of marriage.

With the Emancipation Proclamation, he was no longer a slave but a freeman. He didn't have to walk down a side street in any town for fear he'd be arrested. For the first time in his life, he wasn't looking over his shoulder to see how far Swanson was behind him. When Judge Parker was sworn in as a Judge to the US District Court for the Western District in Arkansas, which included the Indian Territory in Oklahoma, he planned to hire two hundred deputies.

The territory his court was responsible for was enormous, wild and lacking good transportation. Outlaw gangs were numerous. Over a twenty one year career as a Judge, Parker presided over fifteen thousand cases. Of these, the jury found about eighty five hundred guilty. One of his first hires after his appointment was Bass Blake, who'd developed a reputation as a solid citizen, a man competent in the use of firearms and one who could speak many of the dialects of the Indian Tribes in the area. Bass liked Judge Parker the first time they met and served him faithfully. Theirs would be a friendly relationship until Judge Parker died.

His first task was to arrest Sooner Jake, a half Cherokee renegade, who along with the Whitby Brothers went on a murder and robbery rampage, killing eight people. They robbed numerous banks, stores, express offices and railroads in a one year period and anyone who got in their way was eliminated immediately. None of the other deputies serving Judge Parker wanted anything to do with Sooner. He was characterized by them as a natural born killer. Finally, Judge Parker had no choice but to call in Blake. "No one wants to go after Sooner but he's got to be caught. He's killing people whenever he wants. How do you feel about going after him?"

"Judge, it's not a problem. We'll bring him in. Just give me a couple of days."

Bass led a posse that caught the three bandits sound asleep on the ground next to a small creek. He arrested Jake and his gang without firing a shot and transported them to Fort Smith, Arkansas. On the way back, Spooner, though his hands were tied in front of him, slipped off his horse and tried to make it to the river a few hundred yards away.

"Watch the Whitbys and I'll get Sooner" Bass said to the other members of the posse.

Without getting off his horse, he ran down Sooner and hit him over the head with his fist. Sooner tumbled over and Bass waited until he got up and then walked him back to where the other two criminals were being guarded. There was a significant fanfare as the posse rode down the main street of Fort Smith with the three prisoners. Many of the law enforcement personnel had bets that Blake wouldn't return with Sooner. In fact, there were odds that Bass wouldn't return at all. He brought the killers before Judge Parker, who thanked him in public. After the jury found the half Cherokee Indian and the two brothers guilty, Parker sentenced them to hang.

The attorney for Sooner was able to obtain a thirty day postponement of his execution so an appeal could be filed. In the interim, one of the trustees at the jail smuggled a colt revolver into Jake's cell and after shooting a guard, Sooner escaped on the deputy's horse. Blake was at home with his wife and two children when the message came that the convicted murderer had killed a guard and escaped. It took a few days for Bass to get the message from Judge Parker. Its content was clear. "Don't take any chances. If he blinks at all, shoot to kill."

Bass caught up with the escaped man within a few days at a saloon in a small town in southeastern Oklahoma. Blake got lucky. The convicted murderer was sighted coming into Norman and the sheriff telegraphed Judge Parker who let Bass know where his target was. Bass didn't take any chances as he tied his horse three building away from the saloon and walked back to it. Sooner Jake had his back to the front café doors as Bass entered the small two table, one bar saloon with a dirt floor. "I'm Deputy Bass Blake. Don't turn around but put your colt on the bar. You're going back to Arkansas with me."

Jake didn't turn around but kept drinking his beer. "Are you sure you can take me?"

"I did before and besides, I have a gun trained on you. You don't have a chance." Bass replied.

The wanted man put his gun on the bar but continued to stand at the bar until he finished his drink. Then he turned and walked over to Bass, put his hands out and Blake put the cuffs on him. The ride back to Fort Smith was uneventful and a second trial anticlimactic.

Sooner Jake was found guilty again and this time he was hung.

Bass was known for his perseverance and tenacity. He and his posse had a warrant out for two brothers who were wanted for murder. The problem was they couldn't get within ten miles of the brother's hideout because their neighbors, who liked the brothers, shielded them from the authorities. Bass, disguised as a tramp, left the other members of the posse in a field and walked ten miles to the brother's home. He could see that there were no horses tied up out front, so he approached the dwelling using a cane as part of his disguise. When an elderly woman answered his knock at the front door, he asked for food. It was the wanted men's mother who met Bass at the door, fed him and let him sit on the porch until her sons returned. Blake arrested them and walked them back to the posse. The mother was livid and chased after Bass for at least half the distance yelling obscenities at him.

At five foot ten inches tall, Bass Blake could handle himself in any confrontation. The three Baxter Brothers swore vengeance on Bass for wounding one of their kin. The three came upon Blake at the back of a livery stable outside Enid Oklahoma, just before dinner on a summer evening. With their guns drawn, they told Bass they were going to kill him. The young marshal drew and shot two of the brothers in the shoulder and rushed the third brother who was having a hard time pointing his gun. Bass grabbed the gun pointed at him by the third man and pulled it out of his hand. All the way to Fort Smith the three told Blake how they were going to kill him the next time they met. The problem was that the three were found guilty by a jury and Judge Parker sentenced them to hang.

One other story about Bass Blake that was told and retold many times concerned the famous female outlaw, Jesse Wright. It seems that Jesse heard that Bass had a warrant for her arrest. Rather than try to escape from the equally famous lawman, she turned herself into the authorities. Jesse loved to tell how she outsmarted the famous lawman, but she still went to jail for many years.

CHAPTER 12

Augustus Swanson was no dummy. He'd worked for Frank Wilcox for five years and knew that the man didn't forgive nor did he give up on anyone that did him wrong. He'd been in Cuba for almost six months and his contacts told him that Wilcox was in New Orleans and had made inquiries about his former overseer. Swanson had nearly twenty thousand in gold from the cotton sales proceeds he made on Wilcox's behalf. He wasn't going to give any of it back to his former master and at the same time he wasn't going to go anywhere near Frank Wilcox.

He was staying in a small village on the Caribbean about thirty miles from Havana. His life was fairly simple. He'd fish in the morning, take a siesta at noon and have some fun with the local gals in the evening. He knew that he couldn't stay here forever. When he found out that Wilcox had been elected sheriff of the county which included New Orleans, he knew the time had come to leave the friendly island. The question was where? Money wasn't an issue but he knew that he'd have to have some sort of trade to make a living. Some of the Americans that had come to Cuba had mentioned Arizona and California as places where there was a future. Gold had been found in California and statehood was something in its future. The animosity that he felt toward Bass Blake was still with him. He wondered if he'd run across the ex-slave.

He decided to leave one morning and by afternoon, he had passage on a boat to Mexico. Once he reached that country, he made his way up the coast to Texas. Reconstruction was in full bloom in that territory when Swanson arrived. Federal troops were stationed along the border of the state yet the central portion of the large state was mainly unprotected. He made his way to Abilene and took a week to see who was who in the town. He started showing up at one of the local saloons where a lot of the action seemed to be taking place. After a few nights of drinking, he learned who the gang members were in town and what they were doing to make money. Rustling was rampant and gangs of four to six men were making enough money to fill their nights with all the entertainment they sought. He became friendly with two members of one gang and they brought him into the fold. Abilene became a nesting place for all kinds of criminals. Law enforcement was minimal and Swanson fit in perfectly.

For two years the gang, nicknamed the "A Town Bunch" did as they pleased. The cattle herds were large and the ranchos scattered. The ranchers, a law unto themselves, couldn't protect their own herds from the rustlers, who were mainly ex confederate soldiers... It wasn't until 1870 when the town hired Tom Smith as City Marshall at One Hundred Fifty Dollars a month that a semblance of order came to the town. The first thing Smith did was ban guns in the city of Abilene. The outlaw element stated that they wouldn't comply especially since Smith didn't wear a gun. Surprisingly, most of the cowhands went along with the new edict and surrendered their guns to Tom Smith, while they were in town. The exception was Augustus Swanson and his cohort, Billy Taylor. When confronted by Smith in the Lady Luck Saloon, Swanson told Smith to go to hell. Smith left hooked Swanson in the jaw and quickly turned and hit Taylor with his right hand. Both men went down. Smith took the guns away from the stunned gun hands and threw them in jail until the next morning.

Tom Smith grew up in New York and planned to be a prizefighter. When that didn't prove to be lucrative, he went to work for the railroad as a peace officer in Colorado and Wyoming.

The citizens of Abilene, the business owners and the town council all liked Smith. The criminal element knew not to take Smith on when he was in the city, because many citizens would back his play. It was his presence that kept the gangs in check and made Abilene a more livable city for the average citizen, but his tenure was short.

He rode out to the Bar B Ranch one day to settle a fence dispute with the owner of the Crooked R Ranch. On his way he was intercepted by two men, who brutally murdered the lawman. The two were subsequently captured, tried and sent to prison. Everyone knew they were members of the A Town Gang, but it couldn't be proven. With railroad spurs being opened in other Texas towns, the cattle drive bypassed Abilene and the gangs went where the action was. Swanson and his gang immediately moved on. With Texas coming into the union and the Texas rangers being given greater authority, Swanson decided to leave the gang and try his luck in California.

The former overseer was riding the stage to Tucson when it was held up by three masked outlaws. They ordered the four passengers out of the stage, to drop their weapons on the ground and turn their pockets inside out. Swanson didn't like having the tables turned on him one bit. Though the outlaws were masked, he took note of their general build, what they were wearing and any characteristic he could remember.

He'd been careful not to carry too much money with him and relied on the transfer of funds between banks to move his money. Prior to leaving Texas he transferred all his funds to the Territorial Bank of Tucson. After the outlaws left, the passengers got back on the stagecoach and made their way to the big city of Tucson. The stage driver reported the robbery to the sheriff and the passengers were put up at the Tucson Hotel by the stagecoach company and given vouchers for food and drinks. The company promised to make arrangements for the passenger's stolen funds to be replenished and transportation provided to take them to their destination.

Swanson was able to get some of his funds from the bank in town and went to the hotel to freshen up. About an hour later he went to the saloon in the hotel and ordered a cold beer. He wasn't surprised when he saw two men at the bar that could be two of the holdup men. He slowly made his way to the bar and when he saw the expression on their faces when they saw him with his gun pointed at them, he knew they were two of the holdup men...

"Put your guns on the bar and hand over my money pouch." Swanson smiled at the two men.

The two bandits looked at each other and the gun trained on them and tried to bluff their way out of the predicament. "We don't know what you're talking about." The one on the right said.

Swanson hit that man over the head with his gun and he fell in front of the bar. "You're next unless you give me what's mine." The former Alabaman said to the other man.

The second highway man looked down at his companion and immediately reached in his pocket and handed some money to Swanson. "That's all I have. My partner has the rest."

"Get it from him and don't make any mistakes or you're a dead man."

"What are you going to do with us?" the man asked after he gave Swanson all their money...

"Nothing. I got my money back, but I don't know what the sheriff will do when he finds out you're in town."

One bandit helped his fallen partner up and walked him to the front of the saloon. As he turned to go through the café doors, he saw Swanson standing beside him. We gave you your money. What do you want?"

"I want to meet the third man. Maybe I want to join up with you. Did you ever consider that?"

Swanson helped the injured man onto his horse and told the two to follow him down to the livery where he purchased a horse and saddle. "Let's go find the other guy and see if we can make some money. But first I'll take your guns in case your other partner doesn't want to negotiate."

The three stagecoach robbers had a hideout in the foothills about five miles west of Tucson. Swanson tried to engage them in conversation but for the most part the two kept their heads down and were quiet. Swanson made sure they were in front of him all the way there. The shack they lived in was part of a deserted ranch. It didn't appear as though there was any livestock on the ramshackle rancho, but there were remnants of what were once corrals and holding pens. The two men with him named Hank and Jake said there was an active well on the property.

A horse was tied to a railing in front of a broken-down building. Swanson had them call out to the third man as they approached the house. A tall, thin, whiskered man came out on the rotten porch. "Who the hell is this?" he asked Jake.

As they got closer, he could see it was one of the men they robbed on the stage and he reached for his gun. Swanson shot him in the chest and the third man fell over dead. "Well so much for a four-man gang." Swanson laughed.

"I want you two to bury him out back and then come into the cabin. I want to see what's in there and learn what the three of you have been doing to make some money."

A four-legged table with two chairs and a bed next to the back wall took up most of the space in the one room building. There was some semblance of a sink with a pump on top and a potbellied stove in a corner. It was filthier than anything he'd seen including the slave quarters on the plantation. When Hank and Jake returned from burying Jim Slanton, the third man, they stood in front of the table while Swanson sat in a chair facing them.

"How much money did you get from the stage robbery other than mine?"

Hank responded. We probably got sixty dollars and some jewelry other than your money."

"How often do you rob the stagecoach?" Swanson asked Jake.

"Maybe three times a month?"

"Where?"

"Mostly the stages to Nogales. We pick a spot about six miles south of Tucson and hide behind some shrubs. I can show you the spot whenever you want."

"Do you rob anything else?"

"No, Slanton didn't want to." Hank said.

"What do you guys do for money for entertainment?"

"We don't need much."

"Well, I do. I'm going to have a gang. You two can join me or you can move on and I'll recruit some other cowboys. What's it going to be?"

"You haven't told us what the gang is going to do?" Hank asked.

"Well, I'll tell you one thing for sure. We're going to make some money and stay around here for some time. I don't like robbing stage coaches. Sooner or later, there's going to be two or three lawmen in the coach and they're going to blow your heads off. We need to make some money quickly. I saw there was a freight office in Tucson. Where does most of the freight go?"

Hank seemed to be the brighter of the two. "Most of the freight is between Phoenix and Tucson. There's some to Bisbee and Nogales. The three freight lines have three or four wagons each going to the cities each month."

"Are you two under suspicion for any of the stagecoach holdups?"

"I was questioned by the sheriff once, but we wore masks on the holdup and they couldn't prove anything." Hank said

"If we start robbing supply wagons, sooner or later they're going to come looking here. This is a dump. As soon as we can make some money, we're going to fix this place up, stock it with a few cattle and make it look presentable. We're going to look like respectable ranchers if the law ever comes here. If we do this right, we can be in business for a long time. What do you say?"

CHAPTER 13

Over the next week, Swanson spent his time in Tucson analyzing the three freight hauling companies. One of them was owned by a company in Phoenix, another by a local husband and wife and the third by two brothers from Tucson. He became friendly with one of the dispatchers from the company owned locally by two brothers. Over a couple of drinks, which he bought, Swanson was able to get an idea how often each of the three freighters went to Phoenix, Nogales, and Bisbee and how many wagons were in the convoy. Bisbee was in the midst of a building boom and most of the freight shipped there was building materials. Swanson decided to rob a three-wagon shipment to Bisbee next Wednesday.

That Wednesday the three would be bandits came into town and waited until the wagon train was ready to travel. Swanson and the other two had spent the previous two days seeking the best place for an ambush. They'd be outnumbered but if they struck quickly, they could pull it off.

There was a spot about two miles outside Tucson on the Bisbee Road that had an outcropping of rocks on each side. One man could hide behind the rocks on the left of the trail and two on the other side without being seen. They cut down a large tree limb and placed it over the road used by the freighter. When the three-wagon convoy stopped to move the limb, they made their move. There was a shotgun rider sitting alongside the driver on the first wagon, but Swanson quickly neutralized him with a rifle shot to the chest. The man fell off the wagon and probably was dead before he hit the ground. The other two drivers pulled up as soon as they saw the guard fall. The gang disarmed the three men from the wagons and had them walk back to Tucson. When the survivors were out of sight, Swanson and the other two took off their masks and drove the wagons to Nogales. It took them a day shopping the materials before they sold everything plus two of the wagons. They kept the third wagon.

Swanson knew Hank and Jake wanted to spend a couple of days in Mexico having some fun drinking and enjoying the senoritas. So, to keep his men happy, they took a few days off before heading home. Two days with the senoritas was what the doctor ordered. Swanson had the third wagon cleaned and stained so it wouldn't be recognized if the sheriff came to their Rancho. They drove the third wagon through the small town of Arivaca, staying west of Tucson on the way back. When they arrived at the hideout, they split the proceeds three ways. In retrospect, Hank and Jake probably would've passed on the two days in Mexico. As soon as they returned to the hideout, Swanson had them working all day doing repairs to the house and corrals. He told them he planned to buy some cattle after the next job. "Who's going to take care of the cattle?" Hank asked.

"The three of us will take turns feeding them. The cattle give us a good alibi if we're ever questioned about how we're making a living." Swanson's gang would alternate robbing the three freight companies and then mix it up and rob one of them twice in a row. Occasionally, they'd head up to Phoenix and rob one of the larger supply transportation lines. Swanson changed the split to one fourth each with the last fourth used to maintain their homestead. Hank and Jake couldn't see the reason for it but they were making more money than they had in the past and that made it palatable.

Swanson felt they'd pulled off too many robberies and the odds were that one day they'd fall victim to an ambush. Hank and Jake couldn't care less. They wanted to rob something every day if they could. To keep his men happy, the three decided to rob the supply wagons going to Bisbee next Wednesday. After the robbery, everything would be taken to Nogales and they'd spend a couple of days with the senoritas. They were well versed on the route the dispatcher would use and felt confident in their plan. They planned a different holdup point and lay in wait two miles further east.

When they heard the wagons coming down the dust covered road, they put on their masks. Hank and Jake were on one side of the road behind a large boulder; Swanson was on the other side in some tall shrub. As usual, they'd put a large limb of a cottonwood tree across the road and waited for the first wagon to stop. Whatever the reason, the first wagon slowly approached the limb in the road but stopped five yards from the fallen limb. The three bandits came out of their hiding place and yelled at the driver. "Throw down your guns."

Three men jumped out of the rear of the first wagon with rifles and headed toward the three bandits. Five other men came out of the other two wagons and started firing at Jake, Hank and Swanson. The three bandits returned fire but they were outgunned and Hank and Jake were shot in the chest and lay dying.

Swanson was hit twice with rifle fire, and could hear Hank and Jake calling out for him, but he got on his horse and took the road back to Tucson. He veered south and rode west until he picked up the road going north toward his hideout. As soon as he reached the road leading to the rancho, he became faint and fell to the ground. The men from the supply wagons couldn't chase the escaping bandits because they didn't have horses other than those pulling the wagons. They buried Hank and Jake where they lay and took their personals to the sheriff.

Jorge and Maria Hernandez left Mexico for Phoenix with all their possessions. Jorge's brother who lived and worked outside the large city, sent the couple ten dollars to come to his home. The Hernandez' were looking for a new start in their lives with the job the brother said his employer was holding for Jorge. They'd lived in poverty across the border near the outskirts of Nogales all ten years of their marriage. To survive, Jorge would take odd jobs cleaning stalls on ranches and Maria would wash other peoples' clothes. This would be their first trip to America. Jorge was about five feet ten inches tall and weighed one hundred sixty five pounds; he had only a second grade education. Maria was petite, nice looking and standing just under five feet tall; she had an elementary school education.

They were in their third day of the trip to Phoenix when they came upon Swanson lying on the dirt road about five miles from his hideout. Jorge was first to jump down from the wagon and give Swanson some water. Maria took a wet cloth and wiped Swanson's face. He wasn't bleeding from the two gunshot wounds, but there was a lot of dried blood around both wounds. Jorge's wife ripped up a white cloth and fashioned bandages around the two wounds, one in the right shoulder and the other in the right leg.

In Spanish, Maria said, "he's been wounded. Could he be a bandit? Maybe we should leave him with his horse."

"We can't leave him here to die. Perhaps we could leave him at a church when we come to a town."

Since Swanson was unconscious, they couldn't communicate with him, even though they were sure that he could travel. They put him in the rear of their wagon, with the intent of taking him to the next town they came to. They tied his horse to the back of their wagon. Maria planned to ride in the back with Swanson and was using a wet cloth on his face when he awoke and looked at Maria. "Who are you and where am I?"

Maria yelled to Jorge in Spanish that the hombre was awake. Jorge stopped the wagon and crawled back to where the other two were. He spoke a little English. Swanson kept asking where he was and Jorge produced an old map and pointed to where he thought they were. Swanson smiled. "Mia Casa is here." He pointed to a place on the map where his hideout was.

An hour later Jorge drove up to Swanson's cabin and the bandit asked the two to help him into the house. The former overseer remembered that Hank and Jake had been shot; therefore, there was no one else inside the cabin, He was just alert enough to tell the two Mexicans "Ganado, agua y alimentos and then he fell on his bed and passed out. The three Spanish words were for cattle, water and food. Jorge and Maria had a good idea what Swanson meant. Jorge fed the cattle some hay and filled up their trough with water. Maria found the food storage cabinet and made supper for the three, but Swanson didn't wake up. The pump at the sink was working and she filled a pan with water and washed Swanson face again, his wounds and tended to his bandages.

After Swanson squatted on the abandoned rancho, he, Hank and Jake repaired and painted the cabin and expanded its size to include two bedrooms with two beds each. The Mexican husband and wife decided to sleep in the extra room tonight and if Swanson was able to get up and tend to himself tomorrow, they would leave in the morning.

Jorge and Maria were up early, and took care of Swanson's cattle. While Maria was fixing breakfast, Jorge fed and watered his horses and hooked them up to his wagon. They planned to get an early start. The smell of bacon was what woke Swanson. Although he hurt, he got up and threw water on his face and sat down at the kitchen table. When Jorge came into the cabin, Maria served both breakfasts. They attempted small conversations during the meal but mostly they laughed at their feeble attempt to communicate.

Swanson could tell they were ready to leave and they just wanted him to say that it was okay and he could take care of himself. But he had something else in mind. When he got up, he checked to see if his money was still under one of floorboards in his room. It was there and Swanson knew that he could take substantial time off and still be financially solvent. When they were finished with the meal, Maria cleared the table and washed the dishes. Swanson looked at Jorge and handed him ten dollars in coin. "Stay until I'm much better. I'll pay you ten dollars a week."

Swanson pointed to Maria and said, "she cooks and clean and you," pointing to Jorge, "take care of Ganado." The two Mexicans talked to each other in Spanish which was too fast for Swanson to truly understand. It was Maria, who said, "one week and we go."

Swanson made a steady recovery during the week. Both bullets went clean through and with Maria washing and cleaning the wounds daily, he was sure that there'd be no infection. As his health improved so did his interest in Maria. He made sure that Jorge didn't take notice, but every time Maria and Swanson were alone, he'd take liberties. They were small at first but lately he'd rub her bottom when he came near her and occasionally, he'd fondle her breasts. Each time she would push him away or slap him.

But Jorge wasn't dumb. He watched the attention being given to Maria and decided he'd had enough. He was cleaning the corrals when Swanson came up to him. "Jorge, there's another corral down by the dry creek bed that I'd like fixed. The fence is rotting and some of the wire needs to be replaced. Put some of the fence posts, rails and wiring in the wagon and drive down there this afternoon."

Jorge walked back to a pile of fencing near the house and put posts, boards and wire in the wagon and off he went. Swanson smiled.

The three freighters who'd been the victims of Swanson and his gang had a meeting in a private room off the main dining room of the hotel. They'd been competitors since they came to town but now, they felt a kinship, because of the losses they sustained. This was their second meeting since they hired the Pinkerton Agency to see if they could put a stop to the string of robberies. Henry Stewart of the Pinkerton Agency in Tucson conducted the meeting. He had a large map of the area displayed on the wall along with some charts showing where the robberies took place and the incidence of the holdups.

He pointed out to the representatives of the three companies where his agency felt was the most likely place for a holdup of supply wagons based upon what the gang had been doing the past year. With this information he set before the group a plan to ambush the gang. What else could the freighters do but see if it would work. Their first attempt met with failure. The holdup was on the Tucson to Bisbee Road instead of the one they thought, namely, the Tucson to Nogales Road.

Their second attempt resulted in them killing Hank and Jake and severely wounding the third man. Flushed with success, the Pinkertons asked the freighters to let them have two more weeks to see if they could track down the third man who was possibly the leader of the gang. The Pinkerton Agents started talking to the employees of the three freight offices to see if anyone had been asking them a lot of questions about their routes. It took three days but one of the dispatchers told them about a man he had a few drinks with after work. The man, who identified himself as Swanson, asked him a lot of questions about schedules and routes. He described the man as five feet ten inches tall, about one hundred seventy pounds, facial hair and a small scar on his left cheekbone.

The dispatcher had a good memory and a keen eye. Harold Jeffries told the Pinkertons that the man described where he lived. It was off the road going north to Phoenix but lying west of Tucson. He said the man told him that his homestead had been abandoned and he fixed up the house, repaired the corrals and added thirty head of cattle. Over the next few days the two Pinkerton Agents travelled the road going north to Phoenix and started checking all the dirt roads leading both east and west. They planned to be out a week to see if they could find the third man.

Frustration set in after a couple of days until they came over a rise one afternoon and saw what looked like the rancho the dispatcher identified. There were some cattle in the corrals and smoke was coming out of the chimney of a small home. The next morning they watched with binoculars trained on the property. Soon, a Mexican man and woman came out of the house just after ten AM. It was then that they saw a man they thought could be one of the robbers, follow them out of the house.

The two agents didn't know how the two Mexicans fit into this puzzle. They wondered if they were help or part of the gang. Around noon they saw the male Mexican ride off to the east with a wagon full of fencing materials. Soon thereafter the woman came out of the house with a white male right behind her. If looked to the agents like she was running away. When she stumbled and fell the man jumped on top of her and started tearing off her clothes. The agents started to make their move but the Mexican male appeared and started to beat her attacker on the back and legs with a pitch fork handle. The woman got up and ran to the house; she was completely nude. The Mexican dragged the man, who seemed to be unconscious, into the house and literally threw him in the front door.

When the Pinkerton Agents got to the house they tied their horses to the rail out front, took out their guns and cautiously entered the house one at a time. Their suspect was lying on his stomach on a bed in a small room and the male Mexican was consoling the woman in the kitchen; she'd wrapped a table cloth around her naked body and sobbed hysterically. Agent Joe Horn, who spoke Spanish, identified himself and his partner, Agent Mark Hubbard. "We're after a bandit who robbed a stage coach and was shot during the holdup."

The agents witnessed the brutal beating the suspect took and they ignored him while they spoke to the man and woman. The Mexicans looked at the two agents and the male said, "we found the senor lying on a road five miles from here with two bullet wounds." He pointed at the man lying on the bed.

"When he woke, he told us to take him to his rancho. We were going to stay a week to let him recover from his wounds and then leave. He gave us ten dollars in gold." Jorge showed the agents the money.

Joe Horn looked at the coin and handed it back to Jorge. "This looks like the money stolen from the Wells Fargo Stage about six months ago," he told Hubbard.

Swanson wasn't hurt as bad as he let on; he was listening to the conversation in the other room and assessing his options. He knew this day would come sometime and he wasn't without a plan. He got up quietly, shut the door to his room, and bolted it with a two by four.

He took the money from under the floor board, grabbed his holster and rifle and crashed through the bedroom window. He was hurt but he realized he'd be hung if he quit now. His horse was in a lean-to in back of the house. He didn't have time to put the saddle on but with the halter in place he climbed on the horse's back and made his way past the house and out the entrance road until he reached the north access road. He crossed over and made his way to an outcropping about three hundred yards from the north/south road and hopped off.

When Hubbard heard the crash, he broke down the door to Swanson's bedroom and saw the broken window. He rushed back into the kitchen and yelled at Horn. "He went out the back window and is mounting a horse now. Maybe we can get him as he rides by"

Horn followed by Hubbard rushed out the front door and fired at the escaping bandit. One round seemed to hit Swanson but he continued on. The Pinkertons mounted their horses and went after the former overseer. They picked up his tracks as they crossed over the main north/south road but momentarily lost the fleeing bandit.

Swanson knew the Pinkertons would come after him, so he found a spot he liked, got off his horse and lay in wait. Mark Hubbard was the first one he saw. Carefully, the bandit lined up his shot and pulled the trigger. Hubbard fell off his horse and lay in the dirt. Horn pulled up when he saw Hubbard go down, jumped off his horse and dragged Hubbard into some brush. Swanson accomplished what he wanted. He rounded up his horse and made his way west. He'd have to be careful, but he was confident he'd make it to California.

CHAPTER 14

Horn tried to stop the bleeding to Hubbard's shoulder but he wasn't that successful. He had to get some medical attention for his partner or he might die. He thought of the Mexican woman who tended to the man who just shot his partner. Horn always carried a large knife with him and he fashioned a travois out of some of the small branches and tied it to Hubbard's horse. When he was ready, he rolled his friend onto the carrier and made his way back to where he left the Mexicans

The husband and wife were packing and ready to depart when Horn came down the road. The couple rushed to him when they saw the travois and Horn. The husband picked up the fallen man and carried him into the cabin and laid him on the bed Swanson was using. The woman immediately took Hubbard's shirt off and washed the wound. She left for a few minutes and when she returned, she put some compound on the wound and gradually the bleeding stopped.

Horn conversed with the couple in Spanish and asked the woman what Hubbard's chances are. She said he needed to be in a hospital or treated by a doctor. "Can you care for him? I'll pay."

"We have a new job in Phoenix and we're already late." The husband said.

"I could have my company talk to your future employer and explain what's happening. I don't want to move my friend for fear he'll start bleeding again."

The couple looked at each other and nodded. They gave Horn the address of Jorge's brother and said they'd stay a week and that was it. "Do you need some provisions? I can purchase whatever you need at a general store in Tucson. Horn said.

Maria pointed to the supply cabinet. "There are Mucho provisions such as coffee, salt, bacon, potatoes and sugar. We could live here for a couple of months on what is stored here. There're cattle out there that could be butchered if meat is needed."

"I'd like to keep my partner in the single room. Can you and your husband sleep in the other room? I'll sleep on the floor by Hubbard and call you if there's a problem."

Over the next week, Hubbard's condition improved; in fact, he walked around the cabin one time. Maria did a fine job but the week was ending and the couple was preparing to move on. Horn looked around the property. To him it looked like a place where a couple could make a fine home and a good living.

He decided to talk to the couple and present a plan to them to see if they understood it. "Why don't the two of you stay here? You can file on this land and I can help you. In fact, I'll have my agency prepare the paperwork; all you two need to do is sign your names to the filing. The property has a good well, thirty head of cattle and enough feed for the cattle to last a month. The bandit is not going to return. He knows we'll hang him if he does. I think you can grow vegetables and with that number of cattle, you can feed yourselves. All you need is some extra money in case there's a drought. You could sell some of the cattle if you needed money or you could negotiate with someone who has a bull and increase your herd."

It didn't take the couple long to make up their mind. The smile on Maria's face said it all. Horn and Hubbard stayed with the couple for another two weeks. At one point, Horn said that Hubbard was well enough to travel. In fact, Horn was comfortable enough to go into Tucson alone and let his supervisor know what was going on. When he returned, he had the documents the couple needed to sign. He was happy to see that Hubbard was moving well. During the two weeks, Jorge, with Hubbard acting as a gofer, fixed most of the corrals and holding pens; Maria planted lettuce, tomatoes and corn. When the two Pinkerton men said goodbye, Maria kissed both on the cheeks.

The couple watched the two Pinkertons until they were out of sight. While Jorge was having a cup of coffee at the kitchen table, Maria went into Swanson's old room and returned with a paper sack and put it on the table in front of Jorge. "I found this when I was replacing the floor boards in the bandit's room. There's thirty-five hundred dollars here. The man was in a hurry when he left and didn't take all his money. I don't think he's coming back, so I guess this is ours."

The ride back to Tucson by the two partners was slow and deliberate. When they reached Tucson, Hubbard went to see the company doctor and Horn, after filing the paperwork for the Mexican couple, reported to the agent in charge. Within a few days, he, along with two senior agents met with Francis J. Schmidt, the district manager, in his office. Horn covered the entire episode involving Swanson and when he was finished, he made his conclusion. "That bandit is dangerous and probably will go to California and most likely Los Angeles. We're going to process a warrant for murder and send it to our office in LA., along with his description."

"Who's our agent out there?" One of senior agents asked.

"Well, we have a lot of agents in California, but I'm going to recommend they give the file to James J. Jefferson. He's run down a lot of desperados and I think he can handle Swanson. He's worked with the sheriff in Santa Barbara County and a civilian who's helped in the past." Schmidt said.

"Who's that?"

A fellow by the name of Tommy Sanchez, who everyone says, is the fastest gun alive."

Jorge and Maria took Horn's suggestion and made arrangements with a farmer five miles away to bring his bull over for a few months at a time so they could cover the cattle. When Horn came back with the documents he filed on the abandoned property on their behalf, the couple couldn't believe their luck. Never in their wildest dreams could they ever have envisioned what had fallen into their laps. It was nearly one year later that they welcomed a six-pound baby boy who they named Joseph after Joe Horn. They wrote to Jorge's brother and asked if he and his family would like to be partners in a hundred-acre rancho.

CHAPTER 15

The wedding of Silas Smith to Marjorie Rawlins at her ranch may not have been as elegant as the joining of Juan Sanchez and Linda De L'Ortega, but it was just as much fun. Tommy Sanchez was the best man and gave the couple a case of his prized Pinot Noir. Sarah Sanchez was the maid of honor and gave the newlyweds an oil painting of Tommy Sanchez.

Silas had long admired Tommy. It was Tommy who helped him through troubling times, both as a friend and supporter. Years earlier, Silas had been found unconscious by Tommy and Sarah in a desolate canyon south of Santa Barbara. He'd been shot in the back and left for dead. How he survived was a tribute to the man himself and both Sanchez' who acted quickly taking him over harsh terrain during a three-day period and bringing Silas to the hospital in Santa Barbara, where he recovered.

Though his wound was not lethal, he couldn't remember who he was and what he'd been doing prior to being shot. The Sanchez' took him in and employed him at their large ranch in the Santa Ynez Valley, with the hope that he would recover his memory, which never happened. But that wasn't all that had happened to him. He was arrested by the then sheriff and charged with being the mastermind of a train robbery south of Santa Barbara. It was Juan Sanchez who acted as his attorney at his trial held in Ventura. But it was Tommy Sanchez who persevered and wouldn't abandon his friend. He subsequently was able to find the person who committed the robbery and Silas went free.

Although Silas never recovered his memory, he was able to learn that he'd been born Hiram Bookers to a New England shipping family, had sold the family business at a substantial profit and placed the funds in a bank in Santa Barbara after he arrived in California. Why he decided to retain the name of Silas Smith rather than his real name was known only to Silas, Tommy and Sarah Sanchez.

There were at least thirty guests at the nuptials of Marjorie and Silas. They included Jacob Thunder, the new County Sheriff, James Jefferson of the Pinkerton Agency, the De L'Ortegas in addition to all of the Sanchez family. Marjorie and Silas planned to live on the five hundred acres ranch her late husband left her. At the reception Sarah Hansen had a chance to talk to her new daughter-in-law, Linda Sanchez, about the home Juan and she were building on Rancho Del Prado. 'The place is so beautiful, yet we'll only be able to live in it part time. Juan's practice has mushroomed and he's had to hire new associates. Since most of his clients are from Santa Barbara, we must live there the majority of our time."

Sarah was surprised. "He had a thriving practice here in Santa Ynez. What happened?"

"The trial in Ventura where he secured an acquittal for Silas made him well know and consequently people like a winner."

"So, he's given up all of his cases in the valley."

Linda was quick to respond. "He's turned over everything except one case to the junior members of the firm who practice in the valley. It's an interesting case. An elderly woman living in Los Alamos who still retains most of the Spanish Land Grant passed down through her family, is having a boundary dispute with her neighbor. Tensions have been raised, some of the woman's stock has disappeared and three of her employees intimidated. Juan feels that sooner or later, violence will break out if they can't get the disputed boundaries resolved."

At the same time, Juan was discussing this same issue with Tommy Sanchez. "The problem is that when the land grants were issued, some defined the boundaries using Metes and Bounds, while others used relationships such as a number of yards//meters/ acres from a prominent land mark. In this case, some of Mrs. Cota's cattle were grazing on her eastern boundary and were confiscated by her neighbor to the east, Harold Chambers. The next door neighbor said the cattle were on his land. I'm meeting with Mrs. Cota next week at her Ranch along with Mr. Chambers to see if we can resolve the issue "

"Do you want some company?"

"No. That's not necessary. Both parties are going to meet at my client's home, so I believe it'll be amiable even if they don't agree.

Silas and Marjorie left their home the next morning. They took a train to San Luis Obispo and then a steamer to San Francisco where they planned to spend their honeymoon. Their reservations were at The Inn of the Opera House in the opera district. They planned to spend a week. On the third night of their stay, they had dinner on the wharf and decided to walk a few blocks and enjoy the many fine shops. As they stopped on the pier to look at the ocean, they were accosted by two men demanding their money and jewels.

When one of the robbers grabbed Marjorie purse, Silas hit him with a left hook and then turned and struck the other with his right. Both men were down and didn't seem as though they wanted to continue the fight. "Where did you learn to fight like that? Marjorie asked her new husband.

"I learned to box in my former life. I even boxed John L'Sullivan, though I lost."

"What else are you not telling me about your other life?"

"Since I don't remember much of my former life, I can only tell you what I remember. I'll try not to hold back anything that I remember, but I'm as surprised as you that all of a sudden, I know how to do certain things. Let's take a cab back to the hotel. I don't think I've showed you how much I love you." Marjorie giggled.

James Jefferson had read the circular from the office in Tucson, but he hadn't much time to research the matter. He wanted to be at Silas' wedding, since he had a hand in freeing him. He bid his friend Tommy Sanchez goodbye and said he'd see him sometime later.

Juan took the train to Los Alamos on a Tuesday and was met at the train depot by Mrs. Cota's foreman. The ride in a buckboard out to her house located on the seventeen thousand acre rancho, took three hours. After an early dinner Mrs. Cota, sat down with Juan to discuss the negotiations they would have the next day with

Chambers. After an hour, they came up with an agenda and established what their objective was for tomorrow. "I trust you Mr. Sanchez. This land has been in my family since 1841. I came here as a young woman and I feel that I have to protect what my ancestors passed on to me."

"I'll do my best." Was all that Juan would say?

Chambers came with his attorney and although the meeting was professional, nothing was resolved. Chamber's attorney showed Juan their deed and a map showing the boundary between the properties. However, that deed was in direct conflict with the deed and boundary description that Mrs. Cota had. "The fence line when you bought the property was different then compared to now. You arbitrarily moved the boundary. Didn't you question the property line before you moved it?"

"Why should I question my deed? That's the piece of paper that I bought that defines what I bought. I assumed that your client moved the property line to suit herself or that no one had really checked the property line."

"That still doesn't explain confiscating my client's cattle. They had brands on them. Didn't it mean anything to you?" Juan asked Mr. Chambers.

"My foreman said he didn't find any brands on the cattle that were grazing on my property, so he assumed they were strays and put them with our main herd."

"That's a little hard to believe. The two properties together are fenced and it's impossible to have strays."

"I believe my foreman."

"We'll now that you know the real story, why not in the spirit of being a good neighbor, return them to Mrs. Cota?" Juan asked.

"I couldn't do that even if I wanted. Those cattle are mixed in with a larger herd and it's too much work to cut them out."

"One hundred head of cattle are missing. Why not reimburse Mrs. Cota for the misunderstanding. You seem like a man of means, so twenty-five hundred dollars shouldn't impact you. This would be a gesture of good will and a start to resolving the issue, between the two properties." Juan responded.

"You're pretty smooth. I'm not going to be pushed into making a quick decision. What else do you have to discuss?"

"Several of Mrs. Cota's employees have been roughed up by your men. What's that all about?"

"I've given my men explicit orders not to get into scrapes. Her men came looking for trouble and my men had to defend themselves."

Chambers looked to his attorney, "let's go John. There's nothing more that we can do here."

When the two men left, Juan sat down with his client to discuss their next step. "I know your position is sound Mrs. Cota but I'd like to ride out to the disputed area and see if there's a compromise position we can suggest before we start legal action."

With his client's consent he and her foreman rode out to the disputed boundary. The foreman provided Juan with a horse. It took them an hour to reach the fence line between the two properties. Juan had copies of both property owners' maps. Mrs. Cota's fence line had been cut down and Chambers had installed a fence where his deed said the line was. "Who cut her fence down?" Juan asked the foreman.

"Their foreman said his crew did it."

The terrain around the disputed line was flat for about ten miles in all directions. With a clear sky, it didn't take Juan long to see where the potential problem lay. There were two outcroppings of rocks that were visible to him. One was near the existing fence line; the other was at least two to three miles away. One answer to the dispute was that since Chambers used an outcropping relationship to define his boundary, it was possible that he selected the wrong outcropping to establish his boundary.

Just then four men rode up on Chamber's side of the fence to where Juan and Cota's foreman were talking. Each of the four men was armed. The one in the lead was tall and rawboned, two others were of average height and fairly young while the fourth man was graying and had an edge to him. "What are you men doing here?" The tallest of the four asked

"I'm Mrs. Cota's attorney. I met with Mr. Chambers this morning to discuss the boundary dispute." Juan said.

"There's no dispute. Our fence is on the property line. The tall man responded.

Juan saw this as an opportunity to resolve the issue if what he saw was correct. "I wonder if you can cut the fence here so we can take a look at that outcropping about three miles away.' Juan pointed to the distant rocks.

The tall man was quick to respond. "That's not possible. Mr. Chambers doesn't like trespassers on his property. In fact, we've been given authority to shoot any trespassers."

"I can see with that attitude why there's been a dispute." Juan responded.

"I don't think I like your attitude sonny. I can see where you can rile some folks quickly. I suggest the two of you go back to where you came from. It's dangerous out here. There've been people shot and their bodies left to the coyotes."

Just then one of the four on the other side of the fence, fired a couple of shots over Juan's head, his horse bucked and Juan was thrown to the ground. The four laughed out loud and rode off. Juan landed mostly on his left shoulder very hand. He heard something break but wasn't sure if it was his shoulder or his hand. Cota's foreman quickly dismounted and ran to help Juan. "Are you okay?" He asked.

"I don't know. Give me a few seconds."

Juan was stunned and lay on his back for a few moments before he attempted to rise. When he rose, he spoke to the foreman. "I hurt but if you can get my horse and help me into the saddle, I believe I can make it back to Mrs. Cota's. I don't know what we did to provoke them?"

The foreman grabbed Juan's horse, settled it down and then helped his guest mount his horse. Juan could sit the saddle but he was still groggy, so the foreman took the reins to Juan's horse and led him back to the Cota's Hacienda. He helped Juan off the horse and assisted him into the kitchen. The Mexican housekeeper cut off Juan's shirt, cleaned up his face and head and made a sling for his shoulder. She checked his hand and though it hurt, she told him it wasn't broken. Someone gave him a glass of whiskey and the foreman helped him into the guest room.

Mrs. Cota was shocked that her attorney had been assaulted and she cried. Juan told her not to worry; he'd been hurt worse in the past. He fell asleep quickly and woke up at five the next morning. He didn't want anything to eat but took two cups of coffee. Although he hurt all over, he cleaned up and was on his way when he saw Mrs. Cota at the front entrance. "Maybe I should forget about the boundary dispute. I can see you are really hurt and I don't want any more trouble. It isn't worth it."

"You're a nice woman and you shouldn't be treated this way. I must go home but I'll be back; your boundary dispute will be resolved. I promise you."

The trip home was painful, especially the buckboard ride to the train depot in Los Alamos. The train ride was okay, but he was grateful that Rancho Del Prado was just a few miles away. Linda saw him riding down the entryway and rushed out. "Where have you been; we were so worried."

When she saw the sling, she broke down and cried. "What happened?"

Just then Tommy and Sarah came out on the porch. Tommy helped Juan down and led him into the kitchen. His mother got a wet cloth and put it against his forehead, while Linda poured him a glass of cold water and kissed him. Juan drank the water and when he was ready, he told the group that he would tell everyone what happened in a couple of days, but he was hurting too much to talk right now,

Tomas went for the doctor and brought him back to the ranch; Juan's shoulder was broken and his hand sprained. The doctor gave Juan some medication to sleep and helped Tommy put his stepson to bed. Linda was distraught over what happened to Juan and she wouldn't leave his side.

It wasn't until the following afternoon that Juan was able to get up, have some coffee and sit up for a few minutes. "I don't want to talk just yet, give me until tomorrow and I'll fill you in on what happened." Juan said.

Two days later he told them the story, the description of the four men and who shot at him." Tell me more about the one with the gray hair." Tommy asked.

I'd say he's about forty five, maybe five feet ten inches tall, and has a jagged scar on his left cheek. He wore his gun a little lower than the others. Do you know him?"

"I think it's a guy named Charlie Crisp. He's a hired gun. He may be the one that's intimidating your client's employees."

"The scar was really distinctive. I wonder how he got it." Juan asked.

Tommy smiled. He came in second in a shootout about twenty years ago."

Sarah turned to Tommy. "Is he trouble?"

"Without giving an opinion about the boundary, my guess is you have a serious problem and he's there to enforce it." Tommy told Juan.

"You're not going to do anything, are you Tommy?" Juan asked.

"My philosophy is that if you allow someone to intimidate you, they'll just keep pushing. I don't like it when any of my family is shot at. I take it personal even if it wasn't meant that way."

"Can we wait a couple of weeks until my shoulder is improved? I want to be there if there's a confrontation."

"What about the hand?"

"The doctor says it's sprained, but I can use it."

The Smiths had returned from their honeymoon in San Francisco and came for dinner the following evening. After Silas was briefed on what happened, he insisted that he'd be allowed to go with Tommy and Juan. Marjorie was hesitant at first until Silas told her firmly that Juan and Tommy saved his life and any chance he had, he'd be there for them.

Over the next month, Juan's shoulder improved and his hand was fine. When he was ready to ride, he told Tommy and Silas it was time. Tommy sent several of his vaqueros to Los Alamos on different days of the week to see if there was a time that Chambers and his men were in town... It turned out that Chambers and about six of his riders would come to Los Alamos every Wednesday to pick up supplies. Before they headed home, they always stopped for a couple of drinks at the Silver Dollar Saloon in town. Tommy, Silas, Raoul, Juan, Tomas and four Vaqueros went by train to Los Alamos with their horses. Although Silas wasn't part of the family, he refused to be excluded; each was armed with a Remington. Tommy chose his Colt Revolver. They timed their arrival so that they'd be there after Chambers and his crew had at least one beer at the Silver Dollar Saloon.

Tommy sent Tomas and the four Vaqueros around to the back of the saloon. They were to enter the rear door so no one would escape out the back. There was a noticeable silence as Tomas and the four Vaqueros carrying rifles entered from the rear door and stayed there. But when Tommy and the four others walked in the front door and spread out, it was as though there was a funeral service in sessions. Chambers and his men occupied two of the four tables in the room. Chambers, Charlie Crisp and two others occupied one table; the other four

Chambers' men were at a second table. Chambers turned to Crisp and asked who entered. "That's Tommy Sanchez and his men."

"Who's that?"

"You're looking at the fastest gun alive or as many men have called him, death."

"Is he faster than you?"

"Oh yeah. How do you think I got this scar on my cheek?"

"What's he doing here?"

"That was his adopted son this little shit took a shot at. "Crisp pointed to one of the cowboys at his table.

"He doesn't scare me." The cowboy responded.

"You mean Cota's attorney is his son?" Chambers asked.

"Yup."

Tommy walked up to Chambers' table while Silas and the others held back and stood in front of the other table where four of Chamber's men sat. "I didn't know you were in this area Charlie? I can't have any of my family, who are minding their own business be attacked, let alone left out on the range severely injured."

"I didn't have anything to do with it. Though I was with the group; it happened so fast that there was nothing I could do." Just then, the young man who shot at Juan rose and reached for his revolver. Tommy shot him twice, once in the shoulder and once in his gun hand before he even touched his holster. The young man yelled and slumped to the floor holding his hand. Just as quick, Tommy brought his gun back to bear on the other three at the table. Chambers stared in disbelief at what he saw. "Now look here, you can't shoot any of my men and get away with it."

Juan, who was not as fast as Tommy, drew his gun and pointed it at the four at the second table. Tommy glared at Chambers and the man's face turned white. "Charlie, you and the other three who were with you when Juan was shot are leaving town today. Do I make myself clear?"

Chambers stood up. "Who the hell do you think you are? My men aren't going anywhere."

"I don't care if they leave by train or in a pine box. If you continue to object, you'll go with them, either upright or down." Chambers sat down. He tried to stare Tommy down, but the steel grey eyes of the man in black sent a shiver up and down his spine.

"What if we settle the dispute with Mrs. Cota? Would that square us?"

"I have nothing to do with the boundary dispute. That's Juan's business. Whether you settle or not, Charlie and the other three are leaving town and are not coming back. If I have to come back here because any of my family is threatened again, you'll leave town."

The young cowhand that lay on the floor was treated by the bartender. The bullets went through and both wounds were bandaged and he was able to walk. The Rancho Del Prado men waited while Crisp and the other three collected their pay and gear and the Vaqueros walked them to the train going north. Before he left, Tommy had a private conversation with Charlie Crisp. All Juan heard was Crisp say, "I understand."

Silas couldn't believe what he saw. He heard about the fast draw but seeing it in person was beyond belief. He even asked Juan if what he saw was real. "I've seen it many times. He seldom kills anyone but he's so quick that his opponent doesn't know what's happened to him.

Silas walked with Tommy to the train station. "Tommy, the legend doesn't do you justice."

Over the next two weeks Chambers returned the one hundred head of cattle he confiscated and had his attorney meet with Juan to come up with a reasonable settlement for both parties. Juan's shoulder healed and he was able to go back to his practice on a full-time basis.

CHAPTER 16

After three months in Chicago, he decided the Windy City wasn't for him; William Todd took the train to California. In those days, the train trip was four days long but he didn't mind. His late wife and young child were still on his mind; he wondered if he'd ever move on with his life. Like other travelers to the western part of the United States, he took limited funds. The fear of a train robbery was paramount in the traveler's mind even though the incidence of train robberies paled in comparison to the robberies of stagecoaches.

Los Angeles in the late eighteen eighties and early nineties was a robust city of several hundred thousand people. There was a black community that William visited, but he was unimpressed with its status. He came to California at the invitation of a gentleman he made shoes for. This man lived outside Santa Barbara California. William decided to meet with that man before he decided where he wanted to locate or if he really wanted to live out west.

At Tommy Sanchez suggestion, William transferred funds to the Bank of Santa Barbara before he came west. When he arrived in that beautiful city, later known as the American Riviera, he went to the bank, produced letters from his bank in Philadelphia and one from Tommy Sanchez. He informed the bank manager what his trade was and that he may be seeking some financing.

"So, you're the one who made Mr. Sanchez' shoes? When you get settled, I'll purchase a pair of your custom shoes. Let me know." The two shook hands, William got direction to Rancho Del Prado and then took the stage to Santa Ynez.

To his surprise, they weren't robbed and he met a delightful couple who ran the Kinevan Way Station. After a quick lunch all the passengers got back on the stage and were in Santa Ynez four hours later. When the passengers were offloaded at the Central Hotel, he wired the Sanchez that he arrived and asked if they could meet in the next few days. Tommy wired back the next morning that they'd send a carriage for him and he'd be their guest at Rancho Del Prado.

It was Sarah who saw the wagon coming down the entranceway and went out on the porch to greet their guest. She hadn't realized William Todd was black but that didn't matter, he wasn't any darker than her first husband, Crazy Horse. Tomas had driven into Santa Ynez to meet William; he took William's two bags and put them in the guest room in the main house. Tommy was called and came out to greet his guest. "It's a pleasure to greet you William, my condolences about the passing of your wife and children"

It was just after lunch so Tommy invited his guest to see his vineyard and where they made their wine. Tommy was busy with a meeting the next day, but over dinner that night Tommy suggested that Tomas escort William into Santa Ynez. "This will give you an opportunity to see the small town, look at some of the locations and be introduced to some of the merchants by Tomas."

The question was gnawing at him and he had to ask his host. "If you're uncomfortable with me staying at your fine house, I'll understand."

Tommy smiled. I'm half white and half Sioux. I'm referred to by some as a half breed. My wife was married to the Indian Warrior, Crazy Horse and her children are half breeds. I have never judged a man by the color of his skin, only by his character."

When William retired that night, he realized he met an important acquaintance. The family and children were fun to be with and Mrs. Sanchez was positively beautiful. The next morning, he and Tomas rode into Santa Ynez, met the manager of the hotel and most of the merchants. All were positive and welcomed him to their community. "I remember seeing Tommy Sanchez's new boots and told him I'd like to know who made them. I was surprised to learn that you were living in Philadelphia. I hope you join our community." The manager of the hotel said.

They found a couple of buildings that would be suitable and were vacant. Tomas suggested they have lunch at the Lucky Lady Saloon across from the Central Hotel. "They have the best brisket in town."

There were a few cowboys at the bar as they walked in but only a few customers sitting at the tables. Two of the cowboys took a long look at William. He'd experienced that before and assumed there weren't many blacks in the area. Tomas ordered two beers.

They finished their lunch and had another beer each. The bartender came with the beer and asked William where he was from. "I lived in Philadelphia for almost ten years. I make custom shoes, mainly for the horse-riding set. Mr. Sanchez was one of my best customers."

"I saw the boots. I'd like a pair if you decide to set up shop here in town. How long have you known the famous gunman?" Tomas tensed as the conversation drifted to include his patron.

"What do you mean gunman?" William asked.

"He's the fastest man alive when it comes to using a six gun. There never was anyone faster and there probably never will be. His wife also has a history. She was the wife of Crazy Horse the Indian leader of the Battle of The Little Big Horn, where an army of three hundred Americans were massacred."

"I think that's enough Charlie. Give me the bill, we're going now." Tomas got up and William followed him out.

"What's that all about?" William asked.

"Mr. and Mrs. Sanchez have been asked those questions by many of their friends and acquaintances... Rather than bother them again, I'll tell you what I know. If you want to ask them some more about their former lives, that's up to you."

"Tommy is the son of Sitting Bull and a white woman the old man captured by the name of Elizabeth Kelly. Tommy is half white and half Sioux. He learned to use a gun early in his life when he was on his own. Over the past years, he seldom takes out his gun but if he does, he means business. I saw him in action last year when Juan, Mrs. Sanchez' son was hurt by some cowboys in Los Alamos. When he drew his gun, it was a blur. How he can be that fast is a miracle."

"What about Mrs. Sanchez?" Joshua asked.

"She was captured by the Sioux when she was thirteen, subsequently adopted by a Sioux family and forced into a marriage to Crazy Horse, the Indian hero of the Battle of the Little Big Horn. She bore him two children. Juan, her oldest, is an established attorney in Santa Barbara and has been adopted by Mr. Sanchez. They're like brothers. Naiwa, her daughter, is married to Raoul who was my predecessor. She had two children by her first marriage to a Sioux Brave who died and one with Raoul. He and she own the five hundred acre Rancho next to Rancho Del Prado. Mrs. Sanchez is an accomplished painter. Many of her works are hung in the Central Hotel lobby."

"How do the townspeople react to them?" William asked.

"Some act in awe of them, others fear Tommy; others like Tommy and Sarah very much. He's been very generous to the community. At least once a year, he's sworn in as a Sheriff's Deputy to capture someone who's evading the law. He's probably the best tracker in the area."

"Are there many black people in the community?" William was probing.

"Very few, but your skin isn't much darker than mine. You'd probably pass as Mexican."

William had one more question for Tomas. "Do you think a black businessman can survive here and also be successful?"

"I do."

The newcomer took Tomas' advice and with encouragement from Tommy Sanchez, he opened a shoemaker's shop next to the livery on Sagunto Street in Santa Ynez. Not everything went as smoothly as his meeting with the Sanchez' family. For the first few months, the only customers he had were from Rancho Del Prado. Townspeople wouldn't patronize the business. Tommy assumed the reason was that no one ever dealt with a black proprietor. After two months, William shared his concerns with Tommy.

"You had a thriving mail order business prior to coming here. Why not contact your former clients and I'll let my friends in the area know of your capability? In addition, I suggest that we advertise in Santa Barbara and Los Angeles and see what happens. I'm comfortable that you'll succeed and if you need an investor to tie you over for a few months, I'm that man."

The first mail order came one month later. By that time, several of Tommy's and Sarah's acquaintances came to William's shop and ordered custom shoes. Soon some of the cowboys sauntered in and when they saw some of the shoes William was capable of making; there was a steady stream of orders. He found a small house off Sagunto Street within walking distance of his shop and moved in. For the first time in years, he had a smile on his face and knew he made the correct decision to move here.

CHAPTER 17

Franklin spent a month in the nation's capital trying to determine if he wanted to accept any of the positions offered to him. One was in the cabinet; others were with lobbying firms while a group of charitable institutions wanted his name on their letterhead. Franklin Sutter alias Joshua Jones was a hot commodity since his retirement from the House of Representatives.

What he finally decided was to have a complete change in his life. He had enough money to last the rest of his days. What he needed was something he could sink his teeth into. He'd never been out west and the frontier seemed to intrigue him. At least he should take a look to see what it offered.

Train travel was fairly comfortable in the late eighteen eighties and Franklin decided to catch up on all the reading he'd been setting aside for a rainy day. On the first day of his trip, he was seated at a table with two women for dinner. The younger one was the daughter of the late Spanish Ambassador to the United States. She'd been in the states for the past six years and decided to stay in America after her father died. Her name was Maria Conchita Contreras. Her traveling companion was her father's sister and was acting as her chaperon on the trip. The main reason Maria was heading to California was to join her brother who inherited a Spanish Land Grant in a small town near Santa Barbara California.

Franklin was surprised when he realized they spent three hours at dinner and wouldn't have left had not the waiter reminded them that they were the last ones in the dining car. He escorted Maria and her companion to their compartment and asked if they could have dinner tomorrow. Maria smiled, held out her hand and he kissed it. He went to bed that night and couldn't sleep. He was like a schoolboy with a crush on a new girl. After breakfast, he went into the lounge to read but didn't see the young woman that day. He took a chance and went to the dining car at the same time as last evening and she was there. He asked the waiter if he could join the two women. The waiter returned from the table and said they'd be delighted.

He kissed her hand again and paid his respects to her aunt and they took up where they left off last evening. She told him about her father and how he died." I met your father one time. He was an interesting man."

"On which occasion did you meet my father?"

"I was introduced to him by my mentor, Representative Weems."

"Did you work for the congressman?"

"No. I was an associate of his. I served for twelve years in congress representing my home district of Alabama."

"I'm sorry. I didn't realize you were an important man."

"Well, I don't know about that. I'm retired now and looking forward to seeing the west. Where did you say you had property?"

They spent most of the trip together getting to know each other. He shared most things with Maria, except he didn't divulge his ancestry. He didn't know how that would be viewed. If this was something they both wanted, he would tell her then. When they arrived in Los Angeles, he decided to accompany the two ladies to Santa Barbara. Maria gave Franklin the address of her home and asked him to call upon her. He kissed her hand and looked longingly into her eyes.

The man from Alabama stayed at the Arlington Hotel for two weeks and went on a sightseeing tour of the city. He looked at property, ate at fine restaurants and sampled the wine from at least a half dozen wineries. He liked the town and the people who inhabited the area, which were predominately of Spanish origin. He knew that Maria lived in the Santa Ynez Valley, so he took the stage to the town of Santa Ynez. As they were coming over the crest of the road leading to the valley, the stage stopped abruptly and they were ordered out of the coach by three armed men wearing masks.

He'd read about the highwaymen in this part of the country, but he never thought he'd experience them first hand. He and the other three passengers were ordered to surrender all their valuables, which included several pieces of jewelry. Franklin wasn't carrying much currency on his person, but he did have four hundred dollars tucked into a false bottom of one of his pieces of luggage. The bandits didn't seem to be interested in the passenger's luggage. It looked to Franklin that they wanted to make a quick hit and then ride off. They were at least three hours from Santa Barbara. Franklin assumed there weren't law enforcement personnel in the area.

When the robbers rode off, the stagecoach driver asked the passengers to get back in the coach and he'd take them to Cold Springs Tavern run by the Kinevans. The other three passengers were women and it was obvious that the robbery had unnerved them. One of the women threw up outside the way station while the other two received a wet cloth from the proprietor and wiped their faces with it. Franklin introduced himself to the ladies. One of the women was the new school teacher and her name was Sarah Huckaby. The others were Mary Pierce, a nurse to the doctor in Solvang and Naiwa Gutterez, the daughter of Sarah Sanchez. The passengers were treated to a fine lunch paid for by the stagecoach line and the driver assured the four that they'd be reimbursed for their losses.

The stage stopped at the Central Hotel in Santa Ynez. The three ladies were met by their kin and Franklin went into the hotel and took a room for the night. He recovered the cash he was carrying in his valise, tipped the boy who carried the bags to his room and went to bed. He had a long day, but he was on an adventure. He looked forward to tomorrow and what it might bring. Breakfast was served in the hotel's dining room and when he finished, he walked into the lobby to read the paper he picked up in Santa Barbara. The first thing he noticed when he entered the lobby was four colorful paintings of Native Americans.

He studied all four paintings. One was of an Indian Village; another was of two Native Americans, probably a husband and wife. The third was a landscape and the fourth was of a warrior. He went to the desk and asked the gentleman handling registrations about the paintings. "I couldn't quite make out the last name of the artist."

"Mrs. Sarah Sanchez is the artist."

"I think I've heard that name somewhere before. Now it comes to me, I rode on the stage with a woman who said she was Sarah Sanchez's daughter."

"You must mean Naiwa Gutterez. She and her husband have a five hundred acre spread next to Mrs. Sanchez and her husband."

"So, Mrs. Sanchez is from this town. Who's her husband?"

The assistant manager smiled. "She's the wife of the famous gunman."

"You mean he shoots people?"

"He the fastest man alive with a handgun. He's not someone to trifle with. In fact, she's quite a shot herself."

"Is this the only style of painting that she does?"

"I believe that's true. She was the wife of Crazy Horse, the famous Indian who led the attack on the Seventh Cavalry and wiped-out Custer and all his men."

"I take it you don't like the Sanchez?"

"I've spoken too mush. I must get back to my duties. I didn't mean anything at all."

Franklin continued to study the painting and was captivated by the rich colors and distinctive subjects. It was near one o'clock and he asked the assistant manager where he could get a sandwich and a beer. He was directed to the saloon across the street. There were about fifteen cowboys sitting at three of the tables in the only room in the building. He also saw two men sitting at a table in the shadows near one of the walls. Franklin saw a table near them and told the bartender he wanted a beer and a brisket sandwich; He acknowledged the two men at one table as he passed by them.

He finished his sandwich and ordered another beer when there was a confrontation between two of the cowboys at one of the tables. Each had a gun in a holster on their side and the confrontation was starting to escalate. "You can't talk about her like that." One cowboy said.

"She's nothing but a high-priced whore and you can tell your boss I said so."

Just then one of the men at the table in the shadows near him rose and walked to the cowboy who was protesting the name calling. He was a thin man standing about five feet ten inches tall and dressed entirely in black. He slapped the young cowboy, took the man's gun out of his holster and told him to get back to the ranch. The silence was overpowering as the man in black turned and faced the other agitator. Everyone was quiet and everyone was now watching at the confrontation between the two men. "Oh my god, I didn't know you were in town Mr. Sanchez. I didn't mean anything. I just had too many beers. .I don't want any trouble"

Sanchez walked up to the cowboy and glared at him. Within a few seconds, he slapped the cowboy in the face and waited for his reaction. When one wasn't forthcoming, he slapped the young man again. The cowboy looked around at his friends and seemed to be trying to decide on what to do. With the whole room looking at him; he went for his gun. He didn't get even close to touching it when a shot rang out and the cowboy slumped to the floor. He'd been shot in his right shoulder. The man in black holstered his weapon walked over to his table, put down some money and he and his companion left the saloon.

Franklin was mesmerized by the incident and it took him a few minutes before he got up and asked the bartender what happened. "The cowboy called Mrs. Sanchez a whore and her husband, Tommy Sanchez shot him in the shoulder. Sanchez is nice enough, but he doesn't stand for anyone abusing his wife. The cowboy was lucky the man in black didn't kill him."

Raoul and Naiwa had come for dinner. Tommy greeted them and while his wife's daughter went into the kitchen to help, the two men had a glass of wine in Tommy's office. Before they could sit down, Sarah entered the room and announced there would be two additional guests for dinner this evening.

As soon as Sarah left the room, a magnificent carriage adorned with silver plated handles, pulled by two black horses came up the drive and stopped in front of their house. Sarah and Tommy went to greet their guests but Sarah made the introductions. "Tommy, I want you to meet Senor Enrique Contreras and his sister, Maria from Buellton."

The two men bowed and Tommy kissed Maria's hand and escorted them into their home. The others had already been seated at the dining room table as the two men entered the room. Sarah handled the introductions and sat Maria Contreras. next to Tommy.

The brother and sister were quite interested in the vineyard and winery that the Sanchez built. Enrique asked if he could come back some time and view the operation. Tommy and he discussed a date and agreed upon a week from next Friday. Another topic of conversation was the stranger that Maria met on the train. His name was Franklin Sutter, a former US Congressman from the state of Alabama. He travelled west to see if this was a place he wanted to live. Maria invited him to Buellton, but to date he had not responded. It was clear Enrique was a little concerned about a potential relationship between Sutter and his sister. After dinner, everyone adjourned to the living room. The men enjoyed a glass of wine; the women had coffee. Dessert was chocolate covered lady fingers. Contreras was taken with Sarah's beauty and her skill as an artist. He could not take his eyes off the rich colors of the Indian Villages that were hung n the dining room and living room.

"Your paintings are magnificent. I hope I'm not being too bold to ask if any of these are for sale, for I would truly love to have one in our home."

Sarah was flattered. "These are not for sale, but I have several on display in the lobby of the Central Hotel in Santa Ynez that can be purchased."

"I will make it a point to visit the hotel in the next few weeks."

After all the guests departed, the Sanchez' had a glass of wine at their nook in the kitchen. "When did you meet the Contreras?"

"I'd met Maria at the mission church in Solvang last week. We talked for some time and she shared with me that her brother had inherited a ranch in Buellton and that she's been so busy with decorating the house that she didn't have time to meet anyone near her age. What's Enrique like?"

"He seems like a pleasant man. Perhaps a little intense, but maybe that's because he didn't know anyone here. He may thaw out later on. He inherited a five-thousand-acre ranch from his father who died of pneumonia last year. His sister is a few years younger than he and as soon as they address the renovations they plan, he'll consider a suitable husband for her. I was amused at how she lighted up when she raised the issue of the man she met on the train. I haven't heard of anyone like that coming into the valley. Have you"

Two days later Franklin Sutter was admiring Sarah Sanchez's paintings hung in the Central Hotel in Santa Ynez and decided to buy the one of Crazy Horse. He completed the transaction with the hotel manager and went back into the lobby to admire his purchase. Soon thereafter, a Spanish gentleman walked in and talked to the manager and both came into the lobby and he, like Franklin admired Sarah's work especially the painting of Crazy Horse... "The painting seems to be her most popular work." Enrique Contreras said.

No sooner had the manager taken the painting off the wall than Enrique Contreras asked if there was another painting of the same individual. "No sir. This is the only one here." The manager responded.

"May I ask who purchased the painting?"

"Why it's the gentleman sitting here in the lobby."

Enrique walked over to Franklin Sutter and introduced himself. I met Mrs. Sanchez last weekend and admire her paintings, especially the one of the warriors that you just purchased. I hope I'm not impertinent to ask if you would sell it to me. I truly think that is her best work."

"Sir I appreciate your taste but I have looked at this painting for the past three days. This is the one I want. The manager seems to think the artist has painted this subject previously and perhaps would paint one for you."

"Sir may I know the name of the man who bested me today?"

"My name is Franklin Sutter of Alabama and you sir?"

"Enrique Contreras of Buellton at your service. The Spaniard bowed as he introduced himself. It wasn't until later that Franklin put the name with the young woman, he admired on the train ride out west.

CHAPTER 18

Sarah had joined with ten other women to form a group called The Friends of the Santa Inez Mission. Their goal was to provide funding and assistance in renovating the historic mission. Each Wednesday, Sarah was driven to the mission in Santa Ynez by one of their vaqueros. Though there was an occasional robbery between Santa Ynez and Solvang, Sarah had never been stopped. Perhaps no one wanted to be chased down by her husband Tommy and then again it was well known that she was an excellent shot and never went anywhere without her trusty Remington.

Today there were six workers using scaffolding to shore up a section of the west wall of the mission. A large crack running up and down the wall appeared over the past year. Some of the masonry appeared to be crumbling and was becoming a safety hazard. An architect had been hired by the women to recommend a fix. It was he who suggested the scaffolding.

On her weekly visit, Sarah always brought sandwiches and coffee for the workers. The vaquero from her ranch parked her carriage, carried what she brought and placed it on a table away from the foundation. Maria Contreras was already at the site pouring coffee for the itinerant workers. The two women greeted each other and Sarah sat down alongside the young woman.

"Thank you for the dinner invitation last weekend. My brother and I loved your home and felt comfortable with you and your husband. I feel a little embarrassed. I hope I didn't go on too long about the man I met on the train?"

Sarah smiled at her new friend. "I didn't see anything wrong. I hope for your sake that he does come to visit. If he does, please bring him to our home."

At that moment they heard a loud crack followed by a roar. Both women looked up and saw three men falling from the scaffolding near the top of the wall with large chunks of the wall chasing after them. The three landed on their backs with pieces of mortar landing on top of them. They lay under the rubble and didn't move. Sarah and Maria rushed to help but chunks of the wall were too large for them to move. Soon, the other workers were able to pull or roll the debris off the men and yelled at the women to move back. Pieces of the roof were hanging over the side and it was too dangerous to get near the injured men. In addition, a section adjacent to the wall had caved in, leaving a gaping hole in the ground. Sarah yelled for her vaquero to go for the doctor, whose office was but a few blocks away.

By the time the doctor arrived, the other three workers were able to clear most of the mortar off the fallen men, but they didn't move them. The doctor couldn't treat the injured men where they lay so the other three workers carefully moved them to a safer spot. Two of the victims were unconscious, while the third was alert but crying out for help. Two of the men had broken legs while one of the two also had a broken shoulder. The third man was not responding to the doctor and appeared to have internal injuries. The only hospital in the immediate area was in Santa Barbara and would take most of the day to reach. Sarah offered her carriage and her vaquero and

Doctor Bickford loaded the one worker, still unconscious, and sent him to Santa Barbara with written instructions.

It was late in the afternoon and Maria suggested that Sarah stay with her tonight and go home in the morning. Since there wasn't any communication between Solvang and Rancho Del Prado, Sarah was reluctant to worry Tommy. The two women then agreed that Maria and one of her vaqueros would drive Sarah home and that Maria would stay there until tomorrow. Maria's other vaquero would notify her brother of her intentions.

When they arrived at the ranch they were surprised to find that William Todd was with Tommy in his office. They'd been discussing some marketing initiatives that William planned to implement to increase his business. Sarah introduced Maria to William Todd and she could tell the two were pleased to meet each other. Naomi had prepared dinner to include William and told Sarah they had more than enough to include Maria. The four sat down in the nook in the kitchen and enjoyed fried chicken.

Without Maria's brother's presence, the young woman didn't feel as constrained as she had the previous evening. Perhaps it was the company; perhaps it was the two glasses of wine that she consumed. Whatever the reason, she was witty and constantly laughing. "I'm having so much fun tonight. Thank you, Sarah, for inviting me."

The women told of the accident this afternoon at the mission and especially the area next to the northwest portion that left a large hole. Tommy was intrigued as was William and both men suggested they visit the mission tomorrow and see what they could do to help. Maria had the guest room in the house and William enjoyed the one in the barn. Before he retired, William asked what time they were returning to the mission the next morning. Around noon the next day the four arrived at the mission and Tommy drove to the back so they could get a good look at the damage.

Enrique Contreras was already on site when the four arrived and his mouth seemed to be open as William helped Maria down from the carriage. It therefore wasn't a surprise to Tommy that Enrique's greeting to William was more perfunctory than cordial. The three men walked to the wall that crumbled and examined the hole that was present. It was about ten feet in diameter and nearly twelve feet deep. No work had been done at the site since the accident, because the supervisor of the six that had been working yesterday, was one of the injured. Tommy asked the three workers who were unhurt to place some timber around the hole. He wanted to be able to stand on the boards, look down in the hole and assess the damage.

By education, Enrique Contreras was a structural engineer and he wanted to access the damage. He and Tommy leaned down in the hole and removed some of the timber and crumbled rock. Just then the hole expanded and Enrique and Tommy jumped back just in time to avoid being pulled down into the hole.

"Tommy, I think we need to start about ten to twelve feet back from the edge and tunnel into the hole. While the men are digging a deep trench, the tunnel needs to be shorn up so that it doesn't cave in on them while they're digging. I think it's either a sink hole or perhaps there's a hidden chamber in the mission that we've uncovered." Enrique said.

There was plenty of used timber at the mission which would be adequate to shore up the sides of the tunnel. Enrique and Maria decided to return to their home early in the afternoon, where she remained. He brought back three of his workers and under his direction they started the tunnel and every four feet shored up the sides so there would be no further accidents. "Tommy, I suggest that we work until four o'clock today and bring back more workers tomorrow." Tommy agreed to bring three of his hands tomorrow to assist Enrique's

It was such a nice day, that Franklin Sutter decided to rent a rig and driver and visit his new friend in Buellton. He asked his driver if he knew where the ranch was located and when the answer was yes, they drove to Buellton. Maria and her aunt were home when he arrived and any thought that he wouldn't be received warmly was dispelled immediately by Maria's greeting.
"I know it's proper to send a card asking for an invitation, but it seemed a little archaic. I wanted to see you before I left the area. I hope you are not offended?"

"Certainly not. My aunt and I want to invite you into our home and have some tea. I'm sorry that my brother isn't here, but there was a cave in at the mission and he, our workers and some of our friends are trying to correct the situation."

"I saw a group of people at the mission as we drove by, but I didn't take any notice of what they were doing. Perhaps my driver and I could take you back there and I could meet your brother?"

The aunt didn't want to go to the mission. But she knew her headstrong niece would go without her and that would be scandalous. Besides, she rather liked the newcomer and wondered if Enrique would approve of such a union. The four barely fit into the carriage. Sutter and the driver were up front and Maria and her aunt sat in the back.

It was nearly three thirty in the afternoon when Maria and Franklin arrived at the mission. Enrique was in the tunnel trying to assess what needed to be done tomorrow. As he exited the tunnel, he saw Maria and her guest and wondered how many more men she'd introduce to her brother. "Enrique, this is Franklin Sutter from Alabama. He was on the same train as auntie and I when we came west. He served twelve years in the US House of Representatives."

The two men shook hands and passed the time with mall talk. Franklin apologized for buying Sarah's painting out from under him. "Senor Sutter, we're finished here for the day and plan to come back early tomorrow to see if we can reach the hidden room. Perhaps, you could come back tomorrow and we could talk further."

"I've already invited Franklin to have dinner with us this evening and he's accepted. Auntie and I will ride back with Franklin and you can take your carriage. Don't be late. The cook promised to have dinner at five PM sharp." Maria smiled and headed for Franklin's carriage.

The master of the house had no choice but to act cordial toward his guest. He knew that he was suspicious of every suitor that showed up and he knew that he had to relax and allow his sister some leeway in her choice. He learned that his guest was the son of James Sutter who owned Bridlewood Plantation in Western Alabama, which was sold before the war started and the funds placed in a northern financial institution. "Your father must have had some insight that told him the south could not prevail." Enrique remarked.

"I asked him one day how he could know that the south couldn't win and yet he fought for her. He said the south was really an agrarian society and that the industrial might of the north plus their overwhelming advantage in population would eventually wear the south down. He said he grew up in the south and his loyalty was with his friends and acquaintances."

"So, he downsized to a thirty-acre farm and raised cattle and grew vegetables."

"That's exactly what we did and when the war ended, we survived and I ran for congress."

"Do you still own the farm?"

"No, I bequeathed it to one of my employees."

"That's enough Enrique. I'd like to spend some time talking to Franklin. He's really here to see me." She wasn't angry, she was just making a point and her brother understood. He excused himself and left his sister, Franklin and her aunt in the parlor having coffee.

To say that Enrique was shocked that Franklin had called upon his sister while he wasn't there was an understatement. Not only that, but he was forced to offer the man from Alabama lodging for the night. He waited up until Franklin retired for the evening and asked to talk to Maria before she turned out all the lights. Her aunt excused herself and went to bed. "Enrique what was I to do. We don't have any way to communicate with the hotel in Santa Ynez. How was he to see me if he didn't take a chance and come to our home. Auntie was with us the whole time and it was he who suggested that we visit the mission so he could be introduced to you. He's being a perfect gentleman. I wish you would be more friendly to a former US Congressman

Reluctantly, Enrique left with some of his workmen for the mission before Franklin rose. When the man from Alabama did, he joined Maria and her aunt at breakfast and offered to take her to the mission.

The next morning Tommy and Sarah rose early and drove back to the mission with three of their workers, some lumber and enough shovels and picks to complete the job. Surprisingly, William, who'd gone home the night before, showed up at their home around five thirty and joined them.

When Enrique arrived at the mission the next morning, Tommy, Sarah and William were already on site and had unloaded the lumber they brought. The three men started work on the tunnel and Sarah unloaded the food and drink they prepared. Franklin, Maria and her aunt arrived two hours later and soon began to help. Franklin was smitten with Sarah and told her how much he enjoyed looking at her paintings on the wall in the hotel "I want you to know that I purchased one of your works two days ago. It was the one of the warrior chiefs. I think he was named Crazy Horse."

"Thank you. Crazy Horse was my first husband. I have two children by him. My current husband has adopted both."

"I'm a student of history and read about the Sioux Nation, the Battle of The Little Bighorn and the Massacre of Wounded Knee."

"Then you want to have a discussion with my husband, Tommy Sanchez. His father was Sitting Bull who led his warriors that attacked Custer at the Battle of the Little Big Horn. Just so you know, I was married to Crazy Horse at the time of the battle and I viewed it from a ridge close by."

Enrique was in his element and quickly took charge of not only the excavation of the hidden room but also the tunnel being dug to that room. He divided up the work, with his men digging the tunnel and excavating the hole while Tommy's men followed with the shoring. William, Sarah, Franklin and Maria helped where needed. It didn't take William long to understand that if he wanted to be a suitor to Maria Contreras, he would be second in line to his fellow Alabaman.

William learned that Franklin's family owned Bridlewood in Western Alabama and that the Sutters were friends of Frank Wilcox, who owned Hickory Falls where William was a slave. Both men spent some time talking about their previous lives. William was surprised that Franklin didn't own slaves and was very sympathetic to their plight. William liked Franklin even though he was a competitor and vowed that he'd get to know this new acquaintance.

The men realized that they hadn't uncovered a sink hole. It was a small room whose roof had been covered over with mud and some debris. Tommy calculated the room to be ten feet by ten feet and shared a common wall with the north wall of the mission church. When the roof timber over the room rotted, the weight of the dirt that had accumulated over the years made the roof collapse into the hole.

Father Mahoney, the current pastor at the mission couldn't shed any light on the hidden room and was as much in awe at what happened as the others. He spent most of the day researching records but still hadn't found any mention of the room, by the end of the day

With ropes and pulleys, Enrique rigged up a system to bring all the debris and dirt from the room and place it separately from the other dirt and rubbage. He knew that the pastor wanted to examine everything from the room to see if it contained artifacts of any kind. They'd only tunneled about five feet leading to the room on the east side by the end of the day, primarily because they encountered a lot of rock in the soil.

It took the workers three more days before they cleared the dirt and debris from the hidden room and were able to climb down into the room and examine it in the daylight. The room was ten feet by ten feet and eight feet high. The pastor was non-committal on what his research rendered about the hidden room. Franklin Sutter was a constant observer during those three days. He didn't do any of the actual work, but was more than willing to ride into town for something the crew needed. And of course, he spent some time helping Maria and Sarah. Enrique was beside himself, but he didn't know how to handle the situation. There was something about the man from Alabama that bothered him

Tommy, Enrique. William and Father Mahoney examined the room carefully with torches held by two of the workers. Tommy noticed what looked like an opening that had been covered over with mortar in the southwest section of the room. They were able to trace a three-foot wide and eight-foot-tall section. To the three it appeared that it might have been a door leading to the mission.

Rather than continue trenching around the outside of the hidden room, they decided to explore the walls to see if there were any other anomalies. Initially, they didn't find anything that indicated what the room was used for. However, as they were about to vacate the area, Enrique spotted what he thought might be small holes in the wall. As they examined the wall more closely, they found sixteen pairs of holes around the room. The sets were approximately five feet off the ground and two feet apart. Tommy and Enrique looked to the priest for guidance. He was reluctant at first but under probing by the two men, he acknowledged that many of the Chumash Laborers had been chained in the excavated room just prior to the revolt at three missions in 1824.

"I know you are appalled as I at this discovery. Perhaps we should go into my office and I can show you some of the documentation I uncovered as a result of the cave in."

A set of drawings was laid out on Father Mahoney's desk as he led Tommy and Enrique into his office. The hidden room had been constructed in 1820 and was to be used to store some of the produce grown by the mission, but in reality, it was used as a jail. "How could your predecessors have allowed such a thing to exist on sacred ground?" Enrique asked the priest.

"It came upon them quickly. The Spanish Government cut back on supplies and stopped paying their soldiers. The soldiers put the squeeze on the missions and we in turn required the Indians to work longer hours without any increase in pay. We didn't have the resources to continue to pay them and the soldiers at the same time. The Chumash revolted and took over three missions. It's all right here in the summary."

"What happened to those who revolted?" Tommy asked.

"The Chumash at Mission Santa Inez gave up within a day. Those at La Purisima continued to hold their mission for three months while the Santa Barbara Mission held out only three days. Subsequently, all the rebels were pardoned. Mahoney sat down with his head in his hands.

Tommy knew about the abuse of Indians. He was one and still was. "Let's go into the mission. I'd like to see what's below the altar."

The area directly beneath the altar hadn't been explored in many years. In fact, Father Mahoney had never been down there.

The entrance below was at the rear of the altar and was guarded by a large oak door. It was so heavy that it took two of the workers to open the door. You could hear the hinges squeak when the door started to move. When it was open enough to walk through, the smell of musk was overpowering. The stairs were sturdy but there was no light other than the two flares carried by the workers.

They made their way through a lot of clutter, including old furniture, tables and chairs. They found what appeared to be an entrance in the wall directly across from where they thought the wall had been plastered over. There was no mortar to disguise where the opening was and although they didn't have the tools to pound their way through the wall, they identified where the passageway was.

As they were walking outside, Enrique turned to the priest. "What do you intend to do with the hidden room?"

"If I had my way, I take the walls down. I don't think we want to remind ourselves of a past mistake."

"Before we do that, why don't we open the passageway to the hidden room from under the altar? It would be more convenient to enter the mission rather than going the way we just came. If there's anything of value under the altar, it would be easier to remove it that way. We can bring back our men tomorrow and open the room within a few hours. What do you say?"

The priest was quick to respond. "Let's Do It."

CHAPTER 19

Getting through the wall between the hidden room and the main mission structure was quicker than imagined. By early afternoon the workers had removed all the rock and mortar that had been in the passageway. Six workers removed most of the clutter that had been sitting under the altar and put everything on the floor of the hidden room. There were tables, chairs, old pews and barrels of miscellaneous items that were moved.

Most of the tables, pews and chairs were damaged beyond repair and they were moved to the debris pile outside the hidden room. The barrels were emptied on the dirt floor. Some of the items in the barrels were packages of candles, a couple of old candlesticks and some robes and vestments that the priests and altar boys wore. Most of these items were rotted and taken to the debris pile. The good items were placed in the north end of the hidden room.

One of the last items removed had been sitting on a wooden rack, next to the north wall and covered with old cloths. Two of the workers carried it outside and placed it against the far wall of the hidden room. When they removed the cloth covers, they discovered a wooden box approximating six inches thick and three feet square. They opened the box like structure. Inside was a painting covered with two layers of cloths.

Removing the cloths was easy; however, the painting was covered with dust and dirt and in dire need of cleaning. Rather than start the cleaning process to determine what the painting was, Tommy suggested that they look at in the daylight tomorrow and by someone who knew something about paintings, namely his wife, Sarah Sanchez.

"I suggest you take it with you. Otherwise, we'd have to guard it in case it's valuable. What do you think?" Enrique asked.

"I'll take it home and give Sarah a head starts on the painting and bring her and the painting back in a few days." Tommy responded.

Tommy personally unloaded the painting and put it in the barn, after dinner he told Sarah about it. The two walked into the barn and Sarah examined the painting and said she'd look at it in the light tomorrow. William had gone home and said he had a few things on his agenda tomorrow and would check with them the following day to see if he was needed. But Franklin made it very clear that he was interested in the painting and insisted that he help Sarah clean it. "What time do you think you'll start on the painting, Mrs. Sanchez?"

"I have a few early chores and the children to get ready for school, but I think I'll be ready about eight in the morning."

"I'll see you then."

Sarah had gone to sleep thinking about the painting found at the mission. She was up early and walked out into a clear warm day. She had one of the workers put a table at the entrance to the barn and then place the painting face up on it. When she came back, Franklin had already arrived. Armed with a feather duster, several clean cloths and olive oil soap, they started to brush off the dust leaving only smudges of dirt. The varnish had deteriorated-to the point where Sarah couldn't determine what the painting was.

Tommy had breakfast and then joined Sarah and Franklin in the barn. She'd removed the dust and dirt by this time and was trying to decide what the painting was. "Is it worth anything?" her husband asked.

"At this stage I would say no, but I want to wash the painting with this olive oil soap and see if I can add some luster."

Sarah took her time and meticulously cleaned the painting. The first thing she noticed was the amount of paint that came off on the cloth she was using. "Tommy, I think there's a painting under the painting on top."

"How can you tell?" Franklin asked.

She handed him the cloth with all the colors attached. "I want to be careful and not damage the canvas below. Who knows what's hidden behind the one on top."

Three weeks later Sarah uncovered a painting below. It was of a young woman in a pastoral setting. Her clothes were those of an aristocrat and her smile was that of a woman with child. Sarah could see that the secret room wasn't reflected in the painting. "From the paintings I've seen in the churches on the east coast, the scene is a Spanish Pastoral Scene." Franklin was commenting to Sarah. He'd been coming very morning to assist her.

Enrique and Maria were anxious. They hadn't heard from Tommy for weeks and worried that something was wrong, so they drove to Rancho Del Prado. They found Sarah working on the painting in the barn, with Franklin at her side. When they saw the painting, they immediately asked Sarah if she could determine who the artist was.

"No. I was unable to discover that but my knowledge of well-known painters or even masters is limited. We have to find an art historian who could research the painting. That part is beyond my capability."

Enrique was fascinated with the effort that Sarah had made on behalf of the painting and he was curious. "Do you think a local artist painted this?" Enrique asked

"My best guess is that it was someone with more talent than I or any of our local artist."

Enrique persisted. "How can you tell?"

"The strokes are smooth. This artist was confident in his craft. Look at the definition between different fabrics the woman is wearing. It's so precise."

"But your paintings are equally precise."

"It's true that I can be precise, but my consistency isn't there I cover over many of my mistakes with broad bands of color." Sarah smiled back at Enrique.

The attraction between Franklin and Maria was evident to all especially Enrique, who still couldn't quite make out the distinguished visitor. Sarah suggested that the five of them have dinner outside on their rear patio. The weather was warm with a slight breeze in the early evening. "What did you do before you were elected to congress, Senor Sutter?' Enrique asked as they all sat down to dinner.

"My family owned a large plantation before the war, that my father sold when it seemed like the conflict between north and south was real. My father was a remarkable man who saw things as they were and not as the general population wanted them to be. Before my father went to war, he sold our plantation, purchased a thirty-acre farm and kept some of the help to run it. In addition, to show what foresight he had, he deposited the money from the sale of the plantation in a northern bank."

Prior to selling Bridlewood Plantation, I was in training to take over management of the plantation. Before that happened, my grandmother died; soon thereafter my mother passed on. I looked to my grandfather, Jesse Sutter for guidance, but he grieved for his wife and daughter. I could ask him some questions and he'd be very helpful. Other questions, he simply ignored or perhaps he didn't hear me."

"You must have had some help that you could turn to?"

"Our overseer, named Will Thacker came with me and stayed until he died. He was like an uncle to me and very loyal. He was by my side when I transacted much of the farm's business."

"Did you have many slaves?" Enrique asked.

"We had perhaps over one hundred fifty during the time of Bridlewood, but all were freed when my father sold the plantation. I was still a teenager when this was happening. Those slaves who came with us to the farm were freed and hired as employees. I gave the farm to the last two employees who came with us. It was a profitable enterprise that I transferred to them. I believe I know the question you want to ask. Was I ever a slave holder? The answer is no. To go further, my father was never a slave holder, but my grandfather was."

"And your mother?" Enrique was persistent

"She was ill most of my early years, but from her I acquired a love of reading."

This seemed to appease Enrique for now. To be sure the discussion changed to something else. Tommy rose and made a toast to his wife who labored for at least three weeks on the painting found at the mission.

'Since Franklin bought your painting of Crazy Horse, I wonder if you intend to paint his portrait again? Enrique asked.

"I've always enjoyed painting him as a regal warrior. If you'd like such a painting, I'd be glad to do it as soon as I'm finished with this project."

During the same week, Father Mahoney and William came to the ranch and saw what Sarah had uncovered. The library in Santa Ynez has a limited number of books and only two dealing with art. However, Sarah was able to find out about a well know art historian living in Los Angeles so she wrote to him, summarizing what she found and asked his advice.

Two-week later Sarah received a letter from Senor Don Jose Dominquez. He indicated that he's studied in Spain and was very familiar with Missionary art. He was teaching at the Art Academy in Los Angeles now, but would be free in September and was willing to come to the valley and examine what Sarah had uncovered.

CHAPTER 20

Bass Blake had wed an Indian woman and fathered three children. For years, he had a steady position with Judge Parker, but the hanging judge died and Bass needed an income to support his growing family. The only jobs available at the time were short lived due to either the duration of the position or the fact that many who took similar positions didn't survive the term. Many growing towns had need of a lawman or better yet someone who could eliminate the unlawful groups. Startup towns needed someone who could instill law and order quickly, mainly with a six gun, and thereby allow the town to grow and prosper.

Bass heard about a small mining town in Northern Oklahoma that was as wild as could be. Money was flowing in from the mines, while gambling was rampant and the girls plentiful. There were at least one or two killings a week and the town council were beyond their means to control the unlawfulness. Two of the men they hired as town marshals or better known as town tamers were shot dead in the street soon after they started their job.

The ride to the town of First Oklahoma took three days. Rather than meet with the town council immediately, and since no one knew what he looked like, Bass decided to make his way around town talking to anyone he could to determine who the trouble makers were. Although many didn't want to talk to a stranger, there were those in the saloon that after a few drinks would reveal their life history. It didn't take long to get a picture of the problem. The Lazy Lady Saloon owner, named Jack Perkins, was the self-styled boss of the town. He come into town about seven years ago and tried his hand at mining. When that didn't work, he opened a saloon. Some say he had a silent partner who put up all the money, but no one knew who he was. Perkins hired five gunmen with reputations. They generally hung out at the saloon doing Jack's bidding and intimidating customers. The other gambling houses had some protection but they stayed clear of Jack and his boys.

Perkins had a good-sized spread about two miles from town with a herd of cattle numbering around three hundred. The rumor was that Perkins never bought any cattle but was an expert in changing other people's brands to his own. He was married and had no children with a wife who was never seen in town. She'd send some of the cowhands with her housekeeper to buy supplies. Perkins spent nearly all his time with a girlfriend, named Sadie in his upstairs suite at the Lazy Lady

The town council was desperate; yet impatient. With plenty of money, Horace Watson, the head of the council, offered Bass a three month contract to clean up the city. They'd pay Bass five hundred dollars a month plus room and board.

Though the council indicated they expected everything done by tomorrow, Bass was a patient man with a keen sense of survival. "I'm sorry Mr. Watson. I'm not interested in being rushed into solving your problem overnight. It looks like you tried that with the two you hired before me. How did that work out?"

"I know what I'm doing and you don't know my business. I'm going to take my time. If a six month contract at five hundred per month is not acceptable, then I'm out of here."

After three minutes of indecision the town council wrote a contract under the terms Bass wanted and he signed it with one change. If he hadn't resolved the conflict in six months, he had the option of three more months at the same pay to complete the job. He decided to take his time and use a strategy of divide and conquer. He made friends with the other gambling house owners and especially their gunmen. Perkins heard of the council's hire, but figured he had enough men to take care of Bass. Besides, town marshals didn't last too long in the town of First.

His first action came ten days after he arrived. A miner won a lot of money in Jack Perkins' saloon one night at the roulette table. Jack wasn't happy about it. Bass was in the Lazy Lady that night and saw one of Perkins' gunmen trail the miner back to his tent. Bass kept out of sight as he tracked the gunman, who was trailing the miner. Just when it looked like the gunman was ready to shoot the miner in the back, Bass yelled out, "you're covered; drop your weapon on the ground."

The gunman turned quickly and was about to fire but Bass was quicker and he shot the man in the head and the gunman fell over dead. Bass looked around but didn't see anyone, so he made his way back to the Lazy Lady. The miner was oblivious to the killing that just occurred. He was so drunk that he went into his tent and lay down on his bed.

Soon there was a buzz in the saloon about the shooting of one of Perkins' boys. The boss man came out of his upstairs' office and scanned the hall below looking for Bass. When he saw him, he sent one of his girls to bring him up to his office. Bass took his time, had a drink before he climbed the stairs and knocked on Perkins' door. Perkins opened the door and invited Blake into his elaborate office. It was more of a parlor than an office with plush red velvet chairs, a chaise lounge, a large sofa with a desk and chair. There were many pictures of Perkins and dignitaries adorning the walls. The door to his one bedroom suite was closed.

"Wally West was shot in the alley by the miners' tents. What are you going to do about it?"

"I'll investigate. Let's hope there's an eyewitness. Why was he near the miner's tent?"

"I don't watch my men all the time. Maybe he had a run in with a miner."

Bass strolled down to the miner's tent. There were a few miners milling around the dead body. He asked several if they saw the shooting. No one came forward, so he bent down as though examining the body, though he knew how the man was killed. Soon, he walked into the tent of the miner who'd been trailed by the deceased. The miner was still out and there were no firearms present.

Bass reported back to Perkins and told him there were no witnesses and his man was shot in the head. "What are you going to do about it?" Perkins asked.

"I'm going to convene a coroner's court and see if we can find out who did this."

When Bass left the saloon, he saw five of Perkins' gunmen go up to his office. He waited across the street for an hour before the five came outside, got on their horses and rode out of town. Bass followed at a discrete distance, so he wouldn't be seen. About five miles out they cut across the plains until they came on a herd of about three hundred head of cattle grazing in a valley. They stampeded the herd and shot at the three drovers tending the cattle, who subsequently ran off. Bass continued to follow the five until they stopped for the night and set up camp.

By the light of their fire, he watched from some rocks until three of the gunmen went to sleep, leaving two on guard. About midnight, Bass crawled up on each of the two sentries, using his knife to persuade them to go with him back to where he stood watch. After he tied them up, he gave them a choice to leave the area or be exposed to his knife. Both chose to leave and not come back. "So that we understand each other, If I see you in or around the town, I'll shoot you on sight. Do we understand each other?" The two men nodded and rode toward a town twenty miles away.

He waited an hour and when no one got up to relieve the sentries, he made his way back to town. A day later the three remaining Perkins gunmen made their way back and reported to their boss that two of his men had disappeared. The owner of the Lazy Lady asked Bass several times over the next two weeks if he found out who killed Wally West. "Jack, we conducted an investigation, but no one came forward who saw the crime. There's not a clue to the one who did it."

It didn't take Perkins long to replace the three that Bass had coerced, but they were apprehensive and didn't travel anyplace alone. Bass knew if he waited long enough, he do away with the Perkins' group, but would that change things in the town. Would someone else take over and put the town back in the same condition it was before he came here. With the Perkins' gang somewhat subdued, life was less of a threat in the town. In fact, the council met with Bass and Watson suggested that he could leave any time.

But Perkins was not about to let his stranglehold on the town go away. Within a day of the council's suggestion, two miners were shot down in the street by two of Jack's gunmen. Bass was on the scene immediately and asked the gunmen what happened. They said the two miners cheated them at cards and when they were called on it, they challenged the gunmen to go outside.

Bass examined the two dead miners and looked up at the two Perkins' men and took out his gun. "You two are under arrest; the miners don't have any guns."

One of the Perkins' hands started for his gun and Bass hit him over the head with his revolver. He turned to the other gunman, "help your friend up and take him to the jail. You both are charged with murder."

Many of the townspeople had lived under the threat of the Perkins' gang too long and after a few drinks at one of the other saloons in town, they worked themselves into a frenzy. Someone had a rope and the crowd started walking down to the jail to lynch the two Perkins' gunmen. When Bass found out about the threat, he fired a shotgun to disperse the crown and then closed down all the saloons. That seemed to eliminate the impetus of a hanging and by the next morning, those who had initiated the threat, had decided to let the law handle it. Two weeks later the circuit judge made his quarterly rounds and the two gunmen were found guilty and hung the next day

Perkins tried to intimidate the jurors by sending five gunmen to the trial, and perhaps stir up trouble. When he saw Bass armed with a shotgun sitting outside the courthouse with five townspeople who agreed to act as deputies, he decided this wasn't the time to risk everything. There was also a rumor that the two convicted gunmen were going to name Perkins as the one who told them to kill the two miners. However here were witnesses that said Perkins was in his office playing cards when the shooting took place.

After the trial, Bass checked to be sure that Perkins and his gunmen were in town, He decided to visit Perkins' ranch and look at the brands on their stock. As he rode up to the main house, two of Perkins' cowboys came out to greet him and they weren't friendly. "This is private property." One of the wranglers said as he blocked Bass' path with his horse.

When he saw the badge Bass was wearing and he looked in the eyes of the big man, his tone changed. "Sorry marshal, but Mr. Perkins doesn't want anyone visiting here."

Bass pushed through the two riders and with his rifle in hand, he tied his horse to the hitching rail. "Tell Mrs. Perkins, Marshal Bass wants to see her."

The two men hesitated, but one got off his horse and knocked on the door of the hacienda. A small, slightly overweight woman came to the door and after a brief conversation with her workman, she came out and greeted Bass. "What can I do for you marshal?"

"I'd like to see some of your herd. I've had complaints that they belonged to someone else and Mr. Perkins changed the brands. I'd like to see for myself."

"Shouldn't you discuss this with my husband? I know nothing about the cattle. It's unfortunate that you came while Mr. Perkins is in town."

"There was nothing unfortunate at all. I knew I'd have less of a problem with your husband and his gunmen if they were in town. Now if you don't mind, I'd like to see some of the cattle."

At that moment Bass heard a click and quickly turned and fired two shots at each of the two cowboys. Unless you boys want to be six feet under, I suggest you drop your guns and show me the cattle. Both looked at Mrs. Perkins who nodded her consent. "My guess is that sooner or later you're going to have to explain yourself to my husband."

"I suspect so."

There were about twenty head in a large holding pen that Bass examined. He could tell immediately that the brands had been changed. He knew this was but a small sample to make a definitive judgment, but if the brands on nearly three hundred head of Jack's cattle had been altered, he had a major problem to resolve. When he was finished, he said good bye to Mrs. Perkins. "Find out what you wanted marshal?"

"I did Mrs. Perkins. Thank you for your hospitality."

Jack Perkins was not completely dumb. It took him some time but he was sure that the setbacks he encountered over the past three months could be attributed to Bass Blake coming to the town of First. He was livid about the Bass' visit to his ranch when he knew Perkins wouldn't be there. When his wife told him about the visit, he and his men went looking for Bass but couldn't find him.. He knew his men weren't a match for the town marshal, so he looked at another option. He heard about a gunman named Snake Eyes Frank Gurley who was for hire and he sent one of his men to offer Gurley three hundred dollars if he'd come to First and talk to Jack Perkins about a job.

Bass got the city council to pass an ordinance restricting the closing hours of all the saloons and gambling halls to midnight, Monday through Saturday, and closed on Sunday. After the initial furor and multitude of complaints, all the establishments complied, even the one owned by Jack Perkins.

When Gurley arrived in town and met with Jack Perkins, he decided to size up Bass Blake. The black man was bigger than Gurley thought, but a bullet always shrunk any man down to size. Perkins offered Gurley one thousand dollars if he'd kill Blake. The hired gunman decided to catch Bass one night while he was making his rounds around town. As usual Blake checked to make sure the saloons and gambling halls closed at midnight on

Saturday night and that all their customers left. As he was making his way from the Lazy Lady to one of the other saloons, Bass was shot at just after he crossed over the street and was walking up the steps to another saloon. Bass immediately fell to the deck and didn't move.

Gurley took his time and when he was sure everyone was off the street, he made his way to Blake's body. The lawman was on his stomach, so Gurley with his gun in his hand rolled Bass over on his back and the lawman stuck his gun in Gurley's ribs. "You're under arrest. I'll take your gun."

Gurley straightened up, lowered his gun and aimed at Blake. The town tamer was too quick and Gurley was dead before he hit the wooden deck in front of the post office. Jack Perkins was on the scene immediately and although it was dark, Bass could tell the disappointment in his manner. "You'll have to find someone else Jack. This one couldn't get the job done.'

Although there was still an occasional shooting, the townspeople were becoming emboldened and many refused to back down to Perkins' gunmen. One night at the Lazy Lady, a farmer thought he was being cheated at poker. He stood up and demanded his money back. Three of Perkins' men crowded around him and told the farmer to get out and don't come back.

However, several of the farmer's friends gathered around Perkins men and when one of the gunmen reached for his gun, they beat him and the other two with their fists, disarmed them and threw them into the street. The crowd became bigger and louder and soon they started tearing down the roulette and crap tables, breaking the glass above the bar and setting fire to the furniture.

When they heard the increase in crowd noise downstairs, Jack Perkins and two men came out of his office and started down the stairs to the main room with their guns drawn. One of the miners had a whip and he slapped Perkins gun out of his hand and the crowd grabbed all three men, lifted them in the air and threw them in the street. By this time, Perkins' other three men reentered the saloon and were grabbed by the crowd, disarmed and tied up. Someone had brought along a rope and there were many who could be heard saying, "string them up."

Bass arrived with another deputy and after firing his shotgun twice in the air he took out his six gun and said there wouldn't be any lynching. Although some said they were going to do it anyway, none wanted to get in a shooting match with Bass Blake. He and his deputy took Perkins and his five men to jail. A hearing was held two days later presided over by the circuit judge. Other than being fined for starting a riot, Perkins and his five men were released. But his saloon was destroyed by fire and the town council refused to allow him to rebuild, Perkins had no other choice but to leave town. His power hold over the community was broken

His gunmen left and other than two cowboys and his wife, he was alone at the ranch when Bass showed up with ten men. Included in the ten were five ranchers that had their cattle rustled. The ten looked at the brands on a random number of the steers and came to the conclusion that most of the cattle on Perkins' ranch had their brands changed. Bass ordered his deputies to take the cattle to town, place them in holding pens and advertise the lot for sale. Perkins yelled and hollered and threatened Bass, but the town marshal stood firm and the cattle were taken to town. Perkins had a gun in his holster but he didn't draw on Bass.

The cattle were sold and the proceeds divided up on a proportional basis to all the ranchers who submitted a claim to the city council. After another month, Blake's contract was over. The town council thanked him but said they could handle it now. Bass earned three thousand dollars for his effort. Subsequently, two of the townspeople were appointed to the positions of sheriff and deputy.

CHAPTER 21

Don Jose Dominquez arrived at Rancho Del Prado on a Thursday afternoon as per his agreement with Sarah Sanchez. Their guest was about sixty years old standing five feet ten inches tall with a slim build. What set him apart from other men his age was his formidable Van Dyke which was totally gray. At dinner that night he told his hosts about his early struggles as a painter in Spain and then his one major success, a picture of one of Rome's cathedrals. He also covered his credentials as s restorer of fine art, having worked for several museums in the United States.

It wasn't necessary to say that he was eager to start, because he must have told them twenty times, that he couldn't wait to see the painting. Early the next morning, he and Sarah walked out to the barn, took off the cloth protecting the painting and moved the table so it was in a place where there was more light.

"The first thing I plan to do is make a condition's assessment of the painting. That may take a few days to complete. I think you've done a fine job of cleaning off the dust and dirt and uncovering the picture that was hidden. I can still see some flaking on the picture and I don't know whether that needs to be taken off or perhaps we can adhere it to the original painting. Also, there're some small holes and a slight cut in the painting. Most of those can be restored with putty or a composite material I have with me. I brought some solvents that can be used to clean the panting especially if there is some yellowing."

"Is there anything I can do? I'm a painter of Native Americans and I'd be delighted if I could be of some help."

"I would like to document everything I do and it would be helpful if you could take notes and make it into a narrative at the end of each day. I know you're busy with the children and the ranch, but a couple of hours a day would be appreciated. Sometimes it's a two person task to remove the yellow and darkened varnish in order to reveal the artwork as it was originally intended. If the varnish has been removed and the picture must be repainted, it becomes a one person task. It's in the early stages when I'm making an assessment, that I need the most help."

As the weeks passed it became obvious to Tommy that the restorer had a crush on Sarah. That was okay but when she told him that he fondled her breast, it was time for him to go. In addition, he liked to enjoy long lunches with wine at the Rancho and as such the restoration process grinded to a halt. Tommy waited until the artist started work the next morning which seemed to be later and later as the weeks went by. "Good morning Don Jose"

"Good morning patron."

` "What's the assessment of your progress with the painting?"

"It is a slow process and a delicate operation. One cannot set a time for completion."

"Do you think it'll take another month or perhaps less time?"

"I've done many of these restorations and each is different. Restoring a painting is like making love to a woman. You cannot do it too fast and you must be delicate."

"We're coming to our busy season. Sarah can't be spared to assist you anymore and I'm afraid we have house guests that plan to be here; that cannot be changed. All I can give you is another week. If the restoration can't be completed in that time frame, we'll have to complete it next year. I'm sorry but this is a working ranch and things were put in motion some time ago that can't be altered. If you're unable to return next spring, perhaps you can recommend someone who can. Have a nice day." Tommy left Don Jose speechless.

Later that day Dominquez ran into Sarah who was being driven to town by one of the vaqueros. "Mrs. Sanchez, your husband told me this morning that I have to complete the restoration by the end of the week or come back next year. As an artist, I'm sure you understand that is impossible to rush the restoration; it might even impact the painting. Perhaps you could talk to your husband and explain the necessity for me to complete the restoration, no matter how long it takes."

"My husband talked his decision over with me. I was totally in accord. I have a busy day senor, so please excuse me if I have to leave now. Don Jose Dominquez was not entirely stupid. He'd overstayed his welcome and was being asked to leave. The two or three touches to her bottom and once to her breast made his pulse move quickly. He'd hoped that she would reciprocate but she maintained her distance. "Well it might have been worth it." He said to himself.

He vowed that he would work diligently his last week and complete as much as he could. He knew that he would not be returning even if he asked. That was a nonstarter.

Sarah had kept a duplicate copy of the notes she took while Dominquez was going through the conditions of restoration, but Don Jose never raised that threat. Before he left, he gave a clue to the painting's origin. "There was a French Born American Bishop who during a visit to France, suggested to the nobility that they donate paintings to various Catholic Churches in the United States."

Dominquez couldn't identify the artist but he felt that the painting had a European flair to it. The bishop's named was Joseph Benedict Flaget and his diocese had been in Louisville Kentucky until he died in 1850.

In reality, with the departure of Dominquez, the project of determining who the artist was became Sarah's responsibility. With Father Mahoney's help she wrote to the Archbishop in Louisville Kentucky to see if they had a list of the paintings that Bishop Flaget helped bring to the churches in the United States.

Franklin saw Maria Guitterez on several occasions, but always in the company of Sarah Sanchez. It was obvious the two individuals had some chemistry going between them. Enrique was still opposed to any relationship whatsoever and it put a strain on his association with Tommy. He was invited to a three day fishing trip with Tommy and at the last minute begged off. The same thing happened with dinner invitations.

William's business was progressing. Last month he broke even with his income versus expenses and planned to pay back Tommy and another investor this year. His projections though optimistic seemed to be doable. The only drawback was that he was vandalized a couple of times and once a burning cross was planted in front of his shop. Joshua was a pragmatist and understood the reality of being a black man, even if the civil war was over. There were many former southerners in California and many still felt that blacks were inferior to whites and therefore couldn't be successful in any endeavor.

He didn't contact the deputy sheriff who came up from Santa Barbara three days a week when his windows were broken. But when the cross appeared he visited the deputy and filed a complaint. Although the deputy insisted he was working the problem, no one was ever arrested. In fact, no one was interviewed. William told Tommy about the burning cross and the man in black was concerned. Tommy talked to the deputy and got the same response. But it didn't end there. Tommy contacted the new sheriff and voiced his concern. Jacob Thunder assured Tommy he took the matter seriously and would get some action from the deputy or he'd be replaced.

Within two days an arrest was made. Two former southern cavalry men got drunk at the saloon in Santa Ynez and thought it was funny to put the burning cross on the shoemaker's lot. They told the deputy that they didn't mean any harm; they just got liquored up and had some fun. If they were released from jail, they wouldn't do it again.

Tommy wanted them to do some jail time but the jury in Santa Ynez fined them ten dollars each and let them go. Tommy knew that the deterrent wasn't enough; someone else was going to commit a felony against the shoemaker and someone might get hurt.

From years as a minority, Tommy knew that the men had to have some punishment. As Confederate Soldiers, they knew how the blacks had been treated in the south. But this was the west and Tommy wasn't going to allow that type of intimidation to surface here. If it did, then maybe he and his family might be next. The two former soldiers were employed by the Circle Bar B in Santa Ynez to ride fence lines. From his vaqueros, Tommy learned that the two liked to come into town on Friday nights. They generally spent it at the saloon across from the Central Hotel.

On Friday, Tommy rode into town about ten that evening. He knew the cowboys wouldn't leave the saloon before eleven at the earliest. He decided to sit on the porch of the Central Hotel and wait. As he sat down he noticed another person about three chairs away. The individual looked familiar. It was Franklin Sutter. When he recognized Tommy, he moved next to him and bid him a good evening and asked what he was doing here.

"I haven't seen you lately Franklin. Where have you been?"

"I took a trip up the coast and visited San Francisco. It's a lively town. I enjoyed my stay very much, but I don't think I want to live there. You haven't said what you're doing here."

"I haven't, have I?"

"Does it have anything to do with that burning cross on William's front lawn?"

"Let's just say that I have business tonight that I'd rather not discuss/" Tommy responded firmly.

"I know you don't know this, but I was in that saloon when you counseled the man who spoke ill of your wife. I know your capability. I also don't like the idea of the burning cross being used in this area. I like this valley very much. Whatever you have in mind tonight, I'd like to join you."

Tommy smiled but Franklin couldn't see his expression in the ambient light. "I appreciate that and I'll consider your offer in the future. Tonight, I have something in mind that only I can do."

As Tommy rose to move away from Franklin, he saw the two cowboys come out of the saloon, look around and get on their horses. They didn't see Franklin and Tommy as they took the road back to the Circle Bar B.

"Franklin let's go fishing at my place tomorrow afternoon. Let's plan the trip for two days. It will give us a chance to get better acquainted. What do you say?"

"I'll be there at noon tomorrow."

The two cowboys rode through town and then took the trail north to their place. Tommy went directly north. There was a grove of trees about one half mile out of town. He reached the trees in plenty of time. He put on his black cloak, his black hat, grabbed the lance he brought with him and waited.

The two cowboys were singing as they leisurely took the trail home. They stopped initially when they saw someone waiting in the trees up ahead. But when they saw the burning lance, they spurred their horse and galloped as fast as their horses could with the man in black carrying the burning lance coming after them. When he was near enough, Tommy threw the lance so it would land in front of the galloping horses. When the cowboys saw the lance land in front of them, one screamed and turned in another direction. The other rider, along with his horse fell trying to avoid the burning lance. Tommy had his whip out and slashed at the fallen man, hitting him on his rear and then chased the other. He snapped the whip at him several times and in a voice that the cowboy could hear, he said, "take your friend with you and don't ever come back."

He watched as they took the road to Santa Barbara, He waited another hour before returning home.

CHAPTER 22

He was deep in thought next morning over breakfast at the hotel. He 'd been staying at the hotel for several months and had travelled around to all the small towns in the area. He liked the weather, the people and the surroundings in Santa Ynez Valley. He wondered if he liked it enough to make it his home. He knew he was falling in love with Maria Contreras in spite of the obstacles her brother set up. She seemed to like him; he wondered if she liked him enough to be his wife?

The person he most admired was Tommy Sanchez. Here was a man among men. He wanted to go with him last night but that wasn't to be. He seemed like a knight from the times of the Crusades. Franklin wondered if he should share his secret with Tommy and if he did what would that accomplish. Mostly he wanted to sit down with Maria but the way she was raised made that difficult.

It seemed like a coincidence, but Juan and Linda came to the Rancho the same day as Franklin. They wanted to spend a couple of days in their new home by the fish pond. Significantly, they invited Silas and Marjorie Smith to be their guests. Franklin arrived soon after the others. Sarah suggested they all have lunch at the main house. The conversation turned to the painting that Sarah had been working on.

"I did some research in our library and came across the name of someone who might be helpful in determining what we have. It's beyond my capability at this time."

Franklin smiled. "Those paintings you have at the hotel say otherwise. You're a very skilled artist

"I thank you for the compliment, but there are small techniques that you learn under masters that separate you from other artists and I've not been privy to them. You might say I have natural ability but I know I lack some of the techniques to make me better. It's also a fact that I loved the subjects I painted and that perhaps made them better than they would be normally. Enough about me, when's the last time anyone has seen Enrique and Maria?

"I believe Maria would be here more often if it wasn't for Enrique; he's avoiding us. I suspect he has a problem with our relationship going forward. I believe that I'll go to their hacienda this week and see if I can break down his resistance." Franklin said.

Tommy invited Silas and Juan to go fishing with he and Franklin but both declined; their wives smiled. The two men left shortly after lunch and planned to return tomorrow evening. It took them two hours to reach the pond. They immediately set up camp, lit a fire and opened a bottle of Tommy's latest bottle of Pinot Noir.

When they were comfortable, Franklin posed the issue of last evening. "I assume you accomplished what you had in mind last evening?"

"Yes, I believe that situation has resolved itself. I hold my family and friends close. I take exception when someone goes out of their way to cause them harm. William is a nice man, has overcome many obstacles and should be allowed to leave all that behind him. I for one understand a person being singled out for being different What about you Franklin. You hold your background close to the vest. I wonder if you've experienced problems in the past?" Tommy handed Franklin one of his patented cigars.

"Tommy, I marvel at what you've accomplished and I'm in awe of you sometimes, you seem to have accepted that your wife was married to a Sioux Warrior and from all indications still has feelings for him to this day; yet his son and daughter, never mention his name. I'm not ready to let my skeletons out of the closet yet."

"I know my wife loved Crazy Horse; she told me she did. Do I think she still has feelings for him? Yes, I do. But if you ask me who'd she choose if he was alive, I would tell you that she would choose me. How do I know that? She told me. I loved my father Sitting Bull, even though I'm appalled that he took my mother as a prisoner, then as his wife." It's very hard to suppress old feelings."

Though the two men fished the next morning and caught two fish each, that wasn't the purpose of their trip. Tommy wanted to size up Franklin and see if he could determine the true character of the man. Franklin on the other hand was in awe of Tommy and wanted to see if they could become close friends. After two days, Tommy was as much in the dark about Franklin as before.

Archbishop Carver and Sarah traded letters for a couple of months before Carver furnished the name and address of an artist living in St. Louis Missouri. He'd been retained by another church near San Francisco to validate one of the paintings that Bishop Flaget helped bring into the country. After discussing the situation and the fee the artist might charge with Father Mahoney and her husband, she contacted Don Felipe Serano to see if he was interested in coming to Santa Ynez and what fee he'd charge.

Tommy and Sarah realized that the church didn't have the money to pay the artist for his time. Without being asked, Enrique Contreras, Silas and Marjorie Smith and Franklin Sutter agreed to share the expenses with Tommy and Sarah. Serano arrived late in the day in early July and was greeted by Sarah and offered the guest room in the barn. At dinner that night he was introduced to Father Mahoney, Juan and Linda Sanchez, Raoul and Naiwa Fernandez and Silas and Marjorie Smith. For some reason Enrique and Maria didn't attend.

Senor Serano was an affable individual of fifty to sixty years and slightly over six feet with a slender frame. He sported a small mustache and definitely spoke with a Spanish accent. He entertained everyone at the dinner table and kept the conversation light with stories of his travels to remote churches in the west and some of the accommodations he shared with goats, mules and itinerant families. He enjoyed Naomi's cooking and drank very little. He was indeed a welcome change to his predecessor.

The next morning Serano was at work early reading all the notes that Dominquez had written and the conclusions that he reached. Sarah joined him around ten that morning and the two looked at the painting, discussed what restoration was still needed and who the artist might be. "Senor Dominquez' notes are very accurate and I believe he did an excellent job for the amount of restoration he completed. I'll not ask why he didn't finish the restoration. It must have been a difficult decision."

"Let's just say it was an untenable situation that my husband had to deal with. I think he made the correct decision."

"It'll take a few weeks for me to make a reasonable assessment of who the artist is, unless I can find some definite clues in the interim. The one thing I am sure of is that Bishop Flaget had this painting sent here."

"How can you be so sure?"

"I assume the wood under the table was used to box it."

"Why yes it was."

"The bishop had a habit of carving his initial in one of the boards used around the frame before it's shipped." Serano showed Sarah where the initials were.

He flashed a very large smile. "In addition, I brought along a list of the places where he shipped the paintings." Serano opened up a piece of letter sized paper and showed it to Sarah.

"Do you know anything about the bishop? Serano asked.

"No, the first we heard of him was when Senor Dominquez suggested I contact the Archbishop of Louisville Kentucky."

"Bishop Flaget was born in France, went to local schools and studied at one of the many seminaries throughout France. During the revolution, he escaped to America and was sent to Fort Vincennes to manage a couple of churches that were in dire need of help. He seemed to fall in love with the American West. During this time, he met the famous explorer, George Rodgers Clark, who he maintained a friendship with for many years afterward."

He didn't have a dynamic early priesthood but he managed to impress his superiors and make many friends. One of these friendships involved your President, George Washington and another was the famous General, Mad Anthony Wayne. In the seventeen nineties, Flaget was sent to Cuba to establish a college. When that fell through, he supported himself by learning Spanish and becoming a tutor to one of the Spanish noblemen. But what acted as an impetus for the remainder of his life was his friendship with Louis Phillippe, who along with his two brothers was in exile in Cuba. When Louis Phillippe ascended to the throne of France, he remembered Flaget, his kindness and his counsel."

"Flaget returned to the US and became Bishop of Bardstown. He subsequently returned to France, resurrected his friendship with Louis Phillippe and was introduced to many noblemen in the king's court. Thus, the idea of having the aristocracies send paintings to the American West was born."

"It appears you're a fan of the Bishop."

"I've read several books on his life and I admire what he accomplished."

"How are you going to approach this task?"

"I've been an admirer of Rafael for some time and have studied some of his paintings. Recognize that I'm not an art expert; yet I have enough knowledge that I'll try to determine if this could be a Rafael. It certainly is the type of painting he was famous for."

"How do you intend to do that?' Sarah was persistent.

"One of the first things I'll check is whether there's a signature. Next, I always look at the frame to see if I can determine the age of the package. When I look at the painting, I want to see what the quality of the paint is, especially did the artist use quality brushes or did some of the bristles stay on the painting. I'll look at the canvas to analyze whether this was the type used during Rafael's lifetime and see if there're any visible repairs, such as gouges and cuts. Lastly, but probably the most important, I want to examine the brush strokes used and compare them with my knowledge of the master's brush strokes."

Over the next three weeks Serano labored from dawn to dusk and at the end of that time, he asked for a meeting with Tommy and Sarah and all those who sponsored his activities. Sarah sent out invitations. All including Enrique and Maria attended an early Sunday dinner at the Rancho. Tommy wasn't sure but he suspected that Sarah invited Franklin Sutter.

The dinner was served in the large dining room of Rancho Del Prado. The priest, Franklin, Enrique and his sister, Maria Contreras, Silas and Marjorie Smith and the remainder of the Sanchez family sat down at the large table. After a lavish dinner of steak and mashed potatoes followed by apple pie, Don Felipe Serano stood up to address all those assembled. The painting, in question was on an easel next to Serano, so that he could point to it and everyone could see the painting as he talked. Even the children and Naiwa brought in chairs so they could hear what the Spaniard found out. Everyone had seen the painting during restoration, but this was the first time they saw it as the artist did when he completed the painting.

"During the period of fifteen hundred to fifteen thirty AD, there were three painters in Rome who stood shoulders above all others. The three were Leonardo da Vinci, Michelangelo and Raphael. Competition among the three was intense to the point that Michelangelo distrusted Leonardo and since Raphael was a disciple of Leonardo's, he was equally distrusted. Raphael was the least know of the three at the time but he was judged a master by the time he was seventeen."

"The amount of work completed by all three individuals was enormous. Raphael completed nearly one masterpiece a year in addition to the numerous drawings he did. He was one of the best draftsmen of his day and soon after fifteen hundred, Raphael spent most of his time as an architect, though he still maintained a workshop where he tutored young artists which numbered as many as fifty at various times. A Raphael drawing was a precise drawing and his paintings had a serene and harmonious quality. To complete the amount of work he contracted for, there had to be some of his works that were finished by students in his workshop using his drawings."

"I've been fortunate to examine about five of Raphael's masterpieces. This painting has Raphael's style, similar brush strokes and is comparable to one of his paintings he named Saint Catherine of Alexandria and completed in 1507. Yet, it does not have the quality of his other masterpieces. My conclusion is that this is a painting completed in his workshop by one or more of his students from a drawing by Raphael."

Silas was the first to ask the question that probably everyone in the room wanted to ask. "Is it valuable?"

"Most certainly, but it would have to be authenticated by a Raphael scholar, of which I am not. Though I'm sure this painting was completed in Rafael's studio, my certification isn't worth too much."

"But you are certain that it is similar enough to the master's style that it would be worth the cost to see if it can be authenticated." Enrique was quick to ask before Silas did.

"I believe that to be correct."

"This painting has been under the altar for at least fifty years. Is there any damage from the cold or dampness in the cellar?" Sarah asked.

"Nothing noticeable. It's in remarkably good condition."

"What's our next step?" Tommy asked.

"I know the church is short of money. Probably two or three of you in this room are paying my fees. I'd like to stay another month to finish the restoration so it can hang in the church. During that time you can decide whether to have it authenticated. If you can provide room and board for a month, I'll complete the restoration without further charge, other than for materials."

Father Mahoney looked at the others in the room and everyone nodded their head in agreement. "We'd be delighted to have you stay another month with us, Senor Serano." Tommy put out his hand to the Spaniard, while the others at the table toasted him.

CHAPTER 23

The final month of Serano's stay seemed to fly away. Tommy, Silas, Franklin and the restorer spent two days after he was finished fishing at their pond near Juan's new home. It was obvious that Serano thoroughly enjoyed his stay and the longer he worked on the painting the more luster it showed. It was ready to be hung in the mission church. They thanked the Spaniard and asked him to maintain contact.

When it was time to return the painting to the mission, Tommy and one of his vaqueros decided to deliver it. As was his custom, Tommy brought vegetables, wine and a half steer that had been aged to the mission. Father Mahoney liked his steak and wine. Serano had wrapped the painting carefully before he left so there'd be less chance of damage during its transport. Sarah had planned to accompany Tommy when he delivered the painting, but she'd promised Enrique that she would work on another painting of Crazy Horse for their new friend.

The vaquero was driving, Tommy was next to him and the painting was lying flat on the floor of the buckboard next to the cured cow. They'd rounded a curve with the mission in sight when Tommy was shot in the chest and the momentum knocked him from the wagon and he landed on his back and lay still. The vaquero immediately brought the rig to a stop and jumped down to attend to his employer.

As he rolled Tommy over, he felt the muzzle of a rifle against his back and then he was hit over the head and he fell unconscious. Two men moved toward the buckboard and removed the painting. The other one looked at Sanchez to see if he was alive. He cocked his rifle and was ready to put another bullet in Tommy. "He's dead, we need to get out of here before someone comes to see what the shooting was about." The leader of the three said and all three rode north.

It was a few minutes before the vaquero regained consciousness and a few moments more to determine what happened. He looked around and yelled out for help, but no one came. He dragged Tommy to the back of the buckboard and although it was difficult, he lifted Sanchez into the wagon and drove to the entrance of the mission.

The vaquero jumped down and rang the emergency bell out front and Father Mahoney came running up. The vaquero was slightly confused as he tried to explain to the priest that his patron was wounded. The priest examined Tommy and could see the bullet wound and sent one of the mission's labors to fetch the doctor.

It took the doctor thirty minutes to arrive. During the interim the priest took off Tommy's shirt and cleaned the wound. It looked to the priest that the bullet barely missed his heart. When the doctor arrived, he had three labors carry the wounded man into the mission kitchen and place him on the table. He cleaned the wound with alcohol and probed for the bullet. It took nearly an hour of probing but eventually he found the projectile and pulled it out. There was an immediate gush of blood and the doctor worked frantically to stop the flow.

Tommy hadn't regained consciousness and the priest directed the vaquero to go back to Rancho Del Prado and tell Sarah what happened. She heard the buckboard racing down the gravel entrance road. She walked out the front door to see who was coming. When she saw the vaquero racing down the road without Tommy, she became alarmed. The vaquero pulled the team to a halt in front of Sarah and told her what happened. Most of the vaqueros spoke limited English, so Sarah who studied the Spanish language, was able to communicate with them in their language..

She rushed into the house and told Naiwa what happened and that she was going to the mission. She grabbed a coat while the vaquero changed their transportation to a one-horse rig. She grabbed her rifle just in case, and off they went to the Santa Inez Mission. The doctor had Tommy moved to one of the bedrooms in the mission and had transfused a pint of blood into the injured man. Her husband looked pale and although unconscious was breathing normally as she entered the room. The doctor and a nurse were at Tommy's bedside taking tests to determine his status.

When he finished, Doctor Ryan took Sarah into the hall. "Your husband was shot in the chest and fell from the wagon landing on his head. I was able to remove the bullet but he lost a lot of blood; I gave him a blood transfusion. The bleeding has stopped for now, but he has a high fever and I'm sure he has a concussion. His head is swollen and I don't wasn't to probe to see if there's a fracture to his skull. We're bathing him in alcohol to bring the fever down, but we won't know until tomorrow if he'll make it."

A shudder went through her frame when she heard the doctor's diagnosis and she leaned against the wall so she wouldn't fall down. This couldn't be happening to them. Tommy had never been shot and Sarah looked upon him as invincible. She didn't know what she'd do if anything happened to her husband." Do you have any objection if I stay with my husband until he recovers?" Sarah asked the doctor.

"I welcome your presence. I'm sure we can move another bed into your husband's room if you want to stay around the clock."

Father Mahoney arrived and Sarah made arrangements for the vaquero, her horse and rig. The priest thanked her for the vegetables, meat and wine which remained on the wagon. Sarah asked the nurse if she could do anything. "If you want, bathe your husband in alcohol to bring the fever down."

Over the next few days, Tommy remained unconscious and on one occasion his fever spiked and the nurse sent for the doctor, They placed Tommy in a tub of ice and after a few hours the temperature came down. On the fourth day, Tommy opened his eyes and smiled at Sarah. She cried and thanked god. Her husband didn't speak that day and the doctor was worried that he missed something, but the next day Tommy spoke as though there was gravel in his voice. Doctor Ryan came over and said the worst was behind them and Tommy should recover. The swelling had gone down in his head and the doctor ruled out a skull fracture. After another week and continued improvement in her husband's condition, she made the decision to move Tommy to the ranch.

When they returned to the ranch, she let everyone know they were welcome to visit, but she wasn't sure if she'd allow anyone to talk to Tommy. Visitors came on a daily basis, but Sarah held them all off, citing Tommy's condition. Juan and Silas wanted to go after those who perpetrated this crime as did Jacob Thunder the sheriff. But when he questioned Tommy and his vaquero, they were a little fuzzy on the details. Sarah was sure that when Tommy was well he'd remember more.

A month after Tommy returned home, he was walking around outside. Though when he tried to ride his horse, Sarah became hysterical; he opted for a one-horse rig. Juan, Silas. Enrique, Franklin and he went fishing overnight in the pond at the south end of the ranch: Tommy knew that he was nearly recovered. He tried his guns and he hadn't lost a beat though his right shoulder hurt if he was too quick.

When the five went fishing, Tommy loosened up and told them about the shooting. "Before I was shot, I caught movement to my right side. I've tried to remember if I saw anything else and I did. I saw two or maybe three riders shaded by a tree though it could've been only two. For a quick instant I thought I recognized the hats, but I don't know from where and I still don't. I've asked the vaquero, who was with me if he saw what I did; he did not. If what I remember is true, they attacked from my right and I fell out of the buckboard to my left. My vaquero got out on the right side of the wagon and immediately went to help me. He didn't see them approach from the right and come around the wagon and hit him."

"I probably should've shared this information with Jacob Thunder, but he doesn't know this area and the people like we do."

"Anything significant about their dress?" Juan asked.

"Other than the hats, nothing. Remember they were shaded by the big oak tree just at the bend in the road about two hundred yards from the creek. But I still can't match the hats with someone I know or met."

"How about the horses?" Silas asked.

"Too much shade and it was really quick."

"How did they know about the painting?"

"There's a discrete number of people working on the painting but many knew about it. When the wall to that secret room collapsed, many townspeople were at the site while we excavated. The big question was how did someone know we were moving it that day?" Tommy said.

"Let's put our heads together and see if we can figure out who is the most logical person to have leaked it to someone who stole it and shot me. I think we can rule out the five of us, my ranch help, William, Linda, Maria, Sarah and Marjorie; Serano had already left. That leaves Father Mahoney and those at the mission who were preparing to receive the painting."

CHAPTER 24

As Tommy continued his rehabilitation, Tomas, his foreman, took control of the ranch and was coming of age. The man who really stepped up was Enrique. Though he still had a significant problem with Franklin's attention toward his sister, the shooting of Tommy Sanchez had a bonding effect on the two. Next to Silas and Juan, Enrique had been admitted into that exclusive club as a good friend of Tommy Sanchez.

The pastor of Santa Inez Mission had set up a luncheon of civic leaders and retail owners. Enrique attended the meeting in the large kitchen of the mission. Of the twenty-six that attended, two were landowners, five were city officials and the remainder were owners of restaurants and other retail establishments. Since the theft of the painting and the shooting of Tommy Sanchez, there had been an uptick in vandalism and thefts. The purpose of the meeting was to see if they could come up with a plan to stop the robberies and vandalism.

The most vocal critic of law enforcement was the owner of the general store. Henry Spires had lost nearly two thousand dollars in supplies over the past month and he wanted to know what Jacob Thunder, the sheriff was going to do about it. Jacob rose and said they were working the cases. "Baloney, that deputy you have up here three days a week can't find his butt and you know it. I want action and I want it now, not when Deputy Rosario feels like it. Tommy Sanchez wouldn't put up with this epidemic and you know it." The storekeeper said.

"Tommy is still rehabilitating and it wouldn't be fair to ask him to get involved at this time. My instincts tell me he would try to help, but believe me he needs to rest."

"I was only talking hypothetically. I, for one always appreciated him and what he's done for this community. Why not fire Rosario and send up a full time deputy from Santa Barbara until we have the vandalism and theft under control."

Thunder smiled. "I'll take your advice and make the change this week." Most of the twenty-six attendees rose and clapped. Their old sheriff Jack Rodgers wouldn't have acted so quickly. Then again, he always had Tommy Sanchez to rely on.

As the attendees filtered out and stopped to shake the sheriff's hand, Enrique signaled to Father Mahoney that he liked to have a word. After the preliminaries and Enrique assuring the priest that Tommy was going to recover, the discussion turned to the theft of the painting. "I really have no idea who stole the painting and shot Tommy Sanchez." The priest said.

"I agree with you but I want to know if any of your workers showed an unusual interest in the delivery of the painting back to.
the mission."

The priest thought for a minute and shook his head. "Other than the usual, there was no specific interest as to the time and how it would be transported."

"What about some of you parishioners?"

"No one seemed to be that interested in the transport. They seemed to be thrilled at what it would do for the mission."

Pastor Mahoney started to walk away and as though a light went off in his head, he turned back. "There was an unusual statement made by a rancher from Los Alamos. He said it was a good idea that Mr. Sanchez would be bringing the panting to the mission."

"Can you remember who that rancher was?"

"His name is Harold Chambers and he has a large spread in Los Alamos. I don't believe he'd have anything to do with the robbery and shooting. He's a patron to the mission, and a very generous man."

Tommy Sanchez pronounced himself fit a month after the meeting at the mission attended by Enrique. During that month, he Juan, Silas and the self-elected new member to the group, Enrique Contreras met to discuss what the priest had to say.

They discussed whether Chambers orchestrated the theft and after four meetings, the consensus was that he did it. The four eventually   developed a plan to capture Chambers and search his spread for the painting.. "What if it isn't him?"

"He won't be expecting us and I'll apologize for the intrusion, but if he did it, he'll be armed and waiting."

The last time they confronted Chambers was in Los Alamos. They went by train and found him and his men in a saloon they frequented. Tommy didn't believe that plan would work this time. Someone will be watching the train, the saloon and a lookout would keep Mrs. Cota's home under surveillance. "We've got to change everything up and catch them under our terms."

"I want to show you a map of the area. Cota's house is about three miles from Chambers fence where Juan was shot at. Chamber's hacienda is another three miles north and his western fence line borders the road to Santa Maria. If we're to take the Figueroa Mountain Road north until it intersects the east west road to Los Alamos, we come to the fence line directly across from the spot where Juan was shot at."

"Here's my suggestion. We divide up our team. I plan to have us four and fourteen of the Vaqueros travel with us. Juan and Silas will head one team with seven Vaqueros and Enrique and I will head the other team. My team will enter the fence where the east west road intersects the Chambers fence. We'll rewire it so no one can tell we entered there. We'll travel about two miles to be within a mile of Chamber's home and set up a cold camp. The women are preparing food at this time for all of us. Our departure time is six-thirty tomorrow morning. Well stay at this camp at least one night. It may be a fall back position if we run into too much resistance. I want the camp set up to be defensible just in case."

"Juan and his team will follow the Santa Maria Road and enter the fence about three miles north of the east west line to Chambers house. Here it is on the map. They'll set up their camp similar to ours. Assuming that everything goes as planned, the following morning at six well take whatever we can carry and move toward the Chambers enclave. Once we neutralize the sentries, we'll continue to the house. At this point we must assume they know we're there. Juan and his group will operate the same way and by six thirty both teams should be in position surrounding the house and will know by then how much opposition we face. I don't know the exact lay of the land and that's a problem. Remember, the lives of our men are our responsibility and our primary goal is to return home intact, so if we have to fall back, we will. The painting is the second goal and remember it's only a painting and not worth dying over." Tommy looked at each man assembled. "Do I make myself clear?" Each man nodded.

"If all goes well, Chambers and his men will leave town on the next train or they'll be talking to Saint Peter. Juan and I have done this before. That's why were in charge of our teams. If we fall, it's up to you two to get our men home; Tommy was looking directly at Enrique and Silas.. Juan and I are counting on you to see things as we do, As braves, we participated in a number of attacks similar to this and all were successful."

Tomas and the rest of the Vaqueros loaded the pack horses with help from Sarah, Naomi and Linda. They were off at six thirty. The women were apprehensive, but they knew that Tommy and his adopted son were in a warlike frame of mind and their days as braves ideally prepared them for this type of mission.

Near four o'clock, they reached the Los Alamos Santa Maria Road and after a brief dialog, Tommy's group broke off and cut the fence to Chambers' property while Juan and his group continued north. Tommy's group stopped where they planned to set up camp, about one mile from Chambers' home. While Tomas and the remainder of the group set up camp, Tommy and one of the vaqueros crawled north toward Chambers' house to see what the ground was like and if there were any sentries.

About one hundred yards from the front of the colonial style home was a small ravine. If they could reach there without detection, it would be an ideal attack point. There were three buildings to the right of the five thousand square foot, two story home, and two more in the back of the complex. Tommy didn't think they'd be an issue. They spied two sentries in front of the house but stayed low so not to tip them off. He wondered why the sentries were not nearer to the ravine and therefore negate that attack option.

Juan made the same reconnoiter. The two buildings, that Tommy saw was to the left of Juan's position were much closer to him than he wanted, therefore creating a problem. He'd position two more men on his left flank to reduce that defensive disadvantage.

At six the next morning, both teams left their cold camps and made their way to Chambers' house. At six thirty, they launched their synchronized attack. The two best shots with a rifle were Pablo and Francisco. Tommy asked them if they could wound the two sentries. Each said they could and on Tommy's order both sentries fell to the ground and shooting started coming from the three building s to their right. Tommy knew immediately that Juan and his group were under intense fire. Chambers men were not in the house; they chose the three buildings to make their stand. There was no doubt in any of the attackers' mind that Chambers was waiting for them.

With gun fire coming from the two buildings to his left, Juan and his men were forced to fall back. He knew this would put all the burden on Tommy's group, so he had to come up with an option and do it fast. Juan regrouped and assessed his strength. Four vaqueros were wounded and although they could walk, they weren't effective. With Silas passing the word to all his men, he decided to rush Chambers house. They broke in the rear door. Only the housekeeper and a male servant were in there. Juan ordered them to the floor and he, Silas and the other three vaqueros who weren't wounded went to the windows while the four, who were wounded, covered the two hostages. Since the three buildings where Chambers and the majority of his men were holed up were directly across from his home, Juan's men broke the windows in the main house facing those buildings and started firing at them.

Tommy sensed he had to make a move to take the heat off Juan's group. He took four of his vaqueros with him and raced to the three building while firing on the run. They took out three of Chambers men, but two of the vaqueros fell to the ground wounded Tommy and the other two vaqueros grabbed the wounded and continued on until he and the vaqueros reached the side of the nearest building and used it as cover. Enrique couldn't wait and watch Tommy and the two vaqueros take all the fire. He and the other three vaqueros rushed to Tommy's aid. When the seven were together on the side of the building where most of the fire was coming from. Tommy sent Enrique and two of the vaqueros to clean out the other two buildings.

They made an initial assessment of the wounds to the two vaqueros and they weren't life threatening. They put tourniquets around one's arm and another's leg and told them to wait; they'd be back. Tommy and the other three vaqueros went around to the back of the building they were near and broke into the rear door, got behind some hay bales and began an intense fire exchange with the remaining Chambers' men. After an hour when one after another of Chambers' men fell to the heavy fire, their adversary held up a while handkerchief and said they'd like to surrender. "Throw out your guns before you come out or we'll continue until all of you are dead." Tommy said.

Soon, one gun after another was thrown out and five men came into view with their hands up. At this time Enrique came in the back door and Tommy ordered him to go around and enter the building from the front to be sure all of Chambers' men had surrendered. Soon the two front doors were pulled back and Tommy could hear Enrique say. "It's all clear from where I can see."

Juan and his group could see Enrique enter the building they were attacking. They left the house and circled the same building that Tommy was in and helped with the wounded. Five of Chambers' men were dead, four were wounded and five, including Chambers were still alive. On Tommy and Juan's side, seven were wounded, one dead and the rest alive. Chambers' men buried all of their fallen comrades about fifty yards from the main barn and then tended to their wounded.

Silas took charge of their wounded and two of Tommy's vaqueros bundled up their dead friend and packed him on a horse.

It was at the end of the day when they completed all the burying. They sent some of the vaqueros back for their supplies from their cold camps and settled in the house for the night. All Chambers men were attended to and locked in the large bedroom upstairs with guards in the hall, on the roof and outside so no one could escape. One of the vaqueros pointed to the painting they were after. It was hanging on the living room wall across from the fireplace. He wrapped it up and prepared it for travel the next morning.

At dawn everyone rode to the train station in Los Alamos and Tommy gave some parting words to Chambers and his surviving four cowboys. "I told you before that if I came back you would leave town. All of you have a choice. We can kill you where you stand or you can get on that train and never come back. It's your choice. My instincts tell me to kill you now because I believe you'll come back. My best advice is get on the train." No one said anything at the nine. Chambers and all his men that were alive boarded the train and never looked back.

Of the seven Vaqueros from Rancho Del Prado that were wounded, only two were serious enough to be attended to during the night. The other five had minor gunshot wounds. With Chambers and his men banished from their ranch, the question was who was going to take care of his live stock . Juan and four of the vaqueros rode to Mrs. Cota's ranch the next morning to see if she could spare some of her men to help

They had plenty of food and supplies left over so Tommy left the supplies and four vaqueros to help the foreman of Mrs. Cota's ranch take care of Chambers spread for a month or until it sold. Everyone else saddled up and made their way to the train station and then home to Santa Ynez.

CHAPTER 25

Business started to pick up for William Todd, such that he leased the vacant shop next to him and hired two people. Both were Chumash Indians. The surprise to everyone was that one of the individuals was a woman. The male, named Joseph, was hired to cut the leather to a pattern designed by William, while the woman's job was to handle the bookkeeping and marketing. She was high school educated, which was a rarity among the Chumash. Her name was Letti

The new hires worked well with William and within a month, he didn't know what he did without them. Joseph lived with his wife and two boys in a small group of twenty Chumash down by the creek in Santa Ynez. Letti's husband had worked at the mission. One day he became ill and by sundown he was dead. Letti had been sponsored by the mission and was able to go to school and get a diploma from the local high school. She heard about the shoemaker and approached him for work. She needed the job to support the two children she had by her late husband as well as his mother. Letti and her family lived next to Joseph and his family. She'd walk to and from work with him each morning. Sarah and several ladies from the mission made it a habit to deliver food so the small group along the creek could survive. It was she who suggested to Letti to ask William Todd for a job.

The quality of William's product was the main reason that his mail order business had doubled from when he was in Philadelphia. He loved where he was located but knew that a small town such as Santa Ynez couldn't really support his business. Therefore he needed to have someone to concentrate on the marketing aspect of his business. He hadn't run into any major problem since he arrived other than an occasional racial slur and of course the burning cross. Life was pretty good for him and his employees.

Letti's two children took to William and he to them. Within six months the relationship between William and Letti blossomed and William asked her to marry him. He could see that it was futile to continue to pursue Maria Contreras. Letti accepted him and they were married in a Chumash Ceremony. Tommy was William's best man and one of the women who lived down at the creek acted as maid of honor. William thanked Tommy for all his help and especially the small investment he made in the business. Soon William bought a small house near his business and he and his family seemed to be very happy.

While Tommy and Juan were recovering the painting held by Chambers in Los Alamos, Franklin decided to take the initiative and ask Maria to marry him. He visited her for three days in a row and always while her aunt was present. He told her of his love for her and that he was wealthy enough to provide her with a wonderful life here in the valley if she was amiable. She was embarrassed at first but soon felt as he and hoped that they could be wed. "I must have my brothers blessing or I can't marry you."

"You're an adult and can make up your own mind to do as you wish."

"Not in my family. You must honor the way it is and not ask me to go against what my family wants."

As soon as Enrique returned, Franklin sent a courier with a message requesting a meeting with Enrique as soon as possible. Contreras was no fool. He knew the southerner had designs on his sister. He could not point to anything that he disliked about Sutter, but there was something there that bothered him and he was reluctant to agree to a meeting. Rather than answer Franklin, the Spaniard decided to talk with Tommy Sanchez.

After Tommy brought back the painting from Chambers Ranch, Sarah wanted to be sure it was cleaned up before they returned it to the mission. The four principals decided to get together at Rancho Del Prado and celebrate the return of the painting after they honored the vaquero who gave his life in the operation. After the funeral service conducted by Father Mahoney, the vaquero was buried at the mission. The principals drove to the ranch to have dinner. Afterward, Enrique asked Tommy for a private meeting. He asked the others guests to forgive him but this was important.

Enrique told him about the request by Franklin Sutter and the fact that he visited Maria every day they were engaged with Chambers. "Are you upset that he visited her while you were away. The aunt was there wasn't she?"

"That was not a problem to me; I trust Maria to do what's right. There's something about the man that bothers me and I don't know what it is. I look at him and I see two men. The one I've met is very successful and quite personable. There's another one who I don't see and I don't like it. What do you suggest?"

"I like Franklin very much but like you, he's a bit of a mystery. I look in his eyes and I see someone else looking back at me. Why don't I talk to him and see if he'll be forthcoming. Not everyone is perfect and not everyone is forthcoming. There are things about me and what I've done, that I'd rather keep to myself. I don't even ask my wife about her previous life. I let her tell me what she wants. I assume some of her early life was painful and I don't want to raise anything that might make her unhappy. Perhaps Franklin has something that is painful to him and he'd rather not raise it. If you'd like, I'll talk to him, but it won't be an inquisition. If he wants to tell me I'll listen but that's all I'll do."

"My friend I would be grateful for anything you can find out that will ease my mind."

Tommy talked it over with his wife to see what she could add. "Well, the two seem to be in love and it would make a good match. I like them both. Sometimes it's better to leave things in the past, rather than bring them to the surface. Why bring up something that's painful just to satisfy someone else. I've not told you everything about what I did and what happened to me before we met. I assume your life hasn't been a bed of roses either. We love each other and I don't know what I do without you. I hope that's enough for you?"

"You are exactly right."

Tommy sent word to Franklin that he'd like to talk to him at his convenience at a location of his choice. Sutter responded the following day and set Thursday at noon at Rancho Del Prado as the meeting place. Franklin had been taking riding lessons, bought an older

thoroughbred and rode out to the Rancho for his meeting with Tommy. Sarah had prepared lunch for the two men and graciously excused herself after they ate .She and Naomi went out back to do some gardening. Tommy poured each a glass of wine and Franklin toasted him on his success in recovering the painting.
'Thank you."

"I gather you didn't ask me here to talk about the painting. I assume the subject is Enrique and Maria Contreras. Am I correct?"

"You are very astute Franklin. Enrique has a concern that you have a skeleton in your closet that would preclude you from marrying his sister. He asked me to talk to you. However, I am the last one to ask someone to divulge something that may or may not be painful to them. And I don't intend to do that in this case. I do think there is a way out for you. Why not tell Maria what you are reluctant to divulge. If it doesn't bother her, it shouldn't bother Enrique and I'll tell him that."

"If you asked me to tell you what it is, I would."

"That's not ever going to happen my friend. It's none of my business. I like you the way you are. "

The next day Franklin rode his new horse to meet with Enrique and Maria. The master of the rancho was surprised that Franklin had come unannounced. "I'm here to see Maria. Would you please tell her I'm here?"

Enrique almost said that Maria was not at home; however, he went to her room, knocked on her door and told her who the visitor was.

When she entered the room Franklin bowed. "Maria, I do have a secret that I've not shared with anyone. I would like to be alone with you and tell you what your brother has been trying to find out. If what I tell you is offensive and you no longer want to see me, I will understand and honor your request. If what I say does not offend you, then I'll ask your brother for your hand in marriage. I don't intend to ever tell him what my secret is."

Maria looked at Enrique. "I want to be alone with Franklin and hear what he has to say."

Enrique started to object but Maria raised her hand to silence him and she and Franklin went into the library and closed the door. He took nearly thirty minutes to tell her the entire story and when he was finished, she looked at him for a few moments and then opened the door. Enrique and her aunt were waiting in the drawing room and rose when the two entered. "Enrique, Mr. Sutter wants to ask you for my hand in marriage. I have already approved of his request. I expect you to give your blessing. I know his secret and it has no impact on you. If you fail to give your blessing, I'll leave here immediately and marry him without your approval. It's your choice." Enrique sat down and put his head in his hands. He appeared to be crying.

A few moments went by and Enrique Contreras rose, walked over to Franklin Sutter. "I would be delighted to have you in our family as my brother-in-law." The two men shook hands.

On the Sunday when the painting was officially returned to the mission, Father Mahoney announced the engagement of Franklin Sutter and Maria Contreras, with Enrique present. Tommy and Sarah Sanchez, Juan and Linda Sanchez and Silas and Marjorie Smith were present and congratulated the engaged couple. All four couples plus Enrique went back to Rancho Del Prado for wine and sandwiches.

Two months later the couple was married at the mission in a ceremony conducted by Father Mahoney. Tommy was the best man while Sarah was the Maid of Honor. The reception was held at Enrique Contreras' ranch. The next morning the newly married couple took the train to San Francisco for a three week honeymoon. When they returned, they purchased a small spread in Santa Ynez and settled down to married life. Within two years Maria gave birth to a seven pound boy and the following year a six pound seven ounce little girl. Although both children were slightly darker than their mother, no one made notice of the difference in color. All assumed it was from Maria's side.

CHAPTER 26

Although he'd been content with raising his family and managing their 400 acre cattle ranch, he'd recently become restless. His finances were good and his marriage stable. He'd received a letter from William Todd from Santa Ynez, California. He liked the young man and was glad that he was doing well. He promised to visit William some time in the future

Before he started making plans to visit William, he received an urgent message from the Town Council of Stillwater in Northeast Oklahoma. Lawlessness was rampant throughout the town as a result of a land rush that started two months ago. Fraudulent claims were being made, counterfeit stakes were being placed on parcels, homesteaders were being forced off their claims and two settlers had been murdered. Bass was asked to come to Stillwater to reestablish law and order. He wired the council what his fee was and if acceptable he'd be there by the end of the week.

His family was used to Bass being gone on law enforcement business for short periods of time. Before he left for Stillwater, Bass told his wife he'd be gone less than a month and would come right back home when he was done. He made sure they had enough beef and food stuff on hand and off he went. He arrived in Stillwater on Saturday and had a hard time finding a place to sleep. Finally he and the local constable made an agreement and Bass took one of the cells in the local jail as his room while he was in the town.

Working for Judge Parker gave Blake a good feel for law investigation. He immediately started to look into the two murders. The deceased were men by the names of Charley Little and Frank Jones. Each had made claims to separate parcels of land, placed their stake on the parcel and filed the claim with the local clerk. One night they were celebrating at the Crazy Mary Saloon, and then they went outside. They were shot down as they walked across the street.

Since the two were deceased, Bass checked to see who filed on the two parcels after they were dead. The clerk said that Willy Herman and Pee Wee Smith had filed immediately after Little and Jones were gunned down. Herman filed on Little's and Smith filed on Jones. Bass decided to have a talk with the two. The local constable and Bass walked down the main street and entered all the saloons before they found Herman at one of the bars on the street. Bass walked up to Willy and asked him how he filed so soon after Little was gunned down at the Crazy Mary Saloon. "What's it to you?" Herman sneered.

"I've been hired by the town council to solve the two murders and put an end to the thievery of people's claims."

"Are you suggesting that I had something to do with Charley Little's death?"

"I am. It's too convenient. Little gets ambushed and you file within minutes. Yes I think you had something to do with it."

Willy Herman reached for his gun and Bass hit him over the head with his revolver and the man fell to the saloon floor unconscious.. He picked up Herman's gun and he and the constable carried the man to the jail. They went looking for Pee Wee Smith but didn't find him that day, nor the next,

It was three days after Bass arrested Herman that he found Smith at the Crazy Mary. He was having a beer at the bar and was looking in the mirror when Bass came through the café doors. He turned and faced Blake. Apparently, he'd found out about the confrontation with Herman and was ready for Bass. "I didn't have anything to do with killing either Little or Jones. I was at the saloon when I heard that someone was shot outside. I ran out of the saloon and saw the two men who'd just been in here bragging about their claims. I was just smart enough to realize this was a great opportunity, so I ran over to the clerk and filed a claim on the property.

"What's your relationship with Herman? I heard you two ran together."

"You heard wrong. I barely know the guy. He isn't someone I'd ride with."

"I think you're lying, and I'm going to prove it. When I do, I'll come looking for you."

The next morning, after the judge fined Herman and released him, Bass visited the clerk's office and asked him about the two claims. Bass was shown the paperwork; everything seemed to be in order. "Is there a right of survivorship or succession such that the claim once filed, goes to the claimant's kin?"

The clerk went into his desk and took out the ordnance that established claims during the land rush. In the case of Little, there was no heir but when Jones filed, he made a notation that the land would go to his wife and kids if any harm came to him.

"This makes Smith's claim invalid, doesn't it?"

"It would seem so." The clerk responded

"Why didn't you catch this when he filed on Jones claim?"

"I must have missed it."

"How much did Smith pay you to look the other way?"

"I don't know what you're talking about."

"I think you do. I'll put this all together and if I find out you're involved, I'll see to it that you're tried as an accessory to murder."

Bass left the clerk's office and went to the Crazy Mary to have a drink. He asked the bartender who was on duty the night the two men were gunned down. "I was", replied the bartender.

"Was Pee Wee Smith at the bar when the shooting took place?" Bass asked the bartender.

.   "I don't remember," was the reply..

About thirty minutes later. Smith moved in next to Bass at the bar. "I hear you asked the bartender if what I said was true. I don't like any man suggesting I'm a liar."

"That's too bad. You'll just have to live with it. I was hired to find the murderer of the two men and I intend to do just that. Right now, I think you and Herman killed the two men so you could get their parcels."

Smith walked away and Bass knew that he'd have to be careful from now on. Smith was probably a back shooter and that made him dangerous. He had a pretty good idea that Pee Wee Smith and Herman killed Little and Jones. He decided the next thing to check was the counterfeit stakes.

Since the original stakes given out by the state were made by Handy Saw Mill, it seemed reasonable that the counterfeit ones were made by the same company. He met with the owner of the saw mill and showed him the original stakes that were cut by his company. Bass produced a counterfeit one and the stakes were identical including the parcel numbers on the stake. "My guess is that the original stakes and the counterfeit ones were made here in your mill. "

"I don't know anything about that." The owner responded.

"Well, you can't say that and look at the two stakes side by side. They were made here alright."

"Not by me," was all the owner would say.

"Okay, who did you have making the stakes?"

"Bill Travers."

"Get him. I want to talk to him."

"He quit last week and left town."

"Pretty convenient, don't you think? Okay, who did you give the original stakes to?"

"The clerk's office."

Bass walked back to the clerk's office and asked for a list of people who purchased the original stakes. When the clerk furnished that list, Bass asked for the list of buyers of the land put up by the state to include the stake and parcel number. It didn't take him but a half day to figure it out. While Bass was solving the counterfeit stake problem, the local constable was questioning everyone he could find that was at the Crazy Mary the night of the shooting.

The constable along with Bass met with the town council the next morning. "Gentlemen, I believe I've solved the problem with the counterfeit stakes and who murdered Little and Jones. All of this was dreamed up by your town clerk. I'm surprised that he hasn't left town yet. Maybe he's trying to gut it out."

"Both of the original and counterfeit stakes were made at the saw mill by Bill Travers. He gave them to the town clerk. As an official of the town, he sold the original stakes to would be land owners. Then he and his two cohorts, Herman and Smith sold the counterfeit ones at a discount price to anyone who'd buy them. Here's the list of buyers with the original stakes for the lots the state put up. Only half of them appear on the actual land purchase. The other buyers were sold the counterfeit stakes by Herman and Smith. This situation probably wouldn't be a big concern and you wouldn't have called me, if Smith hadn't killed both Little and Jones. We have two eye witnesses who saw Smith kill the two men. Your constable should be promoted to sheriff. He's the one who ran down the witnesses. As soon as we arrest Smith, I'll give you my final report and expect to be paid."

Blake and the constable walked down the street again checking in every saloon but Smith wasn't in any of them. They repeated this two more times before they called it a night. The next morning they interviewed a lot of bar patrons and finally one of the cowboys told Bass that Smith lived in a shack about a half mile from town. The two lawmen rode out to the shack. They were careful as they approached the small house but no one was there.

It was three in the afternoon when they came back from Smith's shack. They tied their horses to the rail and Bass climbed up on the boardwalk that connected all establishments on that side of the street. Smith was coming out of the Crazy Mary Saloon when Bass met him in front. He was startled when he saw Blake. Then he went for his gun but Bass was quicker and he hit Smith alongside his head with his revolver. His last act in the town was to pick up Pee Wee Smith and literally throw him into a cell.

Bass finished his report and met with the city council for the third and last time. "The local clerk needs to be fired and tried as an accomplice. He and Bill Travers from the Handy Saw Mill are the main culprits in this scheme to defraud legitimate landowners. Smith murdered the two landowners and Herman was his associate. You have enough to convict them all. I've done my job. Here's my bill."

CHAPTER 27

Tommy and Sarah were having a glass of wine when a messenger came to the front door to deliver a letter from John Truit, the Manager of the Santa Barbara Bank and Trust Co. in Santa Barbara. Mr. Truit regretfully informed Tommy that Lenny Harris had died in the hospital in Santa Barbara from injuries suffered while plowing some acreage on his farm. Mrs. Frances Bookers had used up most of her funds at the bank attempting to keep Mr. Harris alive. She was seeking some funds from Mr. Bookers to help her over the winter.

This was something out of Silas Smith's life. He'd been born Hiram Bookers and after selling his maritime company in New England, he came out west and bought a thousand acre spread southwest of Santa Barbara and transferred nearly four hundred thousand dollars into a bank in Santa Barbara. After a year of farming, he was lonely and advertised for a mail order bride. Frances a nurse from Boston answered the advertisement, came to Santa Barbara and the two married.

Six months into the marriage Hiram went hunting for deer to supplement their diet and was shot and left for dead by Lenny Harris. The shooter was the mastermind behind a thirty-thousand dollar train robbery near Oxnard CA.. Lenny met Hiram at his camp after Hiram killed a deer. Lenny listened to Hiram talk about his wife and farm and decided to take over his identity after he shot him.

Lenny went to the ranch, subdued Frances and took over the property. In the interim, Tommy and his wife were out hunting and came across Hiram, lying in a thicket, near death. They transported him over rough terrain to the hospital in Santa Barbara, where Hiram recovered, but couldn't remember any of his past. Tommy took him to their ranch hoping that Hiram would recover his memory

The current Sheriff, Jack Rogers was facing a tough reelection and needed some help. He decided that Hiram was the mastermind behind the robbery in Oxnard and arrested him for the crime. Tommy and James Jefferson, the Pinkerrton Detective, investigated. They found out about Lenny Harris, who Silas really was and confronted Harris. After three years Frances, though brutalized by Lenny Harris had accepted him as her husband and had two children by him. Jefferson and Tommy were able to secure the acquittal of Silas without turning in Harris.

After Silas beat the hell out of Lenny Harris, he provided enough money for Frances and Lenny and their children to stay and tend the farm. The condition Frances agreed to was that she wouldn't divulge what her relationship with Silas was. Subsequently, Silas married his current wife Marjorie, without obtaining a divorce from Frances.

Tommy handed the letter to Sarah who looked up after she read it a few times. "What do you think? Is she the type of person that would blackmail Silas?"

"I really don't know. My impression is that she did everything she could to keep Lenny alive and now needs some funds. Silas set aside about five thousand dollars in an account for her the last we met, but that was nearly four years ago. It's easy for Silas or myself to check out how she used the funds. I'd want to verify the need, but I tend to believe her."

"What are you going to do?"

"Well, I have to get hold of Silas and recommend that he and I visit his wife. I don't think it's anything to worry about. If the story ever comes out, she'd have to explain how she sheltered Lenny from the law."

Tommy wasn't sure how dire Frances Bookers' situation was, yet he acted quickly. The next morning he saddled his horse and rode to Santa Ynez to visit Silas Smith. He arrived around ten in the morning and sat down to have a cup of coffee with Marjorie and Silas. They'd recently renovated the inside of their home and were very proud of its condition. Though Tommy was anxious to pass on the information he received from Frances, he was a polite visitor and waited until Marjorie showed him around the home.

Silas sensed this wasn't a social call on Tommy's part. He was anxious for Marjorie to finish so he and Tommy could talk.
The two men took a walk down by the corrals and when they were sure they were alone, Tommy gave Silas the letter. Tommy let him read it and gave him enough time to formulate his thoughts. "I guess I always knew that this part of my life could surface at any time and I'd be forced to deal with it."

"I don't know if it's that immediate. My read on the situation is that she needs help and hopes that you can provide it. If you were to ask me what I'd suggest. I say we take a ride to the farm and talk to her. She impressed me as a level headed woman and unless she's changed, she's not looking to do you any harm."

"That's what I appreciate the most about you. You have a clear head and look at things as they are unless someone surprises you. I think the sooner we go, the better I'll feel. I guess we can go on a week long hunting trip."

"If your wife doesn't want to be alone while you're gone, we have a nice guest room in the house. Sarah read the letter and won't say anything to Marjorie. My adopted son and his wife Linda don't know anything about Lenny or Frances. If it's okay with you, I'll ask my wife to invite her to the ranch while both husbands are off having fun. We better bring a deer back, probably two."

It was as though Marjorie was expecting her husband to go off with his friend on a hunting trip. She was also delighted that Sarah invited her to Rancho Del Prado. With Linda at the ranch this week, the three women planned their agenda.

The two men were off within two days and it took them two more days to reach the farm that Silas owned and allowed Lenny and Frances to use. Frances wasn't surprised when Silas and Tommy appeared at her front door; she was at least expecting Tommy. It'd been four years since the two men had seen her. From the little they saw as they rode in, Frances and Lenny had improved the house, added corrals and planted another five acres.

"How did Lenny die?" Tommy asked.

"Basically, he worked himself to death. It appeared to me that he was trying to make up for all those years when he was a bum. He was up early and worked late. He was so afraid that he wouldn't be the husband and father we expected. He was plowing one of the fields when he stumbled; the horse spooked and kicked him in the head. He didn't have much of a chance to survive but I wanted to see if he could. I hired the best doctors I could find but in the end it didn't matter, other than I spent most of the money you left me. You don't owe me anything Hiram. I won't cause you any trouble. It's my three kids I worry about."

"What do you have in mind Frances?" Silas asked.

"The farm needs two able bodied people to work it. I can't keep up with it by myself and the children are too young. As you might remember, I was a nurse before you and I married. I'd like to resettle in New England and go back into nursing. I've made inquiries and there's a position at New England Medical Hospital that available if I can get there. I'd like to have my three children grow up back east. Once I'm back there I plan to file for divorce from you so you can use your real name, if you want. My uncle is an attorney in Boston; he'll handle all the legalities without any
charge "

"This is a hard life here. I was hoping that you might give me enough money to travel back to Massachusetts and get a fresh start. I believe Lenny and I improved the farm to the point that if you sold it, you would realize a profit. Whatever you decide to do, I won't cause you any trouble, but I can't stay here. Lenny loved this place. I hope you don't mind, but I had his remains buried by the pond."

"None of what happened was your fault. You were caught up in something that was bigger than the two of us and you shouldn't be made to suffer for it. Don't worry about the farm. I've had a good life, why shouldn't you be able to enjoy yours as well. I'll put enough money in your account at the bank to travel to Boston and set up a home. I'll also see to it that you have an annual living allowance for as long as you live. Should I die before you, I'll set aside something in my will. I'm a rich man and when we were married, I intended to have you enjoy my wealth."

Frances broke down and cried and then threw her arms around Silas and held onto him for some time. "I will never divulge our relationship to anyone. Your secret is safe with me."

They stayed overnight in the barn, that Silas built. The next day Silas helped Frances pack while Tommy fetched the Indians who helped at the farm. He made them promise to stay here until the farm was sold. The next day they escorted Frances and her children to Santa Barbara. They spent a day setting up her account and arranging for her travel to Boston. The bank was a little reluctant to advance so much money on Silas' say so. Tommy Sanchez spoke to the manager and funds were made available immediately. They took the family to the train and Frances said she would maintain all correspondence through Tommy. He in turn would transmit the annual payments.

The two men had their work cut out for them. They travelled back to the farm and on the way were able to bag two deer, which they took to Silas' farm. There were enough vegetables in the eight acres to last the three Indians a year and with the two deer, which the Indian men hung in the storeroom, they'd be okay until the farm sold.

On the way home from Santa Barbara, which took two more days, the two men each bagged a deer and while they were cleaning up their camp, they had a cup of coffee and Silas talked out loud. "I love Marjorie but I always wondered what it would have been like if Harris hadn't shot me and left me for dead. I would still be married to Frances and those kids of hers would be mine. It could have been a good life. Let's saddle up and go home." He threw the rest of his coffee on the embers, but Tommy could see a tear on Silas' cheek.

CHAPTER 28

The two bullet wounds slowed him down even though the Mexican woman did the best she could. It was an effort but he decided to check himself into the General Hospital in Los Angeles and have a doctor treat him. One of the wounds was infected and he remained in the hospital for a week He knew he should've had medical attention sooner, but he wanted to distance himself from the Pinkerton Agency. Little did he realize they were on his trail soon after he left the Tucson Area. When he was released, he walked around the main part of Los Angeles. It didn't take him long to realize this town wasn't for him. Augustus Swanson took the steamer to San Francisco.

He had nearly twenty-five thousand of his loot left, mostly from the sale of cotton at Hickory Hills Plantation. Perhaps he put too much money into the abandoned ranch. "Well someone was going to get a good head start with that place. "

He was comfortable that he could pick up his old ways but he was looking for something different. San Francisco was both an elegant city and a place that you could find release of any kind. The bowery attracted him immediately and he spent most of his days getting acquainted and assessing what opportunities were available for a man of his skills.

One night he was having a drink at the bar and a tall heavy-set individual set down at the bar next to him. They acknowledged each other and finally introduced themselves. "I'm Augustus Swanson from Alabama."

"Nice to meet you. I'm Charles Chambers, recently of Los Alamos, California."

"Let's get a table and have another drink." Swanson suggested.

"The way you answered my question seems to indicate that you didn't want to leave."

"Chambers studied his new acquaintance. "Actually, I was forced to leave at the point of a gun. There a former gunman that lives in the area and he rules the roost. Whatever he says seems to be the law."

"Why didn't you hire some gunmen to take him out?"

"I thought I had but you can't believe how fast he is. He told my top gun to get out of town or die right there."

"Well you can always shoot him in the back. That has a way of negating a fast gun."

"Exactly. We did that but he recovered and came after me with the vaqueros who worked for him and his close friends. He killed five of my men and made the rest of us leave on the train or die right there."

"Do you have a valuable property that you left?"

"I have ten thousand acres, a two-story home and about four hundred head of cattle. The best I can do is sell everything. If I come back, he'll shoot me on sight."

"What would you be willing to give to have him go away?"

"Twenty thousand dollars."

"How about twenty=five thousand?"

"I can handle that. But he has to be dead, or I won't pay. I'll give you five thousand up front and the balance when the job is complete."

"I wouldn't want to be suckered out of my money."

"If you're good enough to take care of him, I won't want to mess with you. Swanson smiled.

"There's one last thing before I go down and check the place out. When this is over, I need a place to operate out of. What about your place?"

"No, that won't work. But I'll help you take over the Cota Land Grant and that's fifteen thousand acres. Then again if you do away with Sanchez, you may want his place. He has an extremely beautiful wife."

Through the years the Sanchez Family had only visited their native relatives. Since the shooting of Tommy Sanchez, Sarah raised the thought that they should go on a family vacation. Citing needs to maintain their operation, Tommy was reluctant to leave the ranch for more than a few days at a time. But with Sarah raising the issue, he knew that he'd eventually agree, so the real question to resolve was where.

Some of the destinations such as San Francisco and New Orleans were considered. Finally, both remembered the small fishing village of Monterey to the north. Silas and Marjorie had visited the town on their way home from their honeymoon and recommended it to the family. There was an Inn along the shore that had six or seven rooms and perhaps with advance notice, they could lease all the rooms for a couple of weeks.

Sarah wrote to the Inn and asked if they could rent the complex for two weeks in mid-September. Within a week she received a response that it was available, what the price was and asked her to indicate how many were in the party and how many meals they wanted. Sarah and Tommy decided they'd take the two children and Naiwa making five in the party. Although there were seven rooms at the Inn, the family wanted the entire complex. They made arrangements to leave by train on the tenth of September and come home on the twenty fourth.

Their ranch manager, Tomas took the family in the buckboard to the train station in Los Olivos and agreed to telegraph them if there was any problem. Everyone was eager to go and didn't mind the eight hour train trip. They were picked up by the Inn's caretaker and checked in about six PM.

At the same time, Swanson had completed his business with Chambers and was ready to leave. Chambers had given him
$ 5,000 in cash and a list of men in Los Alamos that he could call upon if he needed assistance. Swanson took the train and probably passed the Sanchez family on his was down the coast, stopping in Los Alamos before he continued on his journey. Chambers had given him three

names of men who used to work for him and would help Swanson. He found two of them at the Saloon in town and they made room for him that night at one of their cabins. Before he went to sleep he had a conversation with the two. "If we went up against Sanchez and his men, how many men can each of you provide?"

Jake Saddler was one of the men Chambers recommend and he answered. "There are ten here that I would say are guys I could go through a door with. There are five more that can do some of the work but are less reliable. Sanchez has fourteen vaqueros at his ranch that he used against Chambers. They're reliable but they'll take less risks than my guys."

The next morning Swanson purchased a horse and saddle, rode to Los Olivos and stayed at the Central Hotel. The next morning he walked around town and that's when he saw William Todd in the shoemaker's shop. There was a woman and a man working inside the same business, so he stayed out of the way so William wouldn't know he was in town. The first question he asked himself was, if William was here, could that scoundrel Bass Blake be far away. Swanson was here to get Sanchez but finding William Todd and perhaps Bass Blake would be a bonus.

He decided to ride out to Sanchez' ranch and see if he could meet the famous gunman and his pretty wife. He rode down their entranceway not knowing what to expect but he wasn't armed so he shouldn't be perceived as a threat. He met the ranch foreman who said that the patron wasn't here right now and he didn't know what his schedule was. "Perhaps I'll stop back tomorrow."

"Who shall I say called on Mr. Sanchez?"

"He won't know who I am. I was asked to say hello by an acquaintance of his."

Swanson rode back to Los Alamos and decided to hire the two he met last night and then pay William Todd a visit.

The Pinkerton Agency had received a memo from the Tucson office on Swanson and they were on the lookout for the bandit in the Los Angeles Area. Swanson pulled a fast one on them and registered at the hospital as George James. They were lucky that one of their agents, named William Trotter, had spent time in San Francisco with his wife and came home on the steamer. He ran into Swanson in the terminal, but didn't recognize him as a wanted man. He didn't know about the freight robberies in Tucson until he was back in the office the next Monday, when he was brought up to date on the outstanding cases the office was handling..

When he saw the flyer from Tucson, he talked to James Jefferson, who was handling the case. "I believe I saw this guy at the terminal on Friday. He was headed to San Francisco. Is there anything you want me to follow up on?"

"No. I appreciate the update but I'll check with our San Francisco office and see if they can find him."

Within a week Swanson was spotted in the Bowery in San Francisco. When the agent tried to make contact, Swanson evaded him and the agent lost him in one of the back allies of the Bowery. That agent followed up over the next two days and learned through informants that Swanson met with a man named Chambers who was from Los Alamos, a small town north of Santa Barbara. One of the Pinkerton Agents received a report that Swanson had boarded the train in the city and was heading south. His ticket showed that he was headed to Los Olivos.

Jefferson talked to his superiors who suggested he go north to the Los Olivos area to see if he could find and take Swanson into custody. They contacted the Federal Department in Los Angeles and asked them if they wanted the Pinkertons to pursue Swanson. Two days later they were given a request to apprehend Swanson.

He'd received a letter from William Todd last month and finally decided to respond. Bass told William in his response that he was grateful for his help when they were both slaves and he planned to come to the Santa Ynez Valley for a visit. His family knew that he became restless after being at home for more than three months. So when he told his wife about his plans to visit the Valley, she said that was fine and asked him how long he'd be gone.

He decided to go by train to Santa Barbara, take the stage to Santa Ynez and then pick up a horse there. When he arrived at the Central Hotel, he left his bags on the porch and walked over to William's shop. The two men hugged and William introduced his wife to Bass and then showed him around the shop. It was near quitting time , so they went and picked up Bass' bags and walked to William's home two blocks away.

That evening the two men recapped their lives since they last saw each other. "There's a gentleman in the valley who helped me a lot when I came here. His name is Tommy Sanchez."

"There's a famous gunman by that name I've heard about."

"It's the same man. He has a ranch about two miles from here. He's a half breed Sioux and his wife was married to Crazy Horse. He's been my benefactor and investor and when I ran into some racial prejudice, he escorted two former Confederate Soldiers out of town. You'll enjoy meeting him."

CHAPTER 29

Though it rained two days in a row, the family wasn't without things to do. They went fishing the first day on a boat in the ocean. Though they stayed close to shore, they were able to catch enough fish for dinner that evening. Since Helga caught the most fish, she sat at the head of the table and constantly told her brother how she caught that many.

The second day there was only a light drizzle and they went to visit the Carmel Mission and see the shrine of Father Junipero Serra. Originally the mission was planned along the south shore in Monterey, but within a short time Father Serra requested it be in Carmel, along the north bank of the Carmel River, with a view of the ocean. The quadrangle complex, which was one of the oldest structures in California went through its most recent reconstruction in 1884.

They'd been here In Monterey a week and the time away from home was being used to spend time together. Too often, they would reach out to accomplish some individual task and the others felt left out. Tommy spent the evenings reading to the two children while Sarah spent time with Naomi. Too often Naomi was viewed as a servant to the family and Sarah wanted to make sure that the older woman was made to feel part of the family and worthwhile.

The next morning they were outside having lunch in the courtyard of the Inn when the pastor at the mission delivered a telegram to Tommy. He read it twice and handed it to Sarah. There were only a few words. "William severely beaten and in hospital."

"We have to go back don't we?" She asked.

"I'm afraid so. Maybe the two Confederate Soldiers came back; maybe it was someone else. The telegram was sent by Silas. He wouldn't go to all this trouble if it wasn't serious."

Tommy and Sarah were sad for William and hoped that he would recover without any psychological scars that the beating might lay on him. Tomas met them at the station in Los Olivos and he wanted to talk privately to Tommy. "There was a raid on Rancho Del Prado last night. About ten men rode down the entranceway and shot up the house and barn. Six of our vaqueros are wounded; one seriously and may not survive. They caught us by surprise. The hacienda was shot up and a fire started in the barn. Although we were caught by surprise, the vaqueros fought valiantly."

On the way to their home Tommy told Sarah what happened at the ranch. "Who do you think did this?"

"I don't know but my guess is that Chambers is behind the attack .He's the only one I know that has tried to kill me."

When they arrived at the ranch and saw the damage to their house and barn, Sarah cried. "Why did they do this to our lovely home?"

Tommy inspected the house with Tomas and found at least twenty bullet holes in the exterior framework. Windows were broken and the interior of the living room had multiple bullet holes in the wall. "Apparently they rode around the house firing into the rooms. Maybe they thought we were at home. Tomas, I want you to look at the hoof prints in the garden. Make a cast of them if you can."

The hay in the barn had burned but the vaqueros had saved most of the interior and it would be restored shortly.

The next morning they had two visitors. One was an old acquaintance and the other was a big black man. James J. Jefferson had been a friend of Tommy, Sarah and Juan's for many years; he was always welcome at Rancho Del Prado. The other man was quiet and waited until Jefferson introduced him. "Tommy I want you to meet Bass Blake of Oklahoma. He's been a peace officer for a good twenty years though most of his work was with Judge Parker."

The two men shook hands and Bass said. "I've heard of the famous gunman for the twenty years I've been in Oklahoma. It's too bad we're meeting under these circumstances. William Todd is a very close friend of mine. He didn't deserve the beating he got."

The three men went into the kitchen just as Juan and Linda arrived. They were at their home on the southern part of the ranch when the attack took place and weren't involved in any of the action. Linda joined Sarah in the kitchen while the four men went into Tommy's office. Juan and Jefferson hugged each other and Juan was introduced to Bass Blake.

"This can't be a coincidence that you two men are here in our valley?"

Jefferson smiled. "I'm tracking a man named Augustus Swanson, who's wanted for murder and robbery in Tucson Arizona. He'd been in Los Angeles and then travelled to San Francisco where he met a man named Chambers in one of those joints on the Bowery. From our informants, Swanson took the train to Los Olivos but a man fitting his description got off the train in Los Alamos. He met up with Zeke Travers and George Ball. Both men worked for Chambers at his ranch in Los Alamos."

"I know you came home because of the beating that William Todd took. I'll let Bass fill you in on the details. He was the one who found William."

"I came here at the end of last week to visit William Todd. We were slaves at a Plantation called Hickory Hills in Alabama before the end of the civil war. I escaped and was tracked by many people, one of which was our brutal overseer, Augustus Swanson. I believe he's the same man that Mr. Jefferson has a warrant for. I met with William last week and was staying at his home. When he didn't come home for dinner, I went to his store. He was lying on the floor in a pool of blood. He'd been severely whipped. I got the doctor, rented a wagon and took him to the hospital in Santa Barbara. He'll recover physically but I don't know about his mental state. His wife is a nervous wreck. She thinks they're coming after her. Whatever you do, I'm in."

The following morning there was a steady stream of visitors at the rancho. Silas, Enrique and Franklin arrived early and Bass Blake an hour later. The group sat in Tommy's office and reviewed their options. Tommy was first to speak. Before we go off in different tangents, I need to assess the status of my vaqueros. Next someone has to check on Swanson. We need to know where he is and how many riders he has. I'm going to ask Sarah to send Tomas in here. He was involved in fighting the raiders."

When Tomas arrived he gave all of them a summary of the raid. "The man many of you think was Swanson came to the rancho several days ago. I talked to him; he said a friend of the patron asked him to stop by and say hello. They galloped down the entryway and fired at the main house. I was in the barn and wasn't armed. Then they rode around the house while firing into the home; some fired at several of our vaqueros. They left as fast as they arrived."

"Many of our vaqueros were wounded.. "Of the six wounded, four can ride but two aren't able. One was shot in the hip and the doctor had a hard time removing the bullet. Another was shot in the chest and although he'll survive, my guess is it'll take at least two months before he can ride. Of the other four, two were winged in the arm and are wearing slings. They're very angry and insist upon going on any retaliatory raid. I couldn't hold them back even if I wanted."

Tommy smiled and patted Tomas on the back. "James, you look like a lawman and, it's fair to say that Swanson knows what Bass looks like. If Chambers is back, that leaves Enrique, Juan. myself and Silas out. I don't know if you want to get involved and I wouldn't blame you if you didn't. But Franklin, we have to either send you to Los Alamos or send one of the vaqueros."

"I may have come late to the dance, but I'm committed to making this valley safe and repay you Mr. Sanchez for your friendship and hospitality. I can go to Los Alamos tomorrow, check out the town and see if Swanson is there. I'd need a description or picture, if you have one?"

"I cannot in due conscience allow Franklin to go alone. He doesn't have the background that some of you have in combat. I will go with Franklin. I don't believe there's anyone there that's seen me before; if they have, that's their problem. I've been in the army in Spain and I was in two skirmishes where men were killed. I must be allowed to go with Franklin. We have become close since he married my sister and if anything happened to him, I'd blame myself."

"Can we expect any manpower from your agency Jim?"

"Soon after I got here, I wired my office and asked for three or four agents. My request was approved and they should be here in two days." Jefferson responded.

"With six wounded vaqueros, that puts us down to eight that are ready, although the six that are wounded can be used as backups." Tommy said.

Silas, Enrique and Franklin were personally in but they weren't sure if their men were anxious to get into a fire fight. The three said they would talk to their workers to see if they'd help.

Dressed as a couple of middle-aged cowboys, Enrique and Franklin rode to Los Alamos and checked out the two saloons the next day. Business was slow and they didn't see anyone that remotely looked like Swanson. Juan had contacted Mrs. Cota and asked if the two could stay at her ranch. She quickly responded that she would be delighted to help.

Two days later the two were having lunch at one of the saloons when Swanson walked in with two other wranglers. He looked around and spotted the two from Santa Ynez but he continued on and the three sat at a table against the wall and ordered beers. Enrique didn't look up but he caught Franklin's eye. "I think we accomplished our objective. Let's finish up and leave here, but keep your gun handy."

About a half hour later Enrique and Franklin paid their bill and went out the front door. Swanson and his two companions followed them out and tried to engage them but the two got on their horses and started to ride out of town. Swanson's group followed them and within a hundred yards caught up to them. Enrique sensed what was going to happen. He immediately turned and faced the three riders with his gun drawn and aimed at Swanson. Franklin was a little slow to catch on but he turned and drew his weapon. "State your business or move on." Enrique challenged the three.

"You both look out of place here. We want to know who you are and what you're doing in Los Alamos." Swanson said.

"That's none of your business. We weren't bothering you, so let us be on our way or were going to blow the three of you out of the saddle. Your choice?"

"You think you can take all three of us?" Swanson asked

"I can take you and the guy on your right. Do you care after that?"

Before the three turned around, Swanson said, "we'll meet again and I'll have my gun out."

The three turned around and rode back to Los Alamos, though they turned several times to look back at Enrique and Franklin. The Spaniard didn't move and he didn't holster his weapon until they were out of sight.

Franklin was impressed. "How did you know they'd back off?"

"I had a gun trained on them all the time: I not only knew how to use it, but I would have. I guess I can tell my brother-in-law that the reason I left Spain was that I had a duel. My opponent died instantly. I'm a deadly shot. Oh I can't draw like our friend Tommy, but I can hit what I aim at."

"Does Maria know about the duel?"

"I took exception to the way she was being treated by a man who was courting her."

Swanson sent a message to Chambers in San Francisco summarizing what he did and who he saw.

When Chambers received the message, he was emboldened to go back to his ranch in Los Alamos. He knew he needed about twenty riders to defend his property, because Sanchez would come back for him. With Swanson in the area, he decided to go back to Los Alamos.

Before he made the move he reconnected with an old gunslinger who needed a job. His name was Freddy Grimes and he had a reputation as one that wasn't afraid of anyone. He'd been in many shootouts and never lost. Even if he couldn't take Sanchez, he'd probably slow him down enough. With Sanchez out of the way or sidelined, Chambers felt the others would roll over and he'd be back running his ranch without the interference from Juan or Tommy Sanchez.

CHAPTER 30

When Enrique and Franklin reported back to the group assembled at The Sanchez Ranch, Bass wanted to go immediately after Swanson. Tommy put his hand on Bass' arm. "Swanson is a killer and needs to be dealt with, but Chambers is the real villain. He has the money and can hire who he wants. Swanson wouldn't be here if it wasn't for Chambers. I believe that Chambers will be back soon and when he does, that's when we should make our move. We know their layout because we took it to them before. I may not go back as far as you do with William, but I was his sponsor here and also his best man at his wedding . I want Swanson as much as you."

"How many guns do you think he can raise.?" Tomas asked.

Probably twenty. I don't think there are more than that in the area. . How many did you say raided us?"

Tomas thought for a minute. "I counted sixteen. Most of them were young. We wounded five of them at least, but they rode off. Maybe some of them won't be part of Chambers group."

Within a week, the ranch foreman for Mrs. Cota reported that Chambers was back on his property and had kicked all of Mrs. Cota's wranglers off his spread. The foreman reported that there were twenty two hands with Chambers. Everyone that met at Rancho Del Prado knew that there was going to be a range war. Tommy decided to ask Jacob Thunder, the County Sheriff where he stood.

"I have only five deputies to police the county, so my deputies can't join you if you go after Chambers and Swanson. The best I can do is go with you and deputize your group. I didn't appreciate you leaving me out the last time."

Mrs. Cota's people were keeping Tommy's group informed. They reported that Chambers and his men were at the saloon in town every Wednesday. About ten would come inside the saloon while ten to twelve waited outside. It was as though they were waiting for someone to come, the foreman reported.

Tommy asked them all to meet at his place on a Saturday. The first thing they realized was that they couldn't match Chambers numbers. "I know they're baiting us but we just don't have the resources to go head-to-head with them. We have fourteen able bodied men including Jacob Thunder who can go to Los Alamos. There are four wounded vaqueros who cannot travel but could help at the ranch if needed."

"We're at a distinct disadvantage. They know we're coming, they control the turf and they have more guns than us." Enrique said.

"Since we know that Swanson is in Los Alamos, I'm willing to go up there and take care of him." Bass told the group."

"Here's our problem. There's only so many ways that we can approach Los Alamos. It's either by train or road and they can have one man watching the train and one man watching the roads. In addition one man can watch our ranch and when he sees activity, they can beat us to Los Alamos by train." Tommy said

"What do you suggest?" Silas asked.

"I'm thinking that we divide up our forces. I think if they have someone watching the ranch, they plan to send another team to raid the place if we take all our men to Los Alamos. When you were there Enrique, did you see at lot of cowboys around the saloon?"

"No. There were three inside and maybe two or three outside."

"I think they're using some of their men to watch us and see what we do. We caught them twice. I doubt that we can surprise them the same way, though I still think we can have an edge. My proposal is that Bass, Jacob Thunder, myself and seven vaqueros go to Los Alamos. Juan, Silas, Franklin, Enrique and Tomas and the four wounded vaqueros will stay here along with the three we have left.. Juan and Tomas know how to make this a defensive stronghold and Sarah is one of the best shots in the area. My suggestion is that Linda, Marjorie and Maria come to the ranch, just in case."

"The group with me will leave at midnight and ride to Los Alamos. I don't believe they'll think we'll come at night. It shouldn't take us more than four hours. We'll pick the back door lock and be in the saloon before its light on Wednesday morning. We'll tie up the owner and bartender when they come to work and put them in the storage room; one of the vaqueros will act as bartender until Chambers arrives with his men. My guess is that he'll have half his men in reserve and send them to the ranch."

"Most of us will be waiting in the storage room. I know I've covered a lot and haven't given anyone an opportunity to agree or disagree with me. I'd like to hear from you now."

"Why bring the women to the ranch?" Silas asked.

"You and Enrique were part of the raid at Chambers ranch. I know he knows who you are and if they come here, they may go to your places as well. .It's a safety issue with me. I'm also counting on my adopted son and my close friends to keep my wife and children safe."

They all agreed with the plan and the three women came to the ranch. Everyone worked to set up defensive positions to protect those staying at the ranch. Tommy and his group left at midnight and entered Los Alamos around four thirty AM. They picked the lock on the back door of the saloon and checked the building out. Around nine o'clock the owner and his bartender came in the front door and were immediately subdued by the vaqueros, tied up, gagged and put in the storage room.

It wasn't until one in the afternoon that Chambers and his men tied their horses at the rail in front and entered the saloon. They were dusting their clothes off when they heard the click of rifles and everyone froze. "Chambers, you and your men sit down at the tables and will have a little talk." Tommy didn't want a shoot out unless he was forced into it.

When everyone was sitting down, Jacob Thunder walked up to Chambers. "Mr. Chambers, you're under arrest for the murder of Felipe Lopez."

"Who the hell is that?" Chambers demanded.

"He's a vaquero who was killed in the raid at Mr. Sanchez ranch by Swanson and his men."

"I don't know who Swanson is. He's not working for me and I didn't send anyone to raid Sanchez' rancho. I was in San Francisco and I can prove it."

"I'm still arresting you." Thunder responded.

No sooner did Jacob Thunder make that statement when one of the men with Chambers rose and reached for his revolver. Tommy Sanchez was alert and shot him in the shoulder before he touched leather. Several of the other men with Chambers started to fire at the Sheriff but Bass and the vaqueros shot all of them and eight men lay on the floor, either dead or wounded. The others including Chambers raised their hands.

Tommy directed the vaqueros to take all the weapons from Chambers group while Bass checked the men on the floor. All were wounded; none were dead. Jacob Thunder went across the street where the train station was and directed the teletype operator to alert the incoming train to stop instead of going through.

Over the next hour the Sanchez group secured all the prisoners and put bandages on the wounds of those who'd been shot. All of Chambers men were escorted to the train when it arrived. Both groups boarded the train.

There was an empty car and all the horses were loaded in that car. When they reached Los Olivos, Tommy left four vaqueros with the sheriff to transport Chambers and his men to jail or the hospital in Santa Barbara.

Tommy, Bass and the remaining vaqueros unloaded their horses and raced to the ranch. They assumed that since only half of chambers men were in Los Alamos, the remainder was attacking the ranch.

Swanson and the other half of Chambers men had camped out on the north road leading out of Los Olivos for three days waiting for Sanchez to make his move. It was three AM when one of the cowhands thought he heard the sound of many horses go by heading north. Swanson woke the men and asked the others if anyone heard the same thing. No one had. He had a decision to make and he felt he had no choice They would go south and raid the Sanchez ranch. It took them three hours to reach the ranch and another half hour to get everyone briefed on what they were going to do.

At six thirty with Swanson in the lead they raced down the entryway and started shooting at the main house as before. Unlike the last time, there was a volley of fire coming from the barn, the house and some hay bales in the middle of the road just past the house. Four of Swanson's riders fell before they were able to turn left behind the bales and go around the house. It was as though they were being tracked because three more riders fell in the rear of the house and Swanson knew they needed to get out of there.

As they came back around the north side of the house to gain access to the main entryway, the shooting was more intense and Swanson didn't look around but raced down the entryway to escape. It was every man for himself. When he reached the main gate, there were only three of the eleven who started down the road left. "Where are we going?" One of the three asked Swanson.

"Let's make our way back to Los Alamos and see how Chambers made out."

They were cautious as they made their way to Los Olivos and then to Los Alamos. They arrived outside of the town where they saw all the men getting on the train. Swanson recognized Chambers and saw that he had his hands tied as did the other Chamber's riders. The real shock is when he saw the big black man in the middle of everything. He knew it was Bass Blake. He could only be here for one thing. He heard about the whipping he'd given William Todd.

Swanson and the other two kept quiet as everyone boarded the train and off it went to Los Olivos. "What are we going to do?" asked one of the two cowboys with Swanson.

"I don't know what you two are going to do, but I'm getting out of here. You can come with me if you want but I'm heading north."

At the end of the raid at the ranch, it was Enrique who ran after the three men firing his rifle at them as they raced down the entryway. He didn't hit them but he was sure they wouldn't return. Tomas sent two of the vaqueros after Swanson and the other two. He told them to stay back so they weren't recognized but to be sure they saw where they went.

Sarah came out on the front porch with her rifle as Enrique returned. Tomas came up to Sarah. "Mrs. Sanchez, none of our people were shot, though seven of their men are dead. Four lay near the barn and three in your backyard. Was there any damage inside the house?"

"There are a few bullet holes in the wall but no one was shot. I saw them when they were abreast of the house and ran to the back. They circled around the house the last time but this time we were waiting for them. Franklin, Juan and Enrique each shot one of the riders." Tomas smiled. He knew that the patron's wife also killed one of the raiders.

Tommy, Bass and the other vaqueros got off the train and immediately raced to the ranch. They were surprised to see that everyone was okay. When they saw the seven dead raiders, they knew they'd been correct in splitting their resources. Tommy could see that Bass and Tomas were in deep conversation and he went up to them. Was Swanson with the raiders?"

Tomas turned to his boss. "He and two others escaped our net but I sent two of the wounded vaqueros to trail them so you'd know where they went. They'll come back as soon as they know what direction they went."

Four hours later, the two vaqueros came down the entryway and reported to Tomas. He immediately went to the main house to inform Tommy who was talking to Bass Blake. After Tomas told them what the vaqueros found out, Tommy turned to Bass. "My instinct tells me the three are headed for San Francisco. He could get lost in that town."

"Not from me." Bass responded.

CHAPTER 31

Bass decided he would go by train to San Francisco. If Swanson and his two cohorts were on horseback, it was likely Bass would arrive before them. Tommy offered to go or send a couple of vaqueros with Bass but he declined. Tommy took the lawman to the train in Los Olivos and on the way they talked.

"I appreciated you joining us in Los Alamos which went better than I thought it would."

"I heard about your fast gun but I just chalked it up to a lot of things that get exaggerated over time. Everything I heard is true. Your instincts are fantastic. I knew Grimes and there were a lot of men that wish they hadn't. He didn't even touch leather. You must have trained early to be that fast."

"My father was Sitting Bull. He told me to practice, practice, practice. It was a way of making it in the White Man's World, which you seemed to have accomplished. I've also heard of your exploits. I know this is personal between you and Swanson and it's something you have to do. I just ask one thing. I'd like you to come back after you finish your business and go fishing with me on our pond. Perhaps we could have William join us."

He arrived in San Francisco early the next morning and checked into the Clarion near the Bowery. He slept through the day but he was sure he had enough time. It would take Swanson at least five days to make the trip by horse. Bass wasn't sure whether he was going to kill Swanson or make him wish he were dead.

The next evening and the two following that, he started frequenting three bars in the famous landmark. Sooner or later, if Swanson came to the great city, Bass would find him and there would be a reckoning.

A week later Bass was across the street from the Golden Gate Saloon in the Bowery when he saw someone who looked like Swanson, with two other men, whom Bass didn't recognize. He carefully looked around and made his way to the saloon. He mingled with the crowd at the rear of the room and looked around. There was Swanson looking directly at him.

Swanson bolted for the side door and Bass had to push himself through about twenty-five people before he reached the same exit. He came out into an alley and looked both ways to see where Swanson went; he was nowhere in sight. Before Bass went in either direction he heard something slam in the building fronting the alley. He went across the alley and opened the door to a three story tenement.

Bass turned right and started down the hall leading to the individual apartments. When he reached the stairs leading to the second floor, the wall to his left exploded and he could hear footsteps going up. He looked around the corner of the wall that had been hit and then gazed up the stairs before continuing. He made his way up, step by step waiting for another burst of gunfire.

As he reached the landing half way up to the second floor, he glanced up and saw Swanson with his gun aimed at him. He fell on the landing as two shots rang out and hit the wall above him. He waited a few seconds and started up again. He could hear Swanson running and assumed he was going up to the third floor. As Bass reached the second floor he peered around the wall to see if Swanson was lying in wait for him. As he moved to the third floor stairs, he hugged the wall to his left and aimed his revolver at the area where the stairs should be.

He heard several loud bangs and assumed Swanson was trying to break the door down to the roof. Bass carefully came up the stairs and saw that the door to the roof was off its hinges. He pushed the door aside and as he stepped onto the roof, two shots rang out and hit the wall to his left. He was so close to the wall that splinters ricocheted off the wall and hit him in the face. He wiped his face off with a rag and noticed that there were several blood splotches on it.

Swanson was hiding behind a chimney on the roof and fired a shot at Bass. He expected more shots, but Bass could hear a click indicating there were no bullets in the chamber; He could hear Swanson run. It seemed to Bass that he was trying to find a way to escape. Swanson was near the edge of the roof and within ten feet of a ladder going over the side. As Swanson made his move toward the ladder, Bass took the whip off his belt and snapped it at Swanson who fell over backwards trying to avoid the whip. Bass continued slashing at Swanson, backing him away from the ladder.

The Oklahoman lawman was merciless and continued to whip Swanson. All the rage for the years he and William were abused by this man was unleashed on him. For over five minutes Bass showed no mercy. Finally

Swanson got to his feet and although he was hit with the lash at least six times he reached the ladder. He grabbed hold of a metal rung and pulled himself up until he was lying on the top of the ladder. It seemed to Bass that he was trying to decide if he wanted to go down the escape ladder. When he reached for a rung further down, he lost his balance and fell three stories to the dirt below, Bass looked down at the prone figure in the alley; Swanson didn't move.

Bass took his time and sat on the top step of the stairs between the second and third floor. The rage was still with him. He was cold and his body was shaking. The realization of what just happened was just starting to dawn on him and he was numb to the gravity of his action. As he sat there, he felt as though he was the only one in the world; he was lonely and depressed. This wasn't the first individual that he killed but it was the first outside of the law He felt a tremendous amount of stress for violating his oath no matter how much Swanson needed killing.

He didn't know how long he sat there. Finally he got to his feet and walked down both flights of stairs and out into the alley. Swanson's body was gone. The first thing that entered Bass' mind was that Swanson had survived and escaped. Then he saw the blood on the dirt. As he was staring at the spot, one of the saloon patron's came out into the alley. "That's where the guy landed who took a dive off the roof. He must've lost all his money."

"What happened to him?" Bass asked the man

"They took him to the morgue."

CHAPTER 32

William returned home two days after the second raid at Rancho Del Prado. During his absence his wife and worker finished all the outstanding orders and were ready for William to work on the new ones that came in while he was in the hospital. He'd been home only a day before he started to get cabin fever; he decided to go into work. The scars left from the unmerciful beating he received were evident in his face and neck. When he took off his jacket, his arms still bore the welts of a severe whipping. Rather than embarrass any of his customer, he covered his arms and neck.

There was a banner on his shop's outside wall saying "Welcome Back William". All during the first day back, his fellow merchants of Santa Ynez were in and out of his shop welcoming him back. At least half of them made orders for new custom shoes. William was overwhelmed at the greeting by his fellow business owners. All expressed sorrow at what happened to him and hoped that the law would catch the scoundrel who did it.

With Swanson out of the way, Bass made his way back to Santa Ynez via the train. His first stop was to see if William was back. Much to his surprise, his old friend was working in his store. He said he had a lot of back orders from the community and his fellow businessmen. When Bass told him that Swanson had gone to see his maker, he smiled and then sat down. "I never wished that any man or woman be killed on my account but I'll make an exception when it comes to that person."

The two men agreed to spend a day together before Bass headed back to his farm in Oklahoma. Bass left his horse in the livery in Santa Ynez while he was gone. He picked up the horse and made his way to Rancho Del Prado. He needed a day of fishing with the famous gunman. Mostly Bass needed someone to talk to. He knew that Tommy Sanchez would understand what he was going through.

Sarah was as gracious as ever and had Tomas take Bass' gear to the guest room in the barn. He washed up and went into dinner. James Jefferson was still a house guest and the three men went into Tommy's office after dinner. Bass was tired and after a glass of wine he excused himself and said goodbye to Jefferson who was leaving in the morning. But before he did, he made arrangements with Tommy to go fishing about ten tomorrow morning.

The two men made their way to the pond on the southern part of the ranch, unloaded their fishing gear and set up a small camp. Juan's house was nearby and he helped unload their equipment. The three fished for three hours in between a couple of glasses of wine and one of Tommy's imported cigars. They caught six good sized bass and Juan excused himself and went back to his house. "Linda's expecting me."

Bass volunteered to cook and Tommy opened another bottle of wine. Bass shared with Tommy where he was brought up and how he escaped Hickory Hills with William's help. Tommy told a fascinated Bass about his childhood with his father, Sitting Bull. After they cleaned up Bass shared with Tommy what happened to Swanson.

"So it was an accident that he fell over the ladder running down the side of the house."

"Technically that's true, but he fell because he was trying to get away from me."

"I'll share with you a story that Sarah doesn't even know about. When I was much younger, I was in love and engaged to a young woman in Mexico by the name of Maria Conchita. We went on a picnic one day and after a few glasses of wine we fell asleep. I was awakened by Maria's scream and then hit over the head by a rifle butt and shot several times. When I awoke, I was back at her father's hacienda. He came looking for us and luckily found us. I learned later that my bride to be was dead; she'd been violated many times. They say it was a miracle that I survived. It took me three months to recover and two months to find and capture them."

"I wanted to kill them for what they did to Maria and me".

"Did you kill them?"

No. I brought them back and gave them to Maria's father. I let him decide their fate. If we'd been married, I would have killed them. I felt that he had first claim on them. You could have killed Swanson at any time. My guess is that you would've brought him back and allowed William the privilege of exacting that punishment."

"You may be right. Something was holding me back and that may have been just that. I enjoyed meeting you and I hope our paths cross in the future. The two men hugged each other. Bass moved into William's house, the next morning

After spending the next two days with William Todd and his family Bass Blake said goodbye to everyone and went back home.

EPILOGUE

They finally found a Raphael expert to authenticate the painting. Miguel Philippe Ortega said the painting was not done by the master but was a very good copy of one of his paintings. His fee was huge but four couples split the cost. It was an excuse to get together again and enjoy a glass of wine.

After his former wife Frances received a divorce in the state of Massachusetts, Silas finally told Marjorie that he'd been married before and had not received a divorce prior to their nuptials. She was embarrassed and was sure they'd have to be married again. Silas told her that only five people in the world knew the story and none of them were going to divulge it. It was Sarah who convinced her not to make it an issue.

Charles Chambers received a two year sentence from the court in Santa Barbara. When he was finally released from prison, Tommy Sanchez was outside the gate to greet him. The Chambers ranch had been sold the previous year to Franklin and Maria. After two years in jail, Chambers was a beaten man. He told Sanchez he was moving back east for good.

Franklin and Maria had a third child who was male and who was black. His parents didn't care one bit nor did his Uncle Enrique who vowed to take his grandson fishing and hunting when he was old enough.

AUTHOR'S BIOGRAPHY

James S. (Jim) Kelly is a retired United States Air Force Colonel with over 100 combat missions during the Vietnam Conflict. Prior to his retirement, Jim was the program Director for a communication program in the country of Iran, working directly with the Shah.

Jim and his wife Patricia own and operate High Meadow's Horse Ranch in Solvang California. Nearly eighty percent of his novels use the beautiful Santa Ynez Valley as a backdrop for his plots.

He and his wife are heavily involved in a charity supporting our troops in forward operating locations. in hostile territory.

To contact Jim, send an e-mail to asyougo90@gmail.com

BOOK SUMMARY

Franklin Sutter was born in Alabama prior to the civil war. His parents were Marsha Lee Sutter, the white daughter of Jesse and Carolyn Sutter and Odelle Jones a black slave on their plantation. However, Franklin is white. His father, Odelle is banished from the plantation and Franklin is raised by his mother. When his mother dies, he's adopted by her brother and becomes heir to the family fortune while still a teenager, with his secret intact. His future travels take him to the seat of the power in the US and thence to California where he meets the legendary Tommy Sanchez, gets involved in a land war and marries into a Spanish aristocratic family, who are not aware of his secret. The climax comes when he's forced to reveal his secret.

INDEPENDENT BOOK REVIEW

Acknowledgements

I would like to thank everyone who has done so much to help me with this project.

Thank you to my editor, Mary Ellen Bramwell. Your insight and knowledge was invaluable.

Thank you to Getcovers for the amazing cover! Thank you for helping me and putting in the work so professionally while you and your country struggled through these difficult times.

Thank you to my beta readers, Stacie Wheelwright, Rachel LeAnn, Jessica Chipps. Thanks for sharing in this great adventure with me!

Also, thanks to the SouthSide Writers for your encouragement and support!